Praise for D. R. Meredith and the Sheriff Matthews Mysteries

"Up in the Panhandle, D. R. Meredith has been quietly adding quality volumes to a genre that is possibly one of the most popular categories in fiction today, the murder mystery. . . . Such complexity of feelings in a character is rare in what often is called 'formula fiction.' "

The Dallas Morning News

"It is one of the delights of Meredith's *Sheriff* novels that she knows the Panhandle country and Panhandle people so well that she can mirror not only what it must be like to be a lawman there but what it *is* like to live there."

El Paso Herald-Post

"Meredith is an artist with words. Her well-rounded characters are vivid, her presentation of idiomatic language makes for realistic dialogue and the almost unknown geographical area seems more than a speck on a large-scale map."

Murder Ad Lib

Also by D. R. Meredith:

MURDER BY IMPULSE*
MURDER BY DECEPTION*
MURDER BY MASQUERADE*
MURDER BY REFERENCE*
THE SHERIFF AND THE PANHANDLE MURDERS*
THE SHERIFF AND THE BRANDING IRON MURDERS*
THE SHERIFF AND THE FOLSOM MAN MURDERS*
A TIME TOO LATE

**Published by Ballantine Books*

THE SHERIFF AND THE PHEASANT HUNT MURDERS

D. R. Meredith

BALLANTINE BOOKS • NEW YORK

 Published in the United States of America by Ballantine Books, a division of Random House, Inc., New York, and simultaneously in Canada by Random House of Canada Limited, Toronto.

Library of Congress Catalog Card Number: 92-97260

ISBN 0-345-36948-3

Manufactured in the United States of America

First Edition: May 1993

To the 7,999 gentlemen and one male chauvinist pig whom I accompanied on the 1984 pheasant hunt in Moore County, Texas.

I am particularly indebted to Stan Folsom, John Grist, Ricky Beach, and Dean Hubbard for their technical advice on the finer points of pheasant hunting as well as for their patience with an unarmed greenhorn.

With the exception of the annual pheasant hunt in the Texas Panhandle, all other events in this novel are fictional, and any resemblance to actual persons or events is entirely coincidental.

PROLOGUE

IN DECEMBER THE LAND LIES FALLOW, A VAST, FLAT, desolate patchwork of dun-colored fields bristling with milo stubble. The wind blows between the shin-high stalks with the rattling sound of dry bones. A few tumbleweeds catch on the dead stalks, then break free to roll across the fields, to lodge finally against fence rows in layer upon layer of withered aggravation. Patches of snow, dust-coated survivors of an early blizzard, hug the shadows cast by an irrigation pump.

To the stranger the land is bleak and ugly and lifeless, in limbo between harvest and sowing.

The stranger would be wrong.

In December the Texas Panhandle prepares for its most lucrative harvest, a crop that requires no seed, no bank loan for operating expenses, no expensive irrigation. Best of all, at least to the farmer's way of thinking, the crop has no price support, so he may charge all the traffic will bear. And the traffic will bear a lot. For two weeks thousands of hunters pay from ten to one hundred dollars per gun per day to walk across stubble fields in temperatures ranging from tolerable to frigid. All this for the privilege of harvesting the ring-necked pheasant.

To the farmers of Crawford County pheasant season means quick, dependable cash in a profession in which income is seldom quick and never dependable. If an occasional head of livestock is mistaken for a pheasant, the farmers accept the loss stoically, while mentally figuring their tax burden and arranging for the dead animal to be turned into steaks, roasts, and hamburger and stored at the local meat locker. They also charge the hunter the market price for the beef on the hoof, meaning the whole animal including head and horns, not the dressed-out beef, which is considerably lighter. A farmer soon learns how to turn a liability into an asset.

To the farmers' wives, pheasant season means long days of cooking, baking, cleaning, and acting as hostess to any visiting hunters to whom their husbands might offer hospitality. It means muddy boots, blood and feathers on the back porch, loose shotgun shells left in shirt and coat pockets, the lingering smell of gun oil, and dirty, hungry men bonded together—for several days or a week—in a pursuit from which the female of the species is forever excluded.

To the business community of Carroll, county seat of Crawford County, it means full motels and busy restaurants. It also means a brisk trade in hunting licenses, shotgun shells, Band-Aids, and liniment for blistered feet and tired muscles, liquor for a drink at the end of the day, and aspirin for the morning after, when one drink has turned into several.

To the hunter, pheasant season means The Hunt, a rite of passage, an endorsement of masculinity, a subconscious surrender to a primitive urge to provide for one's mate by bringing meat to the campfire. That the campfire is now a split-level tract house and the mate more interested in the payroll savings plan than in a dead pheasant doesn't invalidate the male's instinct to hunt. The instinct is controlled, proscribed, limited, licensed, restricted, ridiculed, denied, ignored—but it cannot be smothered. Every December during pheasant season, the masculine ritual of the hunt begins and instinct is satisfied.

At least as old as the hunt is the ritual that precedes it: the social gathering, the party, the bash, the breakfast, or whatever it's called in current vernacular. Traces of this peculiar ritual are found in prehistoric paintings inside ancient caves, on walls of pyramids in the pharaohs' Egypt, and in myths handed down from earliest times. The trappings are different, but the intent remains the same: to prepare oneself mentally and emotionally for the hunt.

Through the eons of time to the very recent past there was also a spiritual preparation. Shamans and priests and ministers called down upon the hunt the blessings of whatever immortal spirit each age worshiped. Today there is no purging of the mind and spirit of evil to attain the favor of the gods. Today there is only food and drink and talk of guns and past hunts. The ritual of The Hunt has weakened.

Unfortunately, man's evil has not.

He came late to the party.

Cigarette smoke already formed a hazy stratus in the air, and ashtrays overflowed. An unsteady hand had already spilled a bowl of peanuts, and glasses filled with the watery remains of drinks dotted the mantel of the stone fireplace. Open bottles of liquor lined the bar, and cans of beer floated in washtubs of melting ice. Voices were louder and gestures more unrestrained as alcohol released inhibitions and each man boasted of the birds he would shoot. The buffet table, earlier covered with buckets of fried chicken and assorted pizzas, was littered with dirty paper plates, leftover wings and backs, and half-gnawed crusts. The guests were mellow, full of camaraderie, relaxed.

And vulnerable.

He stood a few steps from the bottom of the stairs and meticulously surveyed the hundred or more guests crowding the basement party room of the Carroll National Bank. He mentally ticked off a name as he located each man. Conversation with these particular guests would be as entertaining as hunting pheasant. Like the bird, each was perfectly still, doing nothing to draw attention to himself. Each was depending on his protective coloring, his semblance to the other hunters, to save him. As he came closer, all would take wing like the pheasant. Unlike the pheasant, none of his human game would have the distinction of escaping.

He smiled.

The Hunt should be very enjoyable.

He tightened his bolo tie, drawing attention to the huge chunk of polished green turquoise set in silver that formed the clasp. A ring, watchband, and belt buckle were also set with the same rare green stone. It was an ensemble whose price could and did support a Navajo silversmith's family for a year. Unlike the pheasant, Frederick Lee Hansford III had no desire to be overlooked.

He descended the last few steps into the room and clasped the shoulder of a stocky man with thinning red hair. "Brad, you started without me. I'm hurt." He felt the other man flinch and smiled. "But, of course, you had other guests, and I *was* late. A few loans I needed to check. You understand how it is.

We bankers can't really keep bankers' hours, particularly if we want our institutions to remain financially solvent and profitable. Sometimes we have to call in loans, even accommodation loans made to other banks."

Noting the other man's pallor, he smiled again. "As president of Carroll National Bank, I'm sure you can sympathize with my decisions. Now, if you'll excuse me"—meaningless word choice as *he* always excused others from his presence rather than the reverse—"I'll go have a drink."

Stepping around a wizened man dressed in a beige Western shirt and pants and placidly enjoying a cheek full of tobacco, he walked toward the bar. His remaining game were huddled around it for mutual protection. That was unsportsmanlike. He wanted the joy of stalking each one from corner to corner and from group to group.

"Good evening, gentlemen," he said, nodding to each one. "Mr. Johnson, if you're acting as bartender, I'll have a glass of Scotch."

"I'm not," said Ick Johnson, setting an open bottle down on the bar just beyond Hansford's reach.

"I beg your pardon?"

Ick took a sip of his drink, swirled it around his mouth, and swallowed with an audible sound of pleasure. "I'm not acting as bartender. If a man wants a drink, he serves himself."

Hansford smiled. A certain amount of defiance on the quarry's part made a hunt more interesting. "Haven't you heard that politeness pays?"

"It won't this time, will it? So I don't have to mind my manners if I don't feel like it." Ick took another swallow of his drink. "And I *don't* feel like it."

Hansford heard someone behind him expel a whistling breath and knew it was time to make this kill. "How's your hardware business, Ick? Is your gross up from last quarter? I hope so"—he picked up a paper napkin—"because you're too old to go back to being a roustabout in the oil fields." He tore the napkin in two.

Ick Johnson slammed his glass down. It shattered, and ice cubes skittered across the polished surface of the bar. He stared dumbly at the spreading pool of blended whiskey, then turned and shouldered his way through the crowd.

Hansford blotted up the spilled drink, then circled around

behind the bar. "Ick seems to have left without naming a successor." He smiled at the men standing in front of the bar. "I'll take his place"—he smiled again—"as bartender, of course," he added gently. "I wouldn't want any of you to misunderstand me."

"Ain't no danger of that, Mr. Hansford. We all understand you just fine."

"Mr. Adams, isn't it?"

The old man gripped the edge of the bar. "You know damn well who's talking to you. Your daddy's knowed me since Hector was a pup. Been a good friend, too. You sure ain't a-tall like him."

"I'll give my father your regards," he said, pouring a scant inch of Scotch into a glass. "Did you make a good crop this year? But I shouldn't be asking that question during a party, should I? Falling farm prices and rising costs are depressing topics. Almost as depressing as tales of forced farm sales and foreclosures, wouldn't you agree?"

He lifted the bottle of Scotch. "Not the finest brand, perhaps, but it'll do. May I pour you a drink?"

Bill Adams rubbed his hand across his chin. "I got a pack of coyotes on my place been killing my calves. They're honest varmints just doing what's natural to them. They see a calf and they're hungry, they'll kill it. But they sure don't stand around tormenting it first. It's two-legged varmints who do that." He touched the front brim of his hat. "Never mind pouring that drink. I reckon I'd rather keep company with that pack of coyotes than some folks I could mention. Be seeing you."

Rage, like a sudden gust of wind-blown rain against a window, blurred his vision of the old man walking toward the stairs. He took a deep breath, blinked to clear his eyes, and loosened his grip on the bottle of Scotch. That one he would especially enjoy destroying. Not because Adams had called him a coyote—as a banker, he was used to worse epithets than that—but because the old man had compared him to his father.

And found him wanting.

He focused his attention on the last of his prey. He poured drinks for other hunters who wandered up to the bar, even laughed at a few coarse jokes, all the while waiting for his quarry to come closer. And finally, when the crowd in front of the bar thinned down to a single grizzled individual at the far end, the quarry moved closer.

"What do you want here, Hansford?"

"Why, the same as you. I came to hunt." And he tilted his head back and laughed.

CHAPTER 1

"HOW LONG YOU BEEN HERE, SHERIFF?"
Charles loosened his grip on the windowsill and turned to face his chief deputy. "Since about five, I guess. I don't know."

"You want some coffee?"

"I'm not up to Miss Poole's idea of coffee."

Meenie Higgins shifted his wad of tobacco to his other cheek. "She ain't here yet. I made this pot myself. Figured you might need some."

"You did, huh? You taken up fortune-telling, Meenie?"

"Don't have to. I drove by here on my way to breakfast. Your office lights was on and I could see someone in the window. Had to be you. Ain't nobody else in the department as tall. Figured if you was up this early, you needed some company."

Without looking the deputy spat in the general direction of the spittoon. Charles hoped the cleaning crew hadn't moved it. "I'll get that coffee now. When Slim gets here, I'll send him out for some of them egg and sausage biscuits you like. That's something maybe he can do without messin' up too bad." Meenie closed the door behind him.

Charles leaned against the windowsill and crossed his arms. His coat sleeves felt cold and he shivered. How long *had* he been standing in front of the ill-fitting window and staring at the street three stories below? Long enough to give himself a hell of a bellyache, he thought as he crossed the office to his desk. He couldn't stop the stream of pickups, cars, RVs, and every other type of vehicle ever dreamed of by Detroit or its Japanese equivalent. Even if he could, most Crawford County residents would consider such an act as least as unpatriotic as burning the flag. Some might even consider it blasphemy.

He fumbled in his desk drawer for the bottle of antacid pills he always kept there. Uncapping the bottle, he shook out two tablets and popped them into his mouth.

"You ain't supposed to be taking those things. They're bad for your ulcer." Meenie Higgins stood in the doorway with a disapproving look and two mugs of coffee.

"I don't have an ulcer," said Charles automatically, taking one of the mugs and ignoring the disapproving look. "And I don't recall your ever telling me you had a medical degree."

"I ain't. Doc Wallace told me. He thought maybe between me and Miss Angie, we could get you healed up."

"Dr. Wallace has a big mouth, and he exaggerates," said Charles, rubbing his stomach where the ulcer he didn't have was making itself felt. "Did you want something or were you just checking up on me? If it's the latter, you can leave as quietly as you came. Or did you knock and I just didn't hear you?"

"Who put a burr under your saddle?" Meenie asked, sitting down in a wooden armchair and tilting it back to a comfortable angle.

"I don't need any Western metaphors either."

"Then you shoulda stayed in Dallas instead of comin' to the Texas Panhandle. They probably talk a little fancier down there. But you ain't gonna get out of answering my question by insulting me. My skin's tougher than bull buffalo hide. What's botherin' you, Sheriff?"

Charles massaged the back of his neck and considered his chief deputy. Meenie Higgins was the oldest man in the Crawford County Sheriff's Department, somewhere between fifty and forever. Measuring about five feet seven inches in his high-heeled cowboy boots, he was also the shortest. He was several teeth short of a full set, scrawny as an old rooster, chewed tobacco incessantly, never finished high school, never backed down from a fight, made Charles's business his own, and was the finest man Charles had ever known. He was also the most stubborn. He'd sit in that chair until the Second Coming if that's how long it took to get his question answered.

Charles capitulated. It was either that or pick up Meenie and throw him out of the office. "You know what today is?"

Meenie lifted his Stetson and scratched the bald spot on the back of his head. "It's Saturday, but I don't think that's what's giving you a bellyache, so you must be talking about it being opening day of pheasant season. You get wire-edged this time every year."

"If you mean I get nervous, yes! Good God, Meenie! Do you know how many hunters are predicted to be in Crawford County by noon today? Eight thousand! That will damn near double the population of this town."

"I bet the farmers and the Chamber of Commerce are happy. Eight thousand hunters means a pot full of money."

Charles slammed his fist on the top of the desk. "It means a pot full of guns!"

"You can't kill a pheasant with a slingshot."

"I know that!"

Meenie propped his feet on Charles's desk. "Don't borrow trouble, Sheriff. Worst thing that ever happened during pheasant season around here was when one of them Fort Worth bankers Brad Masters invited got caught crosswise in a barbed-wire fence. Doc Wallace sewed him up, and he was back huntin' that afternoon. He wasn't very comfortable sittin' down, but he was good-natured about it. Said a fellow didn't hunt pheasant sittin' down anyway."

The deputy slurped at his coffee with such placid unconcern that Charles gritted his teeth. "Then there was the year a hunter got excited and didn't get his gun up high enough. Peppered old man Adams's brand-new Ford pickup with buckshot. The old man wasn't even peeved. Said you just had to expect a few accidents. 'Course he charged the hunter for the damage."

Meenie closed one eye and peered at Charles with the other. "As for anything serious, you can quit worrying. Crawford County ain't lost a hunter since the first pheasant was let loose in the Panhandle back in Forty-one."

"I presume you mean 1941?"

"Wasn't nobody around here but Comanches in 1841—and they hunted buffalo."

"And not for sport, either," interrupted Charles, consciously unclenching his teeth. Meenie's reasonable tone of voice was endangering his dental health. "They didn't send the carcass to a taxidermist to have it stuffed and mounted to set on the mantel. They ate the meat and used the hide for clothing and shelter. They hunted to survive, not for some half-assed macho ego thing."

Meenie hooked his thumbs in his belt and studied Charles.

"It ain't just the guns that's got you stirred up, is it, Sheriff? You just don't like huntin'."

Charles felt a flash of irritation at Meenie's intuitiveness. "No, I don't. Does that make me a leper?"

Meenie turned his head, expectorated in the general direction of the spittoon, patted his mouth with a folded bandana, and considered the question. "It danged sure makes you different," he finally admitted. "Folks around here figure you can't help that, being raised in Dallas"—he shrugged—"and all the rest of it. Kinda puts you at a disadvantage."

Charles's stern face relaxed into its first smile of the day. His socialite mother would be appalled at hearing a tobacco-chewing cowboy-turned-deputy dismiss her son's privileged upbringing as disadvantaged. But Meenie was right. With the possible exception of his law degree and his brief experience as an assistant district attorney in Dallas, not a damn thing in Charles Timothy Matthews's background prepared him for being a county sheriff in the Texas Panhandle.

"So I'm an oddity," he mused. "But I'm forgiven because I'm an outsider."

Meenie cleared his throat. "That ain't exactly true."

"That I'm forgiven or that I'm an outsider?" he asked, watching Meenie glance around the room as if looking for some way to change the subject. A desk, a few wooden chairs, a battered filing cabinet—these furnishings didn't offer much in the way of conversational gambits. Charles waited for his deputy to admit defeat and answer his question.

Meenie shifted his tobacco from one cheek to the other. "Ain't nothing for anybody to forgive. Nobody in this office has said anything about your not bein' partial to hunting. Being sheriff is an elected office. Ain't no reason to bother folks who vote with something that don't amount to a hill of beans."

"Do you mean I wouldn't have won if the electorate had known I don't like hunting? Do you mean they would have voted for the incumbent—even though incompetent is the kindest thing I can say about him?"

"There ain't no need to raise your voice, Sheriff. Maybe you'd've won anyway—no way of telling—but there wasn't no need of letting the campaign get bogged down in a man's personal beliefs. So long as he don't try to shove them down other folks' throats."

"I'm no hypocrite, damn it!"

"There you go yellin' again. I never said you was, and neither has anybody else. Not talking about something's not the same as lying about it. I think you'll get reelected next time—even if the voters find out you're a little peculiar. You're doing your best considering what you are."

"You make me sound like a two-headed calf."

Meenie scratched his skinny neck. "No, you're more like a pheasant. You ain't native to the Panhandle, but you've settled in and adapted. You're the first sheriff Crawford County ever had that wears fancy suits to work, but you wear them with boots and a Stetson. That's adapting."

"There's one big difference between the pheasant and me," said Charles dryly. "I don't have eight thousand hunters shooting at me."

"There ain't nothing you can do to stop the hunt, so you might as well quit sittin' behind that desk getting worked up over it."

"That happens to be the first thing you've said this morning that I agree with," said Charles, standing up and taking off his suit jacket. "If you can't beat them, join them. Hand me my sheepherder's coat, Meenie. It's fifteen degrees outside, and I don't intend to freeze while I'm tramping through somebody's field."

Meenie looked alarmed, or as close as Charles imagined his tough deputy could come to such an expression. "Now, just a minute. I never said nothing about you going hunting yourself. I don't think the voters will expect that."

"The voters have nothing to do with it, and I'm not going hunting," said Charles, getting his heavy fleece-trimmed coat himself. Picking up his black Stetson from its habitual resting place on top of the filing cabinet and setting it firmly on his head, he opened the door. "If you need me, have Miss Poole use the radio."

Meenie upset his chair in his hurry to follow Charles. "I ain't gonna have to use the radio, 'cause I ain't fixing to let you out of my sight. Let a man who hates hunting loose around a bunch of hunters—and voters—and he's gonna cause more trouble than a teetotaler in a beer joint on Saturday night."

Charles slammed his door and turned around. "What time is it?"

Meenie stepped back and fumbled a pocket watch out of his pants. "It's seven o'clock."

"Damn it! Mabel's still the dispatcher."

"Until Miss Poole comes in at eight."

"It can't be helped. I'm not waiting around an hour until the shift change." Charles drew a deep breath and relaxed his jaw. "Remind me not to grind my teeth. According to my dentist, it's a potentially injurious habit."

"Your teeth gonna fall out?"

"No. My jaw will drop off."

He opened the door again and marched toward his dispatcher's desk with all the enthusiasm of Louis XVI marching to the guillotine. He stared at his dispatcher and gritted his teeth. When he'd been elected sheriff three years ago, he'd inherited battered desks, filing cabinets whose drawers hung halfway, handcuffs with no keys, a jail that hadn't been painted for twenty years, and Mabel Honeycutt and her archaic radio system. His first official act had been to invite the county commissioners to hold their monthly meeting in the sheriff's office. One commissioner had sprained his back when the chair he was sitting on collapsed; another ruptured a hernia trying to pull out a filing cabinet drawer. A locksmith had to be called when still another commissioner handcuffed himself to the radiator. Charles admitted his strategy did get results. The commissioners voted to remodel the county clerk's office and donate the previous furnishings to the sheriff's department. They did authorize one outlay of cash: they paid the locksmith to make new keys for the handcuffs.

Since none of the commissioners had been electrocuted by the old communication system, they didn't see the need for a new one. Which meant Charles couldn't fire Mabel. She was the only person in the entire county who could keep the radio working.

"Mabel," Charles said, clasping his hands behind his back, the better not to strangle her.

Meenie nudged him. "You're grinding your teeth again."

"Yes, Sheriff," she answered in a nasal tone of voice. It was a medical fact that adenoids atrophy at age fifteen. Charles decided Mabel was a case of arrested development.

"Mabel," Charles repeated, leaning over the dispatcher's desk to search the woman's eyes. It was a challenge since the lenses of Mabel's glasses were blurred with a variety of smears, stains, and spots, the nature of which he didn't care to examine too closely. "I want one man to stay in the office and everyone else out in their cars patrolling the county roads. *County* roads, Mabel, not the highway. The Department of

Public Safety can take care of that. I want the patrols to concentrate on the northern part of the county where the farms are located. The ranchers in the southern part can take care of themselves for the duration."

Mabel blinked. "The duration of what, Sheriff?"

"The Hunt," he answered. "Tell the men to check out every field with hunters in it."

"That's every field in the county," interrupted Mabel.

Charles silently counted to ten. "I want them to check for unsafe use of firearms, invalid hunting licenses, and particularly"—he emphasized the word—"particularly, consumption of alcoholic beverages. Anyone who is inebriated and carrying a gun will be invited to spend the afternoon in the tank."

"The tank ain't big enough, Sheriff," said Meenie, pushing his hat to the back of his head and looking worried.

"Then we'll rent the community building."

"Sheriff Johnson never arrested any hunters!" Mabel's voice squealed at exactly the same frequency as the radio set.

Charles waited until the echo of her voice died away. "Sheriff Johnson was too busy cooking calf fries and drinking beer at the noon feed, or charging hunters a hundred dollars a day to hunt his fields to worry about a few accidents. Hunters shooting off toes and fingers or peppering one another in the rump with buckshot didn't count. As long as no one was actually killed, he was satisfied. But he never had *eight thousand* greenhorns with shotguns running around looking for something to shoot."

"You're yellin' again," muttered his deputy.

Mabel sniffed in disapproval. Any attack on former Sheriff Johnson was an attack on God. "They're experienced gentlemen hunters."

"They are experienced bankers, insurance agents, hardware salesmen, and maybe a kid or two on his first hunt. Most of them fire a gun three or four times a year: duck season, deer season, and pheasant season." Charles stopped and drew a deep breath. Meenie was right; he *was* yelling again. "Just do your job, Mabel, and let me worry about the consequences," he continued in a quieter voice. "And pass along my instructions to Miss Poole."

Mabel smiled, or Charles supposed the smirk on her face qualified as a smile. "Miss Poole won't be in today."

She sounded pleased about something—and Charles braced

himself. Mabel had a knack for knowing exactly what irritated the hell out of him.

"Why not?"

"She's going pheasant hunting out on old man Adams's place." Mabel was almost snickering.

Charles reached out to clutch the desk. Surely the world had tilted on its axis. Miss Poole hunting? A sixty-year-old retired spinster schoolteacher hunting? His puritanical day-shift dispatcher hunting? He caught Mabel and Meenie staring at him, Mabel sporting that same smirk. He swallowed. "Well, Meenie, we won't have to check out Mr. Adams's field. Miss Poole won't allow anyone to pop a beer can in *her* presence."

He turned toward the waiting area with its cracked vinyl couch and chairs. "It's too bad we can't clone her, but since we can't, you and I will have to do our best to keep the peace in the other fields, Meenie."

Meenie aimed a stream of tobacco juice at a spittoon as he followed Charles. "The only peace I'm worried about is the *piece* some hunter's going to shoot off your behind when you throw him in the tank for drinking a can of beer."

CHAPTER 2

CHARLES WALKED OUT OF THE COURTHOUSE INTO A north wind so cold it made his teeth ache. Or maybe they still hurt from his clenching them while talking to Mabel. Between the weather and Mabel, his teeth might not last through pheasant season.

He shivered and pulled on his gloves, wishing he had remained in his office. Mabel endangered his teeth; this damn wind endangered every extremity a man possessed. It rattled through the elm trees that lined the courthouse square, whipping off a dead leaf or two that still clung tenaciously to the branches. It pushed a dried tumbleweed down the middle of Carroll Avenue (otherwise known as Highway 87), swirled dirt from the gutters, whistled around buildings, and lashed at the traffic lights with enough force to set them swaying on their cables.

The streetlights were still on, illuminating empty sidewalks and closed stores. All closed but one, that is. The hardware store directly across the square from the courthouse had been open since five A.M. Business was brisk, Charles noticed, turning up his collar against the wind. It ought to be, he thought as he unlocked his car and slid into its frigid interior. Benny's Hardware sold hunting licenses.

"Cold as a gold digger's butt in the Klondike out there," grumbled Meenie as he crawled in the passenger side. "Those pheasant gonna be hunkered down in the stubble. You'll have to kick them in the tail feathers to make them take wing."

"Good for the pheasant," grunted Charles, flicking the heater on high and hoping Meenie would forgo his habit of riding with the car window rolled down.

It was a vain hope. The deputy promptly rolled down the

window and tested the direction of the wind, then settled back against the seat. "Where you aiming to go first, Sheriff?" he asked, shifting his tobacco to his other cheek and spitting out the open window.

Charles pulled his collar higher against the right side of his face to counter the draught from the window. "North, then east, I guess," he said, starting the car and pulling out into traffic. "That's where most of the milo is grown, so that's where most of the stubble fields will be."

Meenie fiddled with his coat buttons, a nervous gesture Charles had never noticed before. "You ain't fixing to hassle them hunters, are you, Sheriff?"

"I'm not planning to hassle anyone, Meenie. Don't worry. I won't alienate any more voters than I have to."

"That ain't what's got me worried." Meenie rubbed his scraggly chin where he was unsuccessfully trying to grow a beard. "You're real rich, ain't you, Sheriff?"

Charles felt surprise, then the familiar suspicion he always experienced when confronted by that question. Too frequently it preceded a request for a loan. Moreover, it made him feel alienated from the rest of society. Like a two-headed calf. Or a pheasant.

"What does that have to do with anything?"

"Don't get your feathers ruffled. I ain't criticizing, but you ain't never been between a rock and a hard place like these farmers. A couple of them have to have a good pheasant crop this season, or they ain't gonna make their land payment to the bank. In other words, the hunters are the only thing between them and the bank takin' their land. Cut them hunters some slack so they don't go off to some other county to do their shooting. Our boys need their money too bad to let that happen."

"Meaning?"

Meenie sighed and pushed his hat back. "Meaning it might not be a hunter that takes a shot at you if you get to pushing too hard."

Charles gripped the steering wheel a little harder and stared through the windshield at the narrow strip of asphalt that ran arrow-straight between the fields, one faintly green with winter wheat, the other beige with milo stubble. The land. The words ought to be capitalized, he thought, because to the men of the Panhandle it was more than dirt, more than a way of life. It *was* life. Every standard, every code, every law, was measured against what was good for the land. He felt cheated suddenly. He had no roots in the land; he was a transplant from the city. There, one measured wealth in stocks and bonds and securities, symbols of power. A man was worth however much he could buy. Here, one measured wealth in bushels of wheat, of corn, of milo or soybeans, or head of livestock, symbols of the land. A man was worth only what he could produce.

"I'm not going to ignore a drunk with a gun," said Charles finally.

"No one's asking you to. But a coupla swigs of beer after two or three hours walking don't make a drunk."

"How about cutting me some slack, Meenie? Give me some credit for not being a complete fool. And by the way, how did you know I was wealthy?"

Meenie managed to spit out the window and throw him a disgusted look at the same time. Charles was glad it wasn't the other way around. "I ain't no fool either, Sheriff. Them suits you wear cost more than I make in a month, and you must pay five or six hundred dollars for your boots. And I happen to know you put your whole salary in a scholarship fund over at the Carroll National Bank."

Charles whipped his head around to stare at his deputy. "How do you know that? Does my banker have as big a mouth as my doctor?"

"I got my sources."

"Isn't a man entitled to any privacy?"

Meenie gave him another disgusted look. "In Crawford County? Sheriff, the only subjects we got to talk about is each other."

"Damn it, Meenie, there are some matters that are nobody's business, like what a man does with his money and how he behaves in the bedroom."

"How a man spends his money and whose bedroom he sheds his britches in are the two things folks talk about the most. Everybody knows you ain't hanging your pants on Miss Angie's bedpost—so that just leaves money. Now, a poor man can't afford to throw his money around like you do, so I figure you gotta be rich, but you don't have to worry. I don't hold your money against you."

Charles started to laugh, but the expression on Meenie's face stopped the laughter cold. His deputy was serious. Not only did Meenie consider a privileged boyhood a disadvantage, but he considered wealth in the same way. It was enough to humble John D. Rockefeller, not to mention Charles Timothy Matthews.

"Then why doesn't everyone in town know I don't like to hunt?" he asked.

Meenie shrugged his shoulders. "That's just peculiar. Money's interesting."

"And sex."

Meenie's face turned pink as he nodded. Charles stifled a chuckle. For a man of his deputy's age, whatever that was, and in his profession, Meenie Higgins was curiously reluctant to utter the word *sex*. Whatever the reason for Meenie's reticence, Charles was grateful it existed. It was the only sure way to shut him up.

Charles cleared his throat and turned on the radio to listen for Mabel's calls to the other units. There was only the hum of static. "Damn it, what a time for the radio to quit. This is car thirty-two. Mabel, are you there?"

Static, then a voice. "Is anybody listening?"

Before Charles could answer, Mabel's nasal voice beat him to it. "This is the Crawford County Sheriff's Department. This channel is for official use only. Please get off the air."

"I know it's the official channel, damn it. That's why I'm using it." The speaker sounded exasperated. Charles could sympathize. Mabel always had that effect on him, too.

"What is your call number?" demanded Mabel.

"I don't have a blasted call number, lady, but you'd better get me Sheriff Matthews before you're another minute older." The voice was past exasperation and approaching frustration.

Charles cut in. "This is Sheriff Matthews."

"You can't just talk to the sheriff like that," protested Mabel, her voice approaching a squeal. "You have to give your call number."

"Mabel, shut up!" There was a final squeal, then silence. "Thank you. Now, please identify yourself and explain why you're using this channel."

"Matthews, is that you?" demanded a voice.

"It was when I looked in the mirror this morning," Charles replied, frowning. There was something familiar about that voice. Or rather, something familiar about the accent.

"This is Lindman—"

"Sheriff Lindman?"

"There ain't but one of us, Matthews," said the voice impatiently.

One was enough, thought Charles. Christopher "Kit" Lindman, Hispanic from his head to his toes except for bright blue eyes and a Norwegian accent inherited from his father, was sheriff of Union County, New Mexico. He was the only man Charles knew who could curse for ten minutes in three languages and not repeat himself. He was also stubborn, opinionated, short-tempered, totally honest, probably wouldn't jail a man for drinking a beer on a hunt, and a good man to have on one's side. But that didn't mean that Charles wanted him roaming around Crawford County.

"What in the devil are you doing in my county, Lindman?" he demanded.

Lindman sighed. Charles swore he could hear a Norwegian accent in even that wordless expression. "I came to bag a few pheasant, but right now I'm sitting on my ass in a Crawford County patrol car watching one of your deputies puke his guts out in the bar ditch. Tell your dispatcher I'd find out what his call number is, except he won't stop puking long enough for me to ask him."

"You're calling me to report one of my deputies is sick?"

"He ain't exactly sick," said Lindman. "He just don't appear to have a very strong stomach. Can't say as I blame him, though. It's enough to make a grown man queasy, and I don't think your deputy is quite growed."

"What in the hell are you talking about, Lindman?"

"I'm trying to tell you, Matthews. There's been a little hunting accident, and one of your fair citizens has blown his head off."

Charles swallowed convulsively and wondered what Lindman would consider a *big* hunting accident. Dressed in Army camouflage clothes by way of Abercrombie and Fitch, the victim lay on his back, staring at the gray, overcast sky. Rather, he would have been staring at it if he'd had any eyes. He didn't have a face, either. A Remington automatic 12-gauge shotgun lay by his outflung right hand. The amount of damage such a weapon could do at close range had to be seen to be believed. The other hunters, about fifteen men, stood far enough away to avoid seeing. Slim Fletcher was still on his knees by the bar ditch. Other than Lindman, only one other hunter seemed in control of both stomach and situation.

"With the assistance of Sheriff Lindman, I was able to preserve the accident scene. Slim was too incapacitated to be of any help." Miss Poole, dressed in bright yellow baggy pants and an insulated jacket and resting the barrel of a lethal-looking shotgun on the toe of her boot, resolutely kept her back to the corpse.

Lindman shook his head. "I can't steal your thunder, Miss Poole. All I did was try to convince that old biddy with the overgrown adenoids to let me holler at the sheriff. You did all the rest. You should have seen her, Matthews. She herded all those hunters away from the body without taking back-talk from any of them. Not that many of them had too much to say. Half look to be city boys. Leastwise, their boots don't have scuff marks on the soles. They're the ones with faces about as green as a three-day-old fish. Of course, that color could be from the chewing tobacco. Farmers won't allow smoking in their fields, so all these boys buy themselves a tin of chewing tobacco for the hunt. Most of them don't chew except once a year. Takes some practice to do it right. Always some who forget to spit. Swallowing tobacco juice will make a fellow look peaked. Then too, I figure some of them might have eaten their whole chew when they saw the victim. Sort of lost track of what they were doing."

He lifted his Stetson and scratched his head. "The rest must be from around here because they're tougher. They all looked a little sick, but they didn't lose their breakfasts. Except your deputy over there. You might ought to call him an ambulance, Matthews. The vet had to shoot the last critter I saw that sick."

"If we can get back to the subject," interjected Charles. His jaw was clenched so hard that his whole head ached.

"Yeah, sure, Matthews. As I was saying, Miss Poole lined up all them hunters like cattle going through a branding chute, and got their names and addresses. You got a real jewel in this little lady." He slapped Charles on the back. "Woman reminds me of a drill sergeant I had in the Marines," Lindman added under his breath.

Charles smiled. It was an unpleasant smile, more in the nature of a wolf baring his teeth, and he knew it. Furthermore, he didn't care. "I know exactly what I have in Miss Poole, Lindman," he said softly. "I have a dispatcher who is pheasant hunting when she should be dispatching." He glanced at his watch, then at Miss Poole. "If you leave now, you'll only be an hour late for work. If you are very, very lucky, you might be able to straighten out the confusion I'm sure Mabel is busily spreading before the end of your shift. Take Slim's patrol car—

and Slim, since he also is supposed to be at work instead of taking pot shots at birds."

Slim staggered to his feet, detoured around the body, and grabbed Charles's coat. "But, Sheriff, I was just going to bust a cap or two before I went to work." His face was dead white under his freckles. Even his blond beard looked bleached.

Charles glared and Slim jerked his hand back as though he'd touched a hot stove. "Go back to the office with Miss Poole, Slim, and don't let me catch you hunting on county time again."

"We're witnesses, Sheriff. Don't you want to take our statements?" Miss Poole asked.

Charles bared his teeth again. "Write them up back at the office, Miss Poole."

"Slim and I can take preliminary statements from the other hunters."

"Miss Poole, the only thing I want you and Slim to take is yourselves back to the office. I've already called other deputies."

Miss Poole looked thoughtfully at Charles. "But if every deputy is here laboriously taking statements in longhand and Slim and I are babysitting the office, who will be patrolling the rest of the county? Who will be checking on those thousands and thousands of hunters? And I do take shorthand."

She touched the knot of gray hair pinned securely at the back of her head as if checking to see if each hair was exactly where she wanted it. Charles had a feeling he was another hair, and Miss Poole had just put him in his place. "All right, Miss Poole, I see your point. You may stay. Slim can go back to town."

Miss Poole touched her hair again. "That would mean Slim and Mabel would be alone."

Charles shuddered. If Mabel created confusion, Slim created catastrophe. The prospect of what the two together could create boggled the mind. "Miss Poole, have you ever been in the Marines?"

"I beg your pardon?"

"Never mind. Just tell me what happened."

Miss Poole pursed her mouth for a moment. Charles knew she was lining up events in one-two-three order. He could almost hear the clink as each event fell into place like beads on a string. "We arrived just at dawn—"

"We?" interrupted Charles.

"The hunters," explained Miss Poole impatiently. "We parked at the other end of the field"—she gestured toward a cluster of cars parked on a dirt road at least two hundred yards away—"and discussed who would block and who would hunt. Someone suggested that the *fuzz* block for the first sweep, so Slim, Sheriff Lindman, and myself drove to this end of the field."

"Block?" asked Charles.

Miss Poole gave him a disapproving look. "You really should learn more about pheasant hunting, Sheriff. It is an annual event in Crawford County."

"So is chicken pox, Miss Poole, but I don't think it's necessary to expose myself to that either."

That gained him an even more disapproving look. "A blocker is an individual who stands at the edge of the field to prevent birds from running field to field. The hunters walk side by side in a line toward the blockers. The birds are caught between the hunters and the blockers and take wing to escape. The hunters shoot at the cocks, or male pheasant."

"You mean a line of hunters fires shotguns toward the blockers?" asked Charles.

"They fire at the birds in the air."

"And the blockers hope the birds are more than head high," observed Charles, thinking a metal helmet and a bulletproof vest ought to be required dress for a blocker.

"That goes without saying. Some blockers do keep a low profile if the hunters don't flush any birds until near the end of the field."

"She means if a bird flies up in your face, you better be belly down in the dirt damn fast," interrupted Lindman.

"Good reflexes are important," agreed Miss Poole.

"And the victim didn't have good reflexes?"

"I have no idea," said Miss Poole. "But good reflexes aren't very helpful if you're careless."

"Meaning what?"

Miss Poole tilted her head back toward the corpse. "He obviously climbed out of his vehicle without being open and empty. His shotgun open and the shell removed from the chamber," she explained when Charles looked puzzled. "No careful hunter ever drives, or climbs in or out of a car with a loaded gun. He must have done so and tripped. His gun discharged and now Crawford County has its first fatal hunting accident."

Charles looked over her shoulder at the victim. His head was approximately two feet from a white Suburban, the vehicle of choice for any Texan who could afford one. "You saw this happen?" he asked Miss Poole.

"No, but I'm reconstructing the scene."

"Lindman, did you see what happened?"

"I didn't see a goddamn thing, Matthews."

"Sheriff," began Miss Poole.

"Slim, did you see the accident?" demanded Charles.

The young deputy swallowed. "I didn't see anything but what was left of him."

Miss Poole tried again. "Sheriff—"

"Then who witnessed the accident? One of the other hunters?"

"No one did," answered Miss Poole.

"What? Are you telling me this man blew away his face and none of you even saw him fall? I know this whole north end of the county sounds like World War III with a shotgun going off every five seconds, but damn it, didn't any of the three of you notice this blast was closer than the next field?"

"Sheriff!" Miss Poole used her most authoritative schoolmarm voice, the one that always made Charles feel as if he were a sixth grader caught throwing spitballs during class.

"What is it, Miss Poole?"

"No one saw the accident because the poor man was already dead when we arrived."

CHAPTER 3

"YOU STILL CARRY THAT BRANDY FLASK IN YOUR HIP pocket, Sheriff?" asked Mrs. Jenkins.

Charles silently passed the flask to the stout justice of the peace. Viola Jenkins was barely five feet tall, had two chins, and a bosom wide enough to set a coffee cup on, with hips to match. Anyone else her size wearing an orange ski jacket and pants would look like a pumpkin. Charles decided she did, too, but a majestic pumpkin.

She lowered the brandy level in the flask by half and handed it back. "I hate pronouncing people dead, Sheriff."

Charles tucked the flask in his pocket and watched Meenie searching the victim's pockets while the Parker brothers, Crawford County's only morticians, loomed like tall, thin vultures over the corpse. "You knew that was part of it when you ran for office."

She stuck her hands in her coat pockets. "Is that why you didn't campaign for me? Did you think I had a weak constitution? I know it wasn't necessarily because I'm a woman because you didn't support my opponent either, and he's a man. At least, he buttons his shirts on the right side and uses the men's room, if that means anything. I'll tell you something, Sheriff. I may look like a marshmallow, but I'm tough. A short woman has to be. Everybody tries to run over her, including taller women. I can take almost anything, but I'm tired of looking at dead bodies. It started last summer with those two murders on the Branding Iron ranch. I figured that outside of a car wreck or two, I'd seen my quota of corpses for my whole four years in office."

She sniffed and wiped her nose on her sleeve. "Well, I figured wrong. First it was that head-on collision north of town that killed five people. Then old man Pace got drunk and wrapped himself around that cottonwood tree. The only damn tree within five miles of his place and he had to hit it. He always did have bad luck. I told my sister so when she married him, but she said hard work made up for luck. Maybe it did when she was alive, but since then it's been a different story. He left his daughter Maggie in a hell of a fix, too. His land was in hock to the bank, and he'd let his insurance lapse."

She looked up at Charles. "You heard Maggie threw in the towel."

Charles nodded. Maggie Pace's story was only one chapter in the tragedy overtaking too many of the county's farmers.

"Turned the land back to the bank, auctioned everything on the place to cover her pa's debts, and came out flat broke," Viola Jenkins continued. "Brad Masters gave her a job over at the bank. Pretty rough having to work for the people that turned you off your land. Brad felt bad about the whole thing. Didn't want to foreclose on her, but I heard he didn't have much choice. It's not official yet, but they've been talking about getting married—so maybe something good will come out of the mess."

She sighed. "Maggie Pace wasn't the only woman badly served by her menfolk. When Cecil McCormick committed suicide, he left his wife with two little kids to raise. She went home to her folks, so I guess she'll be all right. Or as right as she can be having to live with knowing her husband was a coward. Cecil never did have any backbone, or not much anyway, and I guess he couldn't face going bust."

She shook her head. "Murders, suicides, now a hunting accident. Things like that don't happen in Crawford County. It's unnatural." She looked over at the corpse. "I hope this is my last dead body for the year, Sheriff. This is December seventh. Think I can make it twenty-four more days?"

Charles swallowed. He had a sour taste in his mouth and a burning in his belly. Both symptoms recurred when he was angry and violent death always made him angry. "I don't know, Mrs. Jenkins. We've got thirteen more days of pheasant season."

She pulled out an orange stocking cap and pulled it over her graying curls. "Do me a favor, Sheriff. The next idiot that climbs out of a car with a loaded gun pointed toward his head instead of the ground"—she hesitated—"move the body to another J.P.'s jurisdiction. I've had enough bloodletting for a while. I've seen so much of the Parker brothers, I could almost get to like them. *If* they didn't enjoy their work so much. Don't let them charge the county for washing that white hearse. They could've used the second-best one."

She walked toward her old Ford, then turned around. "I did you a favor, Sheriff. Dr. Akin was hunting in one of my fields. I chased him out before I came. He ought to be in Amarillo by now waiting for the body. Seems kind of silly to do an autopsy on a hunting accident—a damn fool could figure out what killed him—but that's the law. I figure Dr. Akin'll do a fast autopsy so he can get back to his hunting."

She climbed into her car, which immediately tilted to the left, and waved. "Remember what I said about the next body, Sheriff." She drove off with the rattle of a faulty muffler that trailed a cloud of black exhaust smoke.

Charles walked over to the corpse. He nodded to the Parker brothers, observing, not for the first time, their long noses and prominent Adam's apples. They truly did resemble vultures. All they needed was a dead tree to perch in.

He stopped at the victim's feet. "Raul, did you get all the pictures you need?"

Deputy Raul Trujillo looked up from a sketch pad. "I think so, Sheriff. Now I'm sketching the location of the body with measurements of everything." His voice had a pleasant lilt, not quite a Spanish accent, but a cadence that Charles had noticed in many native Texans of Hispanic origin.

Charles looked from the Suburban to the body and back again. "Bag the victim's hands, Raul. Tell Doc Akin that I want a paraffin test. I'm sure the Special Crimes Unit in Amarillo will oblige a fellow law enforcement officer."

He turned to Meenie, who was holding a plastic bag containing the miscellaneous items found in the dead man's pocket: billfold, keys, change. "Meenie, haul that Suburban to the county barn, and go over it with a fine-tooth comb."

His deputy turned his head and spat, hitting a dried milo stalk ten feet away. Then he squinted up at Charles. "A fine-tooth comb is about all I got unless you bought us a lab in the last ten minutes. I got a fingerprint kit, a camera, graph paper, a tape measure, and a few paper bags for evidence. We ain't got that fancy equipment. Don't even have a microscope. I can borrow a vacuum sweeper with a clean bag from somebody and vacuum the floorboards, but what do you want me to do with the sweepings? Send them to the Department of Public

Safety lab in Austin? You'd have a long white beard before we heard from them."

"Send them to the Southwest Forensic Institute in Dallas along with a hair sample from the corpse. And Raul, you attend the autopsy and collect any hair and fibers from the deceased's clothes. And a blood sample, of course. Send those to Dallas, too. Fly them down."

"To Dallas!" exclaimed Meenie. "The county commission's gonna pin your hide to the courthouse door when they see the bill for that."

"I'll pay for it. As you pointed out, I'm rich, and I can't think of a better way to spend my money."

"The institute will be closed," said Raul. "It's Saturday."

"They'll open up. I know some people. One of the advantages of a wealthy, disadvantaged childhood is that I know who to call."

"What's eating you? We got a huntin' accident, and you're treating it like murder," said Meenie.

Charles waved his hand at the corpse. The Parker brothers swooped down. "Not yet," he snapped, and they stepped back. "Look at the body," he continued to Meenie and Raul. "If he climbed out of his Suburban with a loaded gun and tripped, why didn't he fall against the vehicle? His feet are approximately nine feet from the car, so presumedly he walked that far before he died. Did he trip over a clod of dirt, so that his shotgun discharged by accident? Or did he deliberately hold the gun under his chin and fire it? Look at the body! Tell me what he did!"

Meenie shifted his tobacco. "I'd just as soon not look again. I didn't have no breakfast, and if I keep lookin' at him, I ain't gonna want no lunch or supper either. As for how he removed his face, I don't know. But I've seen some funny things happen on hunting trips, things you'd swear couldn't happen. But they do."

"And do accident victims fall so neatly, Meenie?" asked Charles, watching his deputy's eyes. "Legs straight, knees and ankles almost touching, left arm by his side. Except for his right arm stretching toward the shotgun, the victim could be laid out for a wake. He didn't crumple from the force of the blast. He was arranged like a stuffed pheasant!" His forehead stung with icy beads of sweat, and he wiped his sleeve over his face thinking that 'hot with anger' was more than a cliché.

Meenie glanced at the corpse, then back at Charles. "I think you're saddling up the wrong horse when you start talking murder. You're kicking like a bay steer because you got a lot of folks with guns running around your stompin' ground. You know what they say about kickin', don't you?"

"No, I don't know, but I'm sure you'll enlighten me."

"Ain't no use kickin' unless you're a mule," said Meenie. "In other words, Sheriff, ain't no use in you complaining. You can't do nothing to change things."

"That's good advice, Meenie. Why don't you take it? Until I know differently, I'm treating this *accident* as a homicide, so quit complaining and examine that Suburban. Have you printed that billfold yet?"

"In this wind?" asked Meenie in disgust. "It'll blow the fingerprint powder to hell and back again. I'll do it in the patrol car. *And* I'll call for a wrecker to haul that car in." He walked off, mumbling to himself.

"Are you ready for the Parkers to take the body, Sheriff?" asked Raul, handing the sketch pad to Charles. "And what shall I tell Dr. Akin about the case?"

"You mean you don't think I'm paranoid?" demanded Charles. "You're not going to argue that this is a hunting accident?"

Raul rubbed his short, thick beard. "There aren't any footprints, Sheriff. And no drag marks, either. No evidence that the victim didn't walk here."

"And no evidence that he did. For God's sake, Raul, this ground is frozen solid. It has been for weeks. A herd of cattle wouldn't leave tracks."

"What if Dr. Akin rules it an accidental death?"

"Dr. Akin has to take into account the circumstances. The unnatural position of the body, for example, and the curious fact that no one seems to recognize it. Not one hunter has tugged on my coat sleeve to tell me this must be so-and-so."

"But his face is gone!" objected Raul.

"This is Mr. Adams's field. I'll make book that he knows every hunter that will be hunting on his property. Why hasn't he come over and told me one of his hunting party is missing?"

"Maybe he just picked this field at random," said Raul. "We have hunters trespassing every pheasant season."

"Then why hasn't anybody asked who the victim is? Why hasn't Mr. Adams asked? Don't you think it's curious that he isn't interested in knowing who's lying dead in his field?"

"I think it doesn't matter what I think. You've decided it's murder and I don't know if even Dr. Akin can change your mind."

"Raul, listen to me. Even if the victim picked this field at random, there is still another interesting question. If the victim wanted to bag the first pheasant of the season, who blocked for him? According to Miss Poole, the pheasant will run from field to field without taking wing *unless* someone blocks for the hunter. Who is the blocker, and why didn't he report the accident?"

The olive-skinned deputy turned to look at the group of hunters. "You're a stubborn man, Sheriff."

Charles shook his head. "No, I'm not. I'm a curious man. Why is everyone so anxious to dismiss this as a hunting accident? You, Meenie, Miss Poole, Mrs. Jenkins."

Raul turned back to Charles, his face expressionless. "Maybe it's better than suspecting your neighbor."

"Even if it means you're protecting a murderer?" asked Charles softly.

Raul's olive-toned skin paled, but his gaze didn't waver. "Haven't we done it before, Sheriff?"

CHAPTER 4

"HOW COME RAUL TOOK OFF LIKE HE HAD A POSSE on his tail?" asked Meenie as Charles slid into the patrol car. "That stiff's gonna be just as dead when he gets it to Amarillo."

"Have you finished with the billfold?" snapped Charles, holding out his hand. His heart seemed to be pounding in his ears.

"Yeah," said Meenie, passing it over. "You and Raul have words?"

"Leave it alone, Meenie." Charles opened the billfold, examined the driver's license, and felt the pounding in his head increase. He dropped the billfold back in the evidence bag, wondering why, of all the fields in all the counties in the Texas Panhandle, did Frederick Lee Hansford III have to die in this field in Crawford County.

He rested his head against the back of the seat and closed his eyes. "You knew who he was, didn't you, Meenie?" He opened his eyes to look at his deputy.

Meenie looked straight ahead, his hands twisting the top of the plastic evidence bag into a knot. He leaned over and spat out the window without marking a target. "Yeah, I reckoned it was Rich Hansford when I saw all that turquoise on his fingers and around his watch band. I saw him at the bank party last night. You couldn't miss that turquoise. I never said nothing to him because I'm particular who I talk to—and he never said anything to me. Probably didn't even know I was there. I'm too poor for him to notice. I figured he'd be hunting old man Adams's fields. He always does because Adams knows Rich's daddy. Besides, I hear Adams ain't in any position to tell him no. Farmers are walking easy around bankers these days—and Rich Hansford is one of the biggest bankers in the Panhandle."

"You think Mr. Adams killed him?"

"I never said no such of a thing! It was a hunting accident. Probably happened because Rich Hansford never followed nobody's rules but his own, even gun safety rules."

"Did you take a page out of his book? Did you decide to make your own rules instead of following the rules of the Crawford County Sheriff's Department? Goddamn it, Meenie, why didn't you tell me who he was?" Charles shouted.

Meenie dropped the plastic bag on the floorboard and looked squarely at Charles. " 'Cause I figured you'd go off half-cocked, start pushing people around—"

"I never push people around!" interrupted Charles.

"—demanding statements from them when they was in no shape to be talking to the law, getting their backs up when there wasn't no cause to do it. Just like you're fixing to do."

"No cause! I have a man with a bloody pulp instead of a face and you say I have no cause!" Charles felt bile rise up in his throat and swallowed quickly. He leaned over and rested his head against the rim of the steering wheel, hoping to relieve the burning sensation in his gut. He fumbled in his coat pocket for his antacid tablets only to discover he'd left them in his other coat. He uttered a four-letter word that jerked Meenie around in the seat.

"You're gettin' your bowels in an uproar, Sheriff."

"You leave my bowels out of this conversation. And the rest of my anatomy too. We're talking about my chief deputy withholding information about a felony."

"It ain't a felony until the pathologist says so. And I ain't withholding any information. I just took my time about telling you."

"You damn sure did, and I ought to take your badge for it."

"Well, I ain't gonna let you because you'd be sorry five minutes after you did it," Meenie said, peering out the window and letting fly with a stream of tobacco juice.

There was a raucous scream as a pheasant took wing. Fifteen shotguns blasted away at the air over the patrol car, and buckshot rattled against its side like hail as a hunter failed to aim high enough.

Charles ducked, then pushed open the door and rolled out. "Goddamn it!" he roared as he hit the frozen ground.

"*Madre de Dios!* Matthews, are you hit?" yelled Lindman.

Scrambling to his feet, Charles took cover against the side of the car and peered over its rooftop in time to see the hunters converge on the dead pheasant. "Lindman! Take those guns away from those crazy idiots!"

Meenie leaned out of the car. "You okay, Sheriff?"

Charles ducked down to stick his face next to his deputy's. "Next time you spit at a pheasant, make sure it's stuffed. And call for that wrecker. We'll finish our conversation later."

Meenie grabbed Charles's arm. "Sheriff, hold your horses just a minute."

"What is it?"

"You don't like guns and you don't like hunting—"

"Damn right I don't, and having to explain to the county commissioners how a brand new patrol car happened to be on the receiving end of a load of buckshot doesn't make me like it any better."

"—and it sticks in your craw that you can't do nothin' about either one of them, so you're fixing to start a fight to get rid of some of your mad. You figure Rich Hansford gives you a good excuse."

Charles stared at his deputy, stung by the criticism. "First you accuse me of pushing people around. Now you accuse me of deliberately starting fights. For God's sake, Meenie, I'm not the town bully."

Meenie scratched his chin. "I'm sorry you took it like that, Sheriff. I guess what I meant was that you got a one-track mind. You get an idea and sometimes you push pretty hard to prove it. Like now. You're gonna push them hunters until they got their backs to the wall—and you ain't for sure yet you got a right to do it."

"It's murder, damn it! The position of the body—"

"I know all about the position of the body, and I don't much like it either, but I know Rich Hansford and you don't. It'd be like that bastard to fall all straight and pretty just to give folks grief. I hope you're wrong, Sheriff, because Rich Hansford made enough ruckus when he was alive. It ain't fair for him to keep causing grief when he's dead."

Charles tilted his head back and gazed at the sky. It was the color of ashes and it looked threatening and cold. Exactly matching his mood, he thought, and neither the sky nor his mood was likely to clear very soon. "Meenie," he said, straightening his hat and wishing he'd worn earmuffs. "You're wrong on two points. First, I know Rich Hansford, and second, you don't hope I'm wrong nearly as much as I do. No one wants the son of a bitch to have shot himself accidentally more than I do."

CHAPTER

5

"CAR THIRTY-TWO." THE CALL ENDED IN A SQUEAL. Uttering another four-letter word that sent Meenie's eyebrows arching in surprise, Charles reached in the car and grabbed the mike. "This is the sheriff. What is it, Mabel?"

"Report to your office immediately, Sheriff."

Charles closed his eyes and counted to ten. "I am reporting, Mabel. What's the problem?"

"The mayor wants to talk to you."

Charles felt a prickling on the back of his neck. He'd had the same sensation about an innocent-looking field in Vietnam. That field had been mined. He suspected Mabel's statement was, too. He cleared his throat. If mine fields could be detoured around, so could mayors. "I've got a dead body, Mabel. Tell the mayor I'll give him a rain check."

"Sheriff, this is very important. It's about the hunters."

"Goodbye, Mabel," he said, and hung up the mike.

"How did you know Rich Hansford, Sheriff?" asked Meenie, his faded blue eyes suddenly bright with curiosity. "I figured you were too rich for him to pick at."

Charles felt his face stiffen into its habitual stern mask. "That's my business."

Meenie squinted up at him. "Anytime you want to talk about it, I'll listen. Things that are your *business* generally give you a bellyache."

"Call the wrecker, Meenie, while I go bully some hunters."

"Ain't you gonna wait for me?"

Charles turned his collar up against the north wind that seemed bent on freezing his ears. "I've already given you a job."

"Don't pay a man to hold out on you, does it? But I never had you pegged as a vengeful man."

Charles clasped Meenie's shoulder. "I'm not vengeful. Someone murdered a man in my county, and I'm angry. Now get your skinny behind into town and check out that Suburban. And the next time you pull a stunt like keeping something from me out of the mistaken idea that I'll act like a crazy man, I'll show you how vengeful I can be." He released Meenie and turned to walk off.

"Sheriff!"

Charles glanced over his shoulder. "You have something else to tell me, Meenie?"

"Yeah. This is pheasant season. Everybody's crazy."

Facing a group of irate hunters ten minutes later, Charles agreed with him. "Gentlemen, please. I know this isn't how you planned to spend the opening day of pheasant season."

"It's sure as hell not," said a red-faced banker from Fort Worth.

"You can't confiscate our guns, Sheriff," said a lawyer from Beaumont whom Charles had already silently labeled *pompous ass*. "My shotgun alone is worth six hundred dollars, not to mention the case. Not only have our civil rights been violated, but we have been subjected to obscene language from this gentleman, and I use the term 'gentleman' loosely." He gestured toward Lindman, who looked unrepentant.

Charles personally thought spending six hundred dollars on a shotgun was more obscene that any profanity he'd ever heard. "I'm sure you all understand the necessity of answering my questions."

"*I*, of course," announced the lawyer, "will be advising these other gentlemen during questioning. I know how difficult it is for you rural law enforcement people to stay informed of the latest court decisions concerning civil liberties. My presence will ensure that proper legal procedure is followed." He nodded to emphasize his point.

"Sawed-off little son of a bitch," muttered Lindman to Charles. "He's just mad because I told him where I was gonna stuff that shotgun if he didn't put it back in the velvet-lined case. Velvet! God Almighty! I bet he wears silk drawers."

Charles walked closer to the lawyer until the lapels of his coat brushed the smaller man's chin. "Sir," he said, dragging out the word in his best imitation drawl. "You are a witness. Therefore, you can not advise any other witnesses. So please refrain from totting up the fees you were planning to collect from these gentlemen. Also, this particular rural law enforcement officer is not entirely ignorant of legal procedure." He raised his voice. "I am aware, for example, that I am within my rights to transport all of you to the sheriff's department to cool your heels until such a time as I can arrange to take your statements."

The other hunters shuffled their feet and mumbled among themselves. Charles smiled. "You might miss the entire day's hunt." The mumbling grew louder. "Or"—he waited several seconds—"*or* Miss Poole can take your statements, type them up this afternoon, and you can drop by my office this evening to sign them. The decision is mine to make. And how I make it depends on the hassle factor. The more I'm hassled, the more inclined I am to haul in the bunch of you."

The lawyer sputtered. "I object to this kind of—"

"Shut your mouth, Roy," another hunter ordered in the soft slurred accent of the deep Piney Woods of East Texas. "Every time you open it, the shit around here gets deeper. Sheriff, the rest of us have been discussing it. We're from out of town, we just came up here to hunt, and we didn't even know about the body until that deputy of yours let out a screech and headed for the ditch. We'll be glad to tell you what we know. It doesn't amount to much, not enough to waste a day's hunting."

The other hunters nodded agreement. All except four men. Local men. Crawford County men.

Charles stepped back, his eyes on the four men. "As Miss Poole calls your name, step forward and tell her if you recognize the picture on the deceased's driver's license. If so, join Mr. Adams and the other three gentlemen. If you do not recognize the photo, then tell Miss Poole when you arrived in town, where you stayed, if you attended the party at the Carroll National Bank, when you left and with whom. Also tell her what you did from the time you got up this morning until you arrived at this field. After that you may continue hunting. But *not* in this field. Deputy Fletcher will be securing the scene until such a time as certain questions are answered."

"May we inquire what questions, Sheriff?"

It was the pompous ass again. "No, you may not," answered Charles in his finest Dallas upper class private school accent. He enjoyed seeing the man's mouth fall open.

Pivoting on his heel, and secretly glad he carried off the action without falling, he motioned to Lindman and Slim and walked toward the other end of the field. "You're in charge, Miss Poole," he called over his shoulder.

"Damn it, Matthews," said Lindman. "That woman never knows when she's *not* in charge. I hope she never moves to Clayton. The town's not big enough for both of us."

"You just have to know how to handle Miss Poole," said Charles, stopping out of earshot of the hunters. And of Miss Poole. "Slim, I want you to search the area around the body first."

"What for, Sheriff?"

"Anything that doesn't belong in a stubble field. Gum wrappers, cigarette butts, buttons, a clod of dirt or mud that doesn't match the rest of the soil, anything but milo stalks."

"I know what I ought to look for, Sheriff. I just wanted to know why I need to look for it. Do you think this is"—he lowered his voice to a conspiratorial whisper—"murder?"

Charles looked into Slim's inquisitive eyes. The deputy was young and impulsive. Ordinarily Charles wouldn't trust him to cross the street without snarling traffic, but Slim wasn't stupid. Besides, he was the only person who hadn't assumed Charles was paranoid. For that, Slim deserved something. "Confidentially, when you're a sheriff and you have a violent death, you have to investigate every possibility, son. Do you understand?"

"Yes, sir!" Slim's eyes were wide, sparkling with expectation, and innocent of the kinds of shadows Charles knew his own eyes held.

"This is a big responsibility, son. Can I trust you with it?"

Slim straightened to attention. "Yes, sir!"

"I'm glad to hear it," said Charles, hoping for the best. Besides, he didn't have a choice. With Meenie searching Hansford's vehicle, Raul at the autopsy, Miss Poole taking statements, and everyone else patrolling the fields, he was touching bottom.

"Sheriff?"

"What is it, Slim?"

The young man cleared his throat. "I know I screw up a lot because, well, things get away from me sometimes. But I won't this time. Even if the victim is Hansford, I'll do my duty." He shoved his hands in his coat pockets as though he didn't know what else to do with them. "I just wanted to tell you, that's all."

"I appreciate that, Slim."

The young deputy nodded, and Charles watched him walk toward the blood-soaked ground where the body had lain.

"They do grow up, don't they, Matthews?" asked Lindman.

Charles nodded. He felt disoriented. Slim was showing an unexpected maturity; Meenie was withholding information; Raul was being obstructive; Miss Poole, the proper spinster, was hunting. Everyone was acting out of character. Maybe it was because of pheasant season. Maybe Meenie was right. Maybe everyone was crazy.

But some things never change, he thought as he and Lindman walked toward the hunters, their boots crunching into the frozen ground. Men were still killing other men.

CHAPTER 6

"MR. ADAMS?"

Bill Adams had a face like the Panhandle during a drought, thought Charles. His skin was brown, dry, and seamed like the earth; his eyes were the blue of a summer sky when the sun had blanched the vividness from it. It was the face of a man who had endured whatever nature and the land had thrown at him. It was also a wary face.

"Sheriff." His voice was as cracked as his face.

"I believe you knew the victim," stated Charles levelly.

Adams squinted up at Charles. "Can't say that I did. On the other hand, can't say that I didn't. Hard to tell when there's no face to gander at."

Charles controlled his impatience. "Perhaps you can be a little more definite about whether or not you're missing a member of your hunting party."

"That's hard to say, too, Sheriff. Sometimes folks show up with a friend I didn't know nothing about. Sometimes I go down to the bank to meet my party and there's a stranger or two wanting to hunt who don't know any farmers personal-like. That's how come I got that loud-mouth lawyer on the place. I didn't like him much, but his money's as good as anybody else's. I figured I could stand him a couple of days." Adams rubbed his jaw. "I might've figured wrong. That fellow wears on a man awful fast."

"I meant a regular member of your party, one that hunts your place every year."

"That's still hard to say. Like I said, I go down to the bank to meet my party. Mostly they all went to the party there the night before and they meet up again in the morning for coffee and doughnuts about six. We leave for the fields about seven, and them that don't make it up in time generally meet out here. I always start with this field every year and everybody who hunts with me knows it. So sometimes they just come on out when they sober up."

The old farmer's story sounded plausible. Charles only saw one problem with it. Bill Adams still hadn't asked the one question that any innocent landowner would have asked: the identity of the body. "Frederick Hansford always hunts your land, doesn't he, Mr. Adams?"

The old man's face didn't change expression, but his body became still. Like a pheasant who sees the hunter and hopes to be overlooked. "Yeah."

"And he was at the bank party last night?"

"I seen him there."

"And you didn't recognize the body as his?"

The farmer's gaze shifted to a point over Charles's shoulder. "I can't say that I did and I can't say that I didn't."

"Just what can you say, Mr. Adams?" demanded Charles, wondering if the old man would admit to knowing his own name.

"I figured it might be Hansford from them rings he was wearing."

"Didn't you think you might ought to tell me?"

Adams shrugged. "I figured you'd find out one way or another. Didn't see no need to stick my nose in."

"At least you've still got a nose. Hansford's is blown all over your field. Doesn't that bother you?"

"Can't say that it does, Sheriff."

"Are you just callous, or did you . . ." Charles swallowed his words. He couldn't prove murder, not yet. Until he could, he had to treat it as a hunting accident. Maybe that was best. Let a murderer think he's safe, and he becomes careless. As Meenie would say: give a man enough rope and he'll hang himself.

"Did I what, Sheriff?" asked Adams.

"Did you witness the accident and just not want to admit it?"

"I saw that body the same time as everybody else did—just after your deputy bolted for the bar ditch."

"How do you suppose it happened, Mr. Adams?"

"You're the sheriff. You're supposed to be the expert."

Charles shifted his feet like a man trying to find a comfortable spot. "I'll tell you something, Mr. Adams," he said in a confidential tone. "If this were murder, then I'd be an expert." He nodded his head. "I've had experience in investigating murder. But this"—he waved his hand toward the other end of the field—"I'm out of my depth. As Meenie, Raul, even Miss Poole, keep reminding me, I'm not a hunter. I've never seen a hunting accident. Now you've been leading hunting parties on your land for how long?"

"Thirty years or more," announced the old man, relaxing a little.

"You've doubtless seen every kind of careless hunter in thirty years' time. Surely you can help me out." He dropped into the vernacular. "How do you figure this happened?"

Adams slapped his gloved hands together, probably to restore circulation, Charles thought.

"I'll tell you what it was, Sheriff," the old man finally said. "It was greed that killed him."

"What!" exclaimed Charles. Out of the corner of his eye he saw Lindman step closer to listen.

The old farmer rocked back on his heels and nodded. "Yeah, it was greed. He was so damn anxious to bag the first pheasant, make the rest of us look like pikers, that he come out here by himself to shoot. Hell, it was probably still mostly dark. He couldn't half-see where he was stepping and tripped. Swung his gun up when he was trying to get his balance, and"—he spread his hands—"that was the end of him."

"I see," said Charles, glancing at Lindman and meeting eyes as expressionless as his own. "There's still one thing I don't understand, Mr. Adams. You think he came out to bag the first pleasant—"

"That's right. He never could stand for anyone to get ahead of him."

"Then tell me, Mr. Adams, who blocked for him?"

The old man started at Charles, his features slack before he tightened his mouth and shook his head. "Sounds to me like you're more of a hunter than you let on, Sheriff. You damn sure flushed me. But it ain't gonna do you no good to bust a cap. I don't know nothing about a blocker."

"Don't know, or won't say?"

Adams grinned reluctantly. "Suit yourself, Sheriff. It don't matter. But it weren't me out here. I was with Brad and Ick and Jess from six o'clock on, waiting for hunters, and old Rich damn sure didn't shoot himself before that. It was still pitch black at six. Couldn't see to shoot a pheasant if you stepped on one."

Charles felt his own face stiffen. "But it wasn't a pheasant that was shot, was it, Mr. Adams?"

"I know you don't think much of the way I'm talking, Sheriff, but I ain't no hypocrite. I didn't much like Rich Hansford."

"He died in my county and I want to know how. Give your statement to Miss Poole. And Mr. Adams," he called as the old man walked away. "We'll talk some more when you come by to sign it."

"Matthews," said Lindman, his bright blue eyes narrowed against the wind. "There's no way it could have happened the way he said. If Hansford was staggering forward to catch his balance, he would've fallen on his face after he shot himself. And if he was about to fall backward, he would've swung his arms out and shot himself in the side of the head or the body."

"I know that, Lindman, and I think Adams knows it, too. He was quick enough to give himself an alibi when I asked about blockers. Let's see what his alibis have to say for themselves."

Lindman grabbed his arm. "Wait a minute. What's this *let's* stuff. I just came up here to shoot a few pheasant, maybe give you a call and jaw a little. I'm not a Texan, and I don't have anything to do with this mess."

Charles debated a minute as whether to appeal to Lindman's good nature, or to be a hard-nosed bastard. He wasn't feeling very kind-hearted today; besides, the New Mexican sheriff owed him one.

"You're a material witness, Lindman." He held up his hand as the other man ripped out a curse. At least, Charles assumed it was a curse. The words were Norwegian, so he couldn't be sure. "I don't want to have to get technical and start talking warrants and arrest and other legal maneuvers. I'd rather keep our relationship on a friendly, cooperative, professional basis."

Lindman looked suspicious. "What are you getting at, Matthews?"

"I'm a little short-handed at the moment. Pheasant season stretches my resources enough without having a full-scale investigation. Now, if you could serve as a special deputy—"

Lindman interrupted with a curse. Charles was sure this time because it was in English. "Matthews, you're just getting back at me for arresting Raul for murder a few weeks back. I admit I was wrong, but I did what was proper at the time. You can't hold that against a man."

Charles grinned. "Are you calling me a vengeful man?"

"Hell, yes!"

"I admit I didn't appreciate your arresting Raul. I appreciated even less your making me a deputy, which in effect turned me against my own man. But I'm not vengeful, just a believer in equal treatment under the law."

"You're vengeful."

Charles arched one eyebrow. "Maybe a little, but I'm also desperate, Lindman. I need your help."

Lindman rolled his eyes toward the heavens. "Damn it to hell, Matthews, but you're a sneaky bastard. Didn't anybody ever tell you to use the carrot *or* the stick, but not both together?" He took off his hat and slapped it against his leg. "All right, I'll help you out, but I don't like it one damn bit. This business smells worse than a feedlot on an August day. Anybody that would blow a man's face off ain't someone I want to mess with. He might start looking to blow mine off next."

"So you think it's murder, too?"

Lindman sighed. "I been down the trail a few times myself, Matthews. That *accident* didn't fool me very long after I got to looking at it. But you ain't got any proof, so I'd advise you to walk quiet. You don't want to scare off the game until your gun's loaded."

"You ever heard of traps, Lindman?"

"Yeah. You set one and I stepped in it."

"Let's see if we can't set a few together," said Charles, walking over to another Crawford County hunter. "Brad, I'm sorry, but I have to ask you a few questions."

Brad Masters's red hair was a fringe around the knitted cap he wore, and his round face looked pinched and cold. He shook Charles's hand, then huddled further into the shelter of a pickup. "Damn freezing day for this kind of business, isn't it, Charles? But I guess there isn't a good day to die."

"I'm sure Rich Hansford would agree with you, Brad," said Charles quietly.

Masters closed his eyes for a second. "So it was Hansford."

"You knew, and you didn't tell me?"

"I suspected. I didn't know for sure. I thought I recognized the Suburban. He always drove it when he came to the bank."

Masters stopped to wipe his forehead. Charles waited silently. Nature cannot tolerate a vacuum and neither can a nervous witness. Silence is a most effective vacuum; witnesses nearly always rush to fill it with words, sentences, whole paragraphs, usually containing information they never would have divulged in a direct interrogation. The method didn't work with every witness, but Charles sensed it would work with Brad Masters. The banker was sweating, and fear made a man sweat as quickly as heat.

"This is such a shock. I, uh, did a lot of business with Hansford. That is, Carroll National did. His bank in Amarillo carried most of our accommodation loans. We'd borrow money from his bank, and loan it to our customers at a higher rate of interest. It's standard practice. A small town bank like Carroll National doesn't have the cash reserves to make the loans our customers require so we borrow from larger banks. Don't misunderstand me. We've got enough assets to cover our loans—we have to, or the banking commission would close us down—but they're not in cash."

Masters rubbed his forehead, a puzzled expression in his eyes. "I don't know why I'm explaining all this. Pretty dull stuff to the average person. You have to know how the banking industry works to understand."

"I have some knowledge of banking," said Charles, thinking of the bank his family owned in Dallas. "And I think your explanation is clear." As far as it goes, he added silently to himself. What Brad didn't say was that, in effect, an accommodation loan gave Rich Hansford a mortgage on Carroll National Bank.

"This is going to be a real mess," continued Masters. "Rich was a good banker but he ran Lone Star National as a one-man show, or as much as he could under the law. His death leaves a lot of things unresolved."

Charles nodded. "At least you're not dancing on his grave like Bill Adams. I'm glad someone has a good word to say for him, even if it's just that he was a good banker."

"I didn't like him, Charles, but I'm sorry he's dead."

Masters had an expressive face, too much so for a banker, Charles thought. Brad Masters wasn't sorry at all.

"I'll need a guest list for the bank party, Brad," he said abruptly.

Masters's face went blank for a moment. "The party?" he asked in a dazed voice. Charles knew that whatever question the banker had expected, it had nothing to do with the guest list.

"Rich Hansford was there, wasn't he?"

"Yes, but so was half the town. I mean, the bank invites a number of people, usually stockholders and other bankers, but everyone brings a guest. The guest list doesn't begin to include everyone who was there. Why do you want it?"

Charles ignored the question because he didn't have an answer that wouldn't reveal more than he wanted revealed. "Who came with Hansford this morning?"

Masters pressed closer to the pickup. "What do you mean? No one came with him."

"How do you know, Brad? Did you talk to him this morning?"

"No! I had to unlock the basement rec room and get things set up. I was there at a little after five, and the hunters started drifting in about a quarter to six. I never talked to Rich Hansford at all this morning."

"Okay, Brad, go give your statement to Miss Poole, and bring me that guest list tonight."

The stocky banker unconsciously expelled a pent-up breath and walked away.

"Interesting," murmured Charles to Lindman. "He doesn't lie worth a damn. He didn't talk to Hansford *this morning.* I wonder what they talked about *last night*?"

"Sheriff?"

Charles turned to face Ick Johnson, owner of Benny's Hardware. No one knew who Benny was, or why Ick named his business after him. It was one of those small town mysteries that was discussed occasionally over coffee at the doughnut shop. It was a dependable topic when there weren't any scandals to gossip about.

"Do you have something to tell me, Ick?" asked Charles.

Johnson clenched his hands. They were large and rough looking with several of the fingers misshaped. He had been an oil field roughneck and his hands showed it. "Did I hear right, Sheriff? Was it Rich Hansford?"

"You got good ears," said Lindman.

"Ick Johnson, this is Kit Lindman, my special deputy."

Johnson's eyes were like hard brown marbles. "I thought Bill Adams said you were a sheriff in New Mexico."

"These demotions happen," said Charles, ignoring Lindman's snarl. "He's my special deputy in this investigation."

"A special deputy for a hunting accident. Who are you trying to kid, Sheriff?"

"Do you have a reason to believe it's not an accident?"

"Little Freddy Hansford the Third," said Ick. "That son of a bitch's hero was J. R. Ewing. Isn't that reason enough?"

"I don't think so, but maybe we ought to talk more about it at my office. If I have a murder on my hands, I need to know it. As far as I know, it's just an unfortunate hunting accident."

"Don't con me, Sheriff. I worked in the oil fields. I've seen cons worked by experts. You're too honest to do it right."

"That works both ways, Ick. Suppose you tell me what you know about Hansford's death."

Johnson looked down at his hands, then back at Charles. "Not a damn thing, Sheriff. I was at the bank at six o'clock like everybody else. Besides, little Freddy was shot. I'd have strangled him. Shooting was too good for him."

Charles looked at the blunt-featured man. "You know I'll be talking to you again, Ick. And that's no con."

Johnson saluted him. "You can damn sure try, Sheriff. Of course, that doesn't mean I'll talk back."

"Oh, I think you will," said Charles softly. "Just to be sure I don't arrest the wrong person."

For the space of a heartbeat Johnson's face was wiped clean of expression. Then he smiled and his brown eyes held a challenge. "It'll be a fascinating conversation, Sheriff." He touched his hat brim in farewell and walked over to join the group around Miss Poole.

Lindman nudged him. "Who the hell is he protecting, Matthews?"

Charles shrugged. "I don't have the faintest idea, but there's obviously someone. And it's someone who has a strong reason for wanting Hansford dead. Otherwise, why would he try so hard to make himself my favorite suspect?"

He pulled his coat collar higher. The wind was blowing harder, gusts that sought out unprotected skin and chilled it to numbness. The last hunter huddled inside his own sheepherder's coat, his hands tucked inside the thick, fur-lined pockets. He looked frozen and miserable. "Jess," said Charles. "I expected you to be leading hunting parties over your own land. What are you doing trailing after Bill Adams?"

Jess Turner's smile vanished as quickly as it appeared. "I got most of my land planted in winter wheat this year. Got cattle running on it. I just have a little over a section that's stubble. Marta's handling that. You know my wife Marta, Sheriff?"

"I've met her at Angie's," said Charles, hearing his voice soften on the last word. He still wasn't accustomed to casual references to Angie Lassiter. Or accustomed to having the right to do so.

"I heard you and Angie was finally gonna tie the knot. Congratulations, Sheriff. The whole county was wondering if you were ever gonna get around to it. Nobody could figure out what you were waiting for."

"I was waiting for the right moment," said Charles, thinking how easy it was to tell the truth and lie at the same time. He had waited for the right moment, not to propose to Angie, but to confess to her. L. D. Lassiter, Angie's first husband, had been a murderer. The brother of one of his victims killed L. D. as he was trying to escape. He, with Meenie's and Raul's help, passed off the murder as an accident. Now someone else was trying the same tactic and he, as sheriff, was committed to stopping him. It was ironic.

"You'll never regret it, Sheriff," said Jess earnestly.

"I'm sure I won't," agreed Charles, conscious of being both truthful and a liar again. He didn't regret covering up both L. D.'s crimes and his murder in order to protect the grief-maddened young man who killed him—and to prevent Angie from living with the stigma of being known as a murderer's wife. And he didn't regret finally confessing what he'd done to Angie because it enabled them to bury L. D.'s ghost. He did, however, regret breaking his oath to uphold the law. He regretted that very, very much.

"Wives are wonderful," continued Jess. "Take my Marta, for instance. She insisted I go hunting with Bill so I wouldn't have anything to worry about except having fun. Said she could take care of the hunters on our place. She even fixed me steak and hash browns for breakfast before I left to meet Bill.

"What time did you meet him, Jess?" asked Charles.

"About six, like everybody else. Marta woke me up and fed me in plenty of time. She knows I don't like to be late. She calls it my phobia. I guess she must've got me up about four-thirty or a quarter to five, and would you believe she'd already been up and set some homemade bread to rise."

Charles would believe it. Marta sounded like such a paragon of virtue, she made him tired. "I'm sure you know by now that the victim was Rich Hansford, Jess. Were you acquainted with him?"

Jess stuck his hands a little deeper in his pockets. "I'm on the board of directors of Carroll National. I've had a few dealings with Hansford."

"Didn't you recognize his body? Didn't you recognize his car? Brad Masters says Hansford drove it every time he came to Carroll."

Jess seemed to shrink inside his coat. "I wasn't sure. I mean, I couldn't be sure. Not with his face gone. And I didn't want to identify him in case I was wrong."

"Why do you suppose he was out here by himself?" asked Charles as he watched Jess's hands ball into fists inside his coat pockets.

"I just can't figure it, Sheriff."

"How did you feel about Rich Hansford, Jess? Did you like him?"

Jess looked directly at Charles. "He was a hard man to like, Sheriff, and I don't think it bothered him much."

"Okay, Jess, go talk to Miss Poole, and next time you think you know something, tell me. If you four men hadn't been so close-mouthed, we could've concluded these talks much sooner. You'd already be hunting again."

Jess wiped his forehead. "I kinda lost my taste for hunting today. I think I'll go see how Marta's doing."

Charles clapped him on the back. "You do that, Jess," he said, leading the man over to the group of men surrounding his errant dispatcher. "Miss Poole, take a break. I need to talk to you."

"Really, Sheriff," she said, marching over to him, "I don't need a break. I just have the four local men and I'll be through. And about time, too. These men are complaining about the cold. No stamina, that's their problem."

Charles put his arm around Miss Poole and led her out of hearing range of the hunters. "I'm impressed with your efficiency. However, I want you to be as inefficient as possible when you take statements from our Crawford County men."

She looked at him as though he'd suggested she commit an unnatural act. "Whatever for, Sheriff?"

"I need to talk to a lady about breakfast."

CHAPTER 7

WHY MARTA TURNER MARRIED HARD-WORKING BUT unexciting Jess was a bigger mystery to Crawford County than what government farm policy would be next year. It was no mystery why Jess married her. Given the opportunity, ninety-nine point nine percent of normal males above the age of twelve would do the same. Marta Turner was a blonde, blue-eyed, Nordic knockout. She belonged on a Caribbean beach saturated in coconut-scented suntan oil, in a European casino dressed in satin, at a Broadway opening night in furs and diamonds. She didn't belong in the Texas Panhandle dressed in faded jeans, men's lace-up hunting boots, and an insulated yellow coat, with wind-burned cheeks and no makeup.

"Why do you want to know what time Jess left the house?" Marta Turner's voice was sultry and deep, with a Panhandle accent so thick it could grow wheat.

"There's been some trouble. I'm checking out all the hunters in Bill Adams's party," replied Charles in as easy a tone as he could manage.

"What kind of trouble, Sheriff? Is Jess hurt?" Her deep blue eyes held a frightened expression.

"No, no. Jess is fine, but one of the other hunters had a little accident." Charles tried not to grimace at his own diction. *Little* accident! He was as bad as Lindman. "I have reason to believe there was a blocker with the victim at the time of the accident, and I need to eliminate all the hunters with Bill. No sense in wasting my time asking innocent men questions, is there?"

"What kind of trouble?"

"One of the hunters was killed."

"Who was it?"

"A banker from Amarillo named Rich Hansford."

Marta folded her arms and turned to watch the line of hunters walking across her field. "I think Jess knew him. What time did it happen?"

Charles circled to face her. "We're not sure until the autopsy, but before seven-thirty when the rest of the hunters got to the field."

She looked down at her boots, then shifted her feet further apart as if bracing herself. "Jess left the house late, Sheriff. I warned him not to drive too fast just so he wouldn't be late at the bank. I bet he didn't listen to me. I bet he got there right at six."

Charles switched to a desperate tone. "Can you remember exactly, Marta? It's important. I know Jess wasn't blocking for Hansford, because he would've reported the accident. Jess is a dependable guy. But I have to treat my Crawford County people the same as the out-of-town hunters, so no one can accuse me of favoritism. You know how much the county needs those hunters. We can't afford for anybody to get incensed and take his money to another county. If I can just say old Jess left his house at such-and-such a time and drove directly to the bank, then everyone will be satisfied."

He studied her face. "How about taking me through your morning, from the time you got up until Jess left? Did you set the alarm? What about breakfast? What did you serve for breakfast? Maybe we can add cooking times."

She licked her lips. "I forgot to set the alarm, so we overslept. I felt guilty, sending Jess off with just cold cereal, but I knew he could get doughnuts and coffee at the bank. It must have been close to six when Jess left. I can't be sure."

"You think about it, Marta, and give me a call at the office." He raised his hat in farewell, "Thanks. I'm sorry I bothered you."

"That's okay, Sheriff," she said, looking down the field and stiffening like a pointer who spotted game. "Hey, you with the green hat! Put that cigarette out!"

He watched her lope across the field. "Well?" he asked Lindman.

Lindman shoved his hat to the back of his head. "You're a sneaky bastard, Matthews. You gonna pick up Turner for a little heart-to-heart?"

Charles rubbed his stomach where the burning had taken on an added intensity. "What for? Because he lied about what he had for breakfast? I don't have a homicide yet. I don't have any proof the victim wasn't alone. I don't even have an approximate time of death. I don't have a damn thing but a sore gut that tells me this is a set-up. I can't haul someone in for questioning on the basis of my bellyache."

Lindman followed him to the patrol car. "What the hell *are* you going to do then?"

"Give everybody rope," Charles answered, turning the ignition. "And see who else hangs himself."

"Sheriff," said Mabel as Charles, followed by Lindman, tried to sneak past the dispatcher's desk.

Charles gave up trying to sneak and rushed for his office. "Terribly busy, Mabel. Don't bother me unless another hunter starts to bleed." He pushed Lindman inside and slammed his door.

A short pudgy man whose black hair was moussed, sprayed, and otherwise anchored to hide a bald spot the size of a saucer on the top of his head, struggled out of Charles's chair. "Sheriff Matthews," he said in a mellow tenor voice that was the pride of the Methodist Church choir. "I've heard some distressing rumors about the hunt."

Charles stripped off his coat and put his Stetson on the filing cabinet. "It's true, Mayor," he said slipping on his gray tweed blazer, straightening the badge that hung on one end of a leather flap, and sticking the other end in his breast pocket.

Mayor Eddie Culpepper bounced from behind Charles's desk. "Sheriff, we in Crawford County realize that you're not from the area, so perhaps you don't understand or appreciate certain local customs."

"Are you rehearsing for the next election, Mayor?" asked Charles.

The plump little man looked as if he'd lost his place in a memorized speech. "Uh, no."

"Then please get to the point," said Charles, sinking onto his chair and propping his feet on his desk.

The mayor drew himself up to his full five feet six inches. Charles thought he looked like Napoleon, but with a slightly larger stomach. "I don't like your attitude, Sheriff. This is a very serious matter."

"I take a dead body seriously myself," agreed Charles.

The mayor's mouth worked soundlessly for a few seconds.

Charles thought he looked like a carp with a fish hook caught in its throat. "A body? A human body?"

"That's usually the kind that gets a sheriff stirred up," interjected Lindman.

"Mayor Culpepper, may I introduce Sheriff Kit Lindman from Clayton, New Mexico. He's here on sort of an exchange program."

"Pleased to meet you, Mr. Mayor," said Lindman, advancing on the little man, his hand outstretched.

The little man retreated. "A dead body. Oh, my God. Was it a hunter?"

Charles's feet hit the floor with a thud as he stood up. "Of course, it was a hunter. What else have we been talking about?"

The mayor wrung his hands. "I came to tell you that you can't, absolutely can't, throw hunters in jail for having a drink or two. It's not the way we do things in Crawford County."

"I don't know who the hell your *we* is, but I can tell you how *I* do things. I arrest drunks with guns, whether they are hunters or not. I already have one tragedy and, if humanly possible, I don't intend to have anymore." He led the mayor toward the door. "Now why don't you scoot back over to city hall and draft a statement for the newspaper, something about extending our heartfelt sympathy to the widow and family of the deceased."

"Who was the deceased?"

"Rich Hansford."

The mayor staggered back and put his hand over his heart. "Oh, my God," he moaned. He pulled a handkerchief out of his pocket and blotted his forehead. "Was it a natural death?"

"Only if you consider a shotgun blast natural," answered Charles.

The mayor groaned again. "I told him to be careful, not to push so hard. He wasn't doing anything illegal, just being a hard-nosed banker, but some people in town didn't see it that way. I tried to explain to them that Rich wasn't being vindictive, but he had a responsibility to his bank's stockholders."

Charles put his arm around the rotund man and lead him over to one of the wooden chairs. "Take it easy, Mayor. Can I get you a cup of coffee, a glass of water?"

"Oh, this is terrible, just terrible," said Culpepper, clutching his handkerchief to his chest.

Charles perched one hip on his desk. "I know this is a shock to you. I hate to ask questions when you're upset, but I will need a statement."

Culpepper jerked his head up. "Statement?" he asked, his tenor voice approaching the soprano range.

"Background information, Mayor. State of mind and intent of the deceased, that sort of thing. Lindman, if you would take notes please."

"I—I want my lawyer."

Charles folded his hands and rested them on his thigh. "I guess if you were part of Hansford's nefarious schemes, I can't allow you to incriminate yourself. I am disappointed in you, though. I never thought you were the kind of man to make money at the expense of your neighbors. I know the town will be disappointed, too, when they hear about it. You know how hard it is to keep a secret in a small town. I guess it won't bother you too much, though. I heard you weren't planning to stand for reelection."

"That's not true!"

Charles arched one eyebrow. "You were planning to run? I wouldn't take bets on your chances. Voters don't understand about hard-nosed bankers. Too bad. You weren't such a bad mayor."

Culpepper waved his fists in the air. "No! No! I meant I wasn't involved in Hansford's schemes."

"Then I don't understand. Why are you afraid to give me a statement without your lawyer? You're not a suspect. You're not under arrest. By the way, those are the two circumstances under which you can legally refuse to talk to me. Otherwise, lawyer or no, you'll have to answer my questions."

Culpepper wiped his head, rearranging his hair into stiff spikes in the process. He sank back against the chair, looking deflated, as if he were a child's blow-up toy with a slow leak. "I have an oil well service business, just a small one, and not very prosperous with the oil market the way it is. Rich Hansford came by day before yesterday with a proposition. He wanted to buy into my firm. I wanted to know why. I mean, I'm just barely making a living. There's not enough profit for two people. He was foreclosing on some property here in the county and he was negotiating some oil leases. Drilling was supposed to start after the first of the year. He wanted a firm like mine to contract to service the wells. He was willing to pay me top dollar for a share, plus arrange a loan to expand. It was a good deal for me."

"I take it you didn't owe the bank anything on your business?" asked Charles, exchanging glances with Lindman.

"My business was free and clear," said the mayor proudly.

"In other words, Hansford couldn't foreclose on it, so he had to buy it," commented Charles.

"You don't understand, Sheriff," said Culpepper. "Hansford had no choice. Payments were overdue on these various properties. A bank has a responsibility to its stockholders."

"And I bet Hansford was the biggest stockholder," muttered Lindman under his breath.

"What did you say?" asked the mayor.

Charles frowned at Lindman. "He said it would be illuminating to know who the stockholders were."

"Hansford is," said the mayor. "But he can't run the bank all by himself. He has to have a board of directors who are stockholders."

Who probably owned the very minimum amount of stock the law requires in order to serve on the board, Charles thought. Knowing Rich Hansford, he would bet that the banker wouldn't relinquish any more control than the law absolutely demanded. "Who were the property owners who were about to be tossed off their land?"

The mayor wiped his head again. "I don't know all of them."

"Tell me the names you do know," demanded Charles, his voice more harsh than he intended.

Culpepper looked around the room like a prisoner searching for a way to escape. "Please."

"Tell me!"

"Ick Johnson."

"Ick's not a farmer," said Charles.

"But he knows the oil business. And most of the independent drillers around the Panhandle. Rich was afraid he would . . ." The mayor's voice trailed off as if he just realized the significance of what he was saying."

"Afraid he might set up a rival business?" asked Charles.

"I'm sure that had nothing to do with Rich's foreclosing on Ick. Besides, Ick was behind in his payments on one business. He couldn't borrow anymore to set up a new one."

"Nothing like getting rid of the competition," observed Lindman. He ripped out a Norwegian curse that Charles was sure described Hansford in very unflattering terms.

"Whose property was Hansford planning to lease to the oil company?" Charles asked.

"He wouldn't tell me who."

"Anyone else?"

"Jess Turner."

Charles got up. He felt old and tired and disillusioned. And sick, but not the kind of sickness a doctor could cure. He felt sick of the whole human race. "Okay, Mayor. If you'd wait outside, I'll have someone type your statement and you can sign it."

Culpepper rose and walked to the door with an uneven gait. He turned to look at Charles. "I was a fool, wasn't I, Sheriff? He had the Devil's own tongue, and I believed every word until just now when I heard myself repeating what he'd said. Whoever killed him just might have saved my soul." He closed the door behind him.

Lindman stuck his pen in his pocket and got to his feet. "You didn't tell him Hansford was murdered."

Charles circled around his desk and sat down. "I guess he thought Hansford was too mean to die otherwise. Type the statement, will you, Lindman? I don't trust Mabel—and I've got a call to make."

"First I'm a deputy, then I'm a typist. If I stick around your county very long, Matthews, I'll be mopping floors."

"You know what they say, Lindman. Humility is good for the soul," remarked Charles as he picked up the phone and dialed. Lindman muttered something distinctly profane as he left.

Charles tapped his fingers on the desk as he listened to the phone ring. "Come on, damn it, answer."

"Pathology here." The voice betrayed impatience.

"Dr. Akin?"

"Of course." Dr. Akin never identified himself when answering the phone. As the only forensic pathologist in the entire Panhandle, he didn't think it was necessary. Who else would a caller want to talk to?

"This is Sheriff Matthews."

"I recognized your voice, Charles, and I want you to get off my back. Performing an autopsy on a body from Crawford County is always a challenge. This body is no exception. I need more time. Do you know what a mess the head is in? I haven't even got to the organs, not that they have anything to do with the cause of death." He hesitated. "I don't think. I never like to make snap judgments where one of your bodies is concerned. One of these days I'm going to prepare a paper for the College of Forensic Pathology: 'Environmental and Sociological Factors Determining Extraordinary Causes of Death in Homicide Cases Originating in Crawford County, Texas.' I'll try to pin the whole phenomena on a contaminated water supply, or the way the natives comb their hair. Either one's as good an explanation as any."

"Dr. Akin, do I have a homicide or not?"

"Didn't I just say so?" asked the pathologist testily. "Some days I think you're losing it, Sheriff. You just don't seem to pay attention."

Charles reminded himself that Dr. Akin was brilliant, one of the most skilled pathologists in the country. But he irritated the hell out of Charles on most occasions. "I apologize, Dr. Akin. Blame it on the season. Suppose you tell me again, and in words of one syllable, please. I don't have my medical dictionary handy. Now, the cause of death was a shotgun blast to the head."

"No."

Charles gripped the phone harder. "What?"

"The shotgun blast didn't kill him. He'd already been dead, oh, maybe an hour. That's a seat of the pants guess, Charles, but the seat of my pants is better than most pathologists'. Time of death is around five this morning, plus or minus an hour. Damn hard to be sure under the circumstances, but if I entered all the variables in a computer—temperature of the body, air temperature, wind chill, degree of rigor—I reckon that infernal machine would give me an eighty to ninety percent probability that I'm right. When I examine the contents of his stomach, that may pin it down a little closer. Provided you can prove when he had his last meal."

"Dr. Akin," said Charles desperately, "what killed him?"

"Oh, it was the twenty-two slug fired at close range."

"A twenty-two? A pistol?"

"I presume a pistol was used. A twenty-two rifle is a possibility, but a handgun is more likely. The murderer was close—I found stripling on a bit of facial skin the shotgun blast didn't obliterate—and getting close with a rifle is awkward. Unless you sneak up behind someone—and our victim wasn't shot from behind. Ordinarily a bullet that size would've gone right out the other side of the cranium—skull to you—but the murderer had some bad luck. The bullet entered the right side of the face, hit a gold crown on an upper molar, which slowed its velocity. Gold will take the starch out of a bullet about as fast as anything, just in case you're curious."

"Not really," said Charles, swallowing down the bile that threatened to choke him as he imagined the incredible pain Hansford suffered before he died.

"To continue," said Akin with the relish of a man who enjoyed his work. "The bullet took a forty-five degree angle toward the back of the skull and lodged just under the scalp. An hour later, maybe, someone came along and blew his face off to hide the damage. If he'd angled the shotgun more so the blast would've taken the top half of the deceased's cranium, I might, *might*, have had a little more difficulty determining cause of death. The best bet would've been for the murderers to have removed the head. Then you'd be running around like a chicken with its head cut off"—the pathologist chuckled at his play on words—"looking for a maniac with a saw, instead of a garden-variety killer. Anything else you need to know, Sheriff, or can I finish up so I can get back to my pheasant hunting?"

Charles shuddered. "Don't let me keep you from today's blood ritual. What's one more hunter among the eight thousand already in the county?"

"Eight thousand?"

"Yes, and all trying to blow the head off a beautiful bird."

There was silence on the other end of the line, then Akin's thoughtful voice. "You know, Charles, the SWAT team from the Amarillo P.D. gave me a bulletproof vest as a joke last year. I believe I'll wear it. With eight thousand hunters, the probability of someone getting shot is pretty good."

"Someone already has been, Dr. Akin. Or had you forgotten?"

CHAPTER 8

CHARLES WALKED ACROSS THE GREASE-SPOTTED CEment floor of the county barn. "Found anything, Meenie?"

His deputy backed out of the Suburban. Fingerprint powder clung to his bushy eyebrows and filled in the grooves of his face. He shifted his tobacco and spat at a beetle running for cover behind a stack of boxes. "You might say that." Pushing his hat to the back of his head, he stood glaring at the car, a welter of plastic bags and brown paper sacks filled with evidence almost hiding his feet. "Yeah, you just might say I did."

"Well? If it isn't a secret, I'd like to know."

"Someone tried to clean up the car, but I found blood smears on the steering wheel, the window, the driver's seat, and the floorboard. I figure he fell forward against the steering wheel and dripped blood. The floor mat's gone. I reckon the murderer figured it'd be easier to take it than to clean it."

"So Hansford was killed in his car, and the body moved to the field."

"That's what it looks like, unless he had a nosebleed or a cut finger and got out of the car under his own steam, then somebody plugged him."

"Meenie, don't you ever agree with anybody about anything?"

"I don't make a habit of it. Besides, you don't need somebody tellin' you you're right all the time. Not good for a man. Sure not good for a sheriff. Somebody's got to poke holes in a case so you'll know where the weak spots are."

"Before you poke more holes, tell me what else you've found," said Charles in exasperation.

"Mud clods on the floorboard on the passenger side, which ain't much help. How you gonna prove which field it came from?"

Charles grinned. "Easily. I look for the one field that isn't frozen."

"And hope you find it before the weather warms up and the whole county turns to mud," said Meenie, with a gloomy look at the bag holding the offending mud. "I found one thing that's maybe better."

"Damn it, tell me! Getting information out of you is like pulling teeth."

"It's a feather."

"Great! I can check all the pheasant bagged during the day and arrest the hunter whose bird is missing a feather. The D. A. is going to love that."

"Ain't from no pheasant. If I was guessing, I'd say it was a quail feather."

Charles took off his hat and slapped it against his leg. "A quail! I can't get away from the damn birds. If it isn't pheasant, it's quail. Where are the canaries and cockatoos?"

"They'd be better. Leastwise, not everybody has one," observed Meenie. "Every farmer around here has quail in his pastures."

"All your cases like this one, Matthews?" asked Lindman, eyeing the grocery sack evidence bags. "Over-killing a corpse, scattering quail feathers during pheasant season. Doesn't anybody commit a simple murder?"

"I've heard all the jokes about Crawford County homicides I can take from the pathologist."

"What's that you say about over-killing?" interrupted Meenie.

"It seems somebody shot Hansford in the head, then the same individual or someone else dropped by the scene an hour later and blasted him with a shotgun."

"I guess maybe somebody wanted to make sure he didn't recover," observed Meenie, leaning around Charles to spit at another target. "Got it."

Charles grimaced, but didn't turn to see what Meenie had hit. "I said, no jokes. I've lost my sense of humor about this case."

"You don't never have one during pheasant season," said his deputy. "Your face would sour milk."

"Leaving my face out of this conversation, did you come up with any fingerprints?"

Meenie wiped his face with a red bandanna. "Some, for all the good they're gonna do you."

"Meenie, another character trait I don't have right now is patience. Why aren't the fingerprints going to help?"

"Ain't no blood-stained fingerprints, just prints in the places where you'd expect them: the dash, the door handles, windows, steering wheel. Most of them are smudged as hell, which figures since nobody with any sense is going out in this weather without gloves on. Wind chill's been below zero for a week. You might be able to prove Joe Blow was in that car, but they don't prove he was doing something he oughtn't to be doing. And you got to identify them prints before they'll do you any good at all. If they ain't on record in Austin, or in Washington, you're up the creek without a paddle. You can't go around demanding that folks let you print them if they're not under arrest. Violates their civil rights."

"A conversation with you is enough to make Pollyanna suicidal. I've called another deputy to take the evidence bags to Amarillo. Raul can put them on the plane to Dallas with whatever turns up at the autopsy, Meenie. There's another depressing conversation I've postponed—and I need you and Lindman for moral support. I have to notify Hansford's next of kin."

"That would be his daddy and his wife," said Meenie. "Old Fred Hansford the second lives out on the Bar H Ranch, just outside the county line on the road to Amarillo. The Hansfords got to the Panhandle too late to claim a pile of land like old Charlie Goodnight and Bugbee and that bunch, so they had to be satisfied with a small spread, sixty or so thousand acres. Not big enough to really pay. They got into banking and oil instead. They're worth a lot more today than them founding ranchers with their bigger spreads."

He picked up an armful of evidence bags and started for a patrol car that pulled in behind Charles's. "In spite of that, I think it always stuck in Rich Hansford's craw that his family didn't own the biggest ranch in the Panhandle. He never did like somebody else havin' more than he did."

"He found a unique remedy, Meenie. He foreclosed on everybody's land."

"You know something, Matthews," said Lindman as he and Charles collected the rest of the evidence bags and piled them in the back seat of the other car. "From what all I hear about this Rich Hansford, the more I think you ain't got a murder—you got a public service killing. Somebody did the public a favor by killing that bastard."

Charles watched the other patrol car lay down a trail of rubber as its driver took off for Amarillo. "I doubt that his father will agree with you, Lindman. Parents are notoriously blind where there children are concerned."

Forty minutes later Charles decided that not all parents possess blind spots. Frederick Lee Hansford II decidedly did not.

Seated in a motorized wheelchair, his hands and feet grotesquely twisted and knotted with arthritis, the old man's voice echoed from the high ceiling and plastered walls of the ranch house living room. "I told Rich that treating folks like dirt was going to get him killed. Listen to an old man, Sheriff. Pushing folks who are already in a bind is dangerous. They're going to fight back not only because it's natural, but because they don't have anything to lose. Rich never would listen to me."

The old man heaved himself straighter in his wheelchair. Pain deepened the furrows on his craggy face as his swollen joints protested the movement. A Hispanic man nearly as old as Hansford started toward him. "Go 'way, Manuel. I'm not helpless yet. Make yourself useful by running out to the guest house and waking up my daughter-in-law. It's time decent folk was up. Besides, I guess she ought to be told she's a widow. Might make her getting up a little easier."

"Rich and your daughter-in-law lived here at the ranch?" asked Charles.

Hansford removed a thin, brown cigarette from a silver case set with turquoise. He saw Charles studying it and peered up at him. "Looks like something a pimp would carry, doesn't it?" he asked, slipping it back in his pocket. "It was a Christmas present from Rich. He always gave things he liked. Didn't matter what someone wanted. I guess it made shopping easy."

He lit his cigarette and inhaled deeply, letting the smoke trickle slowly from his mouth as he continued. "To get back to your question. No, Rich never lived at the ranch, not since he got old enough to move away. He and my daughter-in-law spent a night or two every month, and sometimes she'd come by herself, but Rich had a guest house built. This old place wasn't fancy enough. Anyway, they'd drive out from Amarillo, spend a night, and check up on me, try to push me into a nursing home. I'm not as easy to push as some folks. Besides, as I told Rich, I'm not bothering them living out here. Manuel is here in case I get bad, and his wife cooks and looks after the house. We manage."

"That isn't the point, Dad," said a soft musical voice. "It's how you manage. Tacos and beans and those horrible hot peppers aren't a proper diet."

Hansford frowned. "That daughter-in-law of mine"—he gestured toward the doorway behind Charles—"according to her, everything I eat either clogs up my veins or stops up my plumbing. I've been eating what I want to for nearly seventy years. I'm not changing now." He slapped the arm of his wheelchair with a gnarled hand. "Quit worrying about my belly and come meet these gentlemen. This is my daughter-in-law, Virginia Acton Hansford. Virginia, that fellow nearest you is Kit Lindman, and the galoot next to him is Deputy Meenie Higgins. They both work for this gentleman here, sheriff from Crawford County, Charles Matthews."

Charles heard the soft inhalation that meant Virginia Hansford had drawn a deep breath. He drew one of his own before turning around. "Hello, Ginny," he said, and heard Meenie bite off an exclamation.

She inclined her head in acknowledgement. "Charles, you're looking well."

"So are you, Ginny." She was, too, thought Charles. Her height was the only average thing about Virginia Hansford. Her hair was silver-blonde and perfectly groomed, her skin flawless, her features perfect, her figure fashionably thin. She was a tribute to the art of cosmetology and the benefits of a rigid diet and exercise program. She was also very nearly Charles's age of thirty-eight, but she would hold time at bay as long as there were plastic surgeons and hairdressers. To Virginia Hansford, aging was in bad taste.

"Rich mentioned you two know each other. Slipped my mind. Old age steals as much from the mind as it does from the body," said Hansford, looking from one to another curiously.

"We were acquainted in Dallas," replied Charles with a frown. It was a subject he didn't want to discuss.

"The sheriff came to tell us Rich is dead, Virginia. Somebody shot him."

Virginia closed her eyes for a second before sinking into a chair. "Oh, my God."

Lindman awkwardly patted her shoulders. "It was quick, Mrs. Hansford. He didn't suffer."

She ignored him, looking over at Charles with expressionless blue eyes. "What happened?"

Charles cleared his throat. He and Virginia had played this same scene before, and he hated giving her the details of this murder as much as he had the details of the last one. "Rich was shot with a twenty-two while sitting in his car sometime between four and six o'clock this morning. The body was later removed from the car and the face mutilated by a shotgun blast."

Virginia sucked in a breath. "A shotgun blast. But why would anyone do that?"

Charles shrugged his shoulders. "To make it look like an accident. At least, we think so."

"Of course, it's pheasant season," said Virginia as if she'd forgotten. "Are you sure it wasn't an accident? Perhaps the first shot was an accident and someone panicked. God knows, Rich was overdue. He hunted geese in Canada, moose in New England, deer in Colorado, duck, turkey, quail, and pheasant wherever one hunts those particular birds. The law of averages was bound to catch up with him."

"It was murder," said Charles. "Did Rich have any enemies?"

Virginia tilted her head back and laughed, a humorless sound that ended in a hiccup. Charles caught his breath as another image superimposed itself over her features. He stepped toward her, his lips forming another name, one he hadn't spoke in four years.

"Are you being facetious, Charles?"

The image disappeared at the sound of Virginia's voice, leaving behind a sense of yearning that both surprised and sickened him. He had buried the past, and damn whoever killed Rich Hansford for inadvertently opening up the grave.

"Sheriff, you all right?"

Charles seized on Meenie's question like a lifeline. "I'm fine. Just a headache from standing out in the cold this morning. Happens every year during the first cold snap. Virginia, who were Rich's enemies?"

"Name someone, Charles."

"Did he mention anyone in particular who was angry with him?"

She shook her head. "Not to me, but we didn't talk about who hated him."

"Bill Adams," interjected Fred Hansford. "He was going to foreclose on Bill Adams, or rather he planned to force Brad Masters to do it. Bill's note, along with several others, had been signed over as security for the accommodation loan Carroll National owed Rich's bank."

"How many payments had Bill missed?" asked Charles.

"One, and another one was due Monday."

"Rich Hansford was going to throw a man off his property for missing one payment?" asked Charles in disbelief.

The old man hunched his shoulders. "It was legal. Might not have been right, but Rich never worried much about what was right, just what was legal."

"Why the hell didn't you step in and stop him, Fred?" demanded Meenie. "He was runnin' roughshod over everybody. Don't you own part of Lone Star National?"

Hansford sank back in his wheelchair, his face gray. "I couldn't, Meenie. When my wife died, she willed all her stock to Rich. That gave him controlling interest, and he forced me out. Oh, I'm still on the board of directors, but Rich did what he wanted. I could cause him some grief, but I couldn't stop him."

Meenie spat at the glowing embers in the fireplace. "Somebody sure as hell did."

Hansford looked down at the glowing end of his cigarette. Suddenly he ground it out in an ashtray built into the arm of his wheelchair. "Rich!" He spat the name out in disgust. "He always was a spoiled little bastard. Too good to be called Fred like his granddaddy and me. Never trust the third generation, Sheriff. The blood's run thin."

He covered his face with his swollen, knotted hands, but not before Charles saw tears seep out of the old man's eyes. "I'm sorry, Mr. Hansford."

The old man lowered his hands. Tears made wet streaks down his face. "I reckon you think Virginia and me are hardhearted and unnatural, talking about Rich like this. It's like someone died who's been sick a long time, and you're just glad he's finally out of his misery."

Charles thought it more likely that Rich Hansford's death

put a lot of other people out of their misery. "Were you and Virginia here at the ranch early this morning?"

Hansford jerked his attention back to Charles. "Are you asking us for an alibi, Sheriff?"

Charles nodded. "I'm sorry, but this is a homicide investigation. I have to know."

Hansford stuck his hands out. The fingers were swollen and crooked, the ends of several twisted to overlap the next. "Look at me, Sheriff. I can hardly get out of this chair to answer nature's call. I'm too crippled up to drive. Don't think I could hold a gun anymore, much less pull the trigger. As for Virginia, she wouldn't kill anybody. She might get her hands dirty."

Virginia sat up straight, her spine hardly touching the back of her chair. "I was sound asleep at four o'clock, Charles."

"In the guest house?" he asked, wishing he were questioning someone else. Anyone else.

"She drove in from Amarillo about one or 'round about there—had a party or some fancy doings she couldn't skip—dropped in to tell me she was here, and didn't leave again, Sheriff," said Hansford. "I can vouch for that. I don't sleep much anymore—hurt too damn bad most of the time—and I would've heard her car. No way to get from the guest house to the road except driving by this place. You're going to have to look closer to home. I'm sorry about that. Those are your folks in Crawford County, and it's hard to distrust your own. But I'll expect you to do it. Rich might've had a mean streak a yard wide, but he was my own and I want his murderer caught."

He leaned his head against the back of his wheelchair and closed his eyes. "I'm tired, Sheriff, and I want to be alone. I'm going to get out all my old photo albums and look at pictures of Rich when he was still calling himself Fred. Maybe then I can mourn my son. So if you don't have anything else to say, Manuel will show you out."

"Goodbye, Mr. Hansford." He tipped his hat to Virginia. "Goodbye, Ginny. I'm sorry."

She smoothed her pale blue woolen skirt over her knees. Charles shivered as the ghostly memory of another woman making the same feminine gesture smothered him like a shroud.

"I'm sorry, too, Charles. I'm sorry about so many things."

Virginia's voice, her words, her blue eyes blurry with tears—all so reminiscent of another—were too much. He turned and blundered through the door, welcoming the frigid air of a Panhandle morning. Maybe it would refreeze those parts of his soul that had begun to thaw.

CHAPTER 9

CHARLES SIPPED HIS COFFEE, PLEASED TO SEE THAT his hands were no longer shaking. He was back in his office with its battered furniture, the yellowed map of Crawford County in its customary place on the wall behind his desk, the old radiators clanging and wheezing as the ancient furnace in the basement three stories below pumped steam through its network of pipes.

He was Charles Timothy Matthews, sheriff of Crawford County.

Memories of what he had been, *who* he had been, were safely buried once more. He was back in control again.

He picked up the typed statements, shuffled them, cut them, sorted them into two piles, then shuffled them again. It didn't matter how he shuffled, cut, or sorted; the facts remained the same. The only people in the hunting party with any connection to Rich Hansford, and thus any motive to kill him, were the four Crawford County hunters: Bill Adams, Brad Masters, Jess Turner, and Ick Johnson. Four respected citizens, directors of the Carroll National Bank, all in some way threatened by Hansford, and all except Jess without an alibi for the time of the murder. Adams was a widower, Brad was divorced, Ick was a bachelor. No one could support their claims to being home in bed during the critical time. As for Jess, his alibi wasn't worth the paper it was written on.

Shoving the papers to one side, he laced his fingers together behind his head, and glanced resentfully at Lindman. The New Mexican sheriff was tilted back in one of the wooden chairs, his feet propped on the edge of Charles's desk, his hat over his eyes, and snoring with every breath. Charles would swear the man even snored with an accent.

He leaned back in his own chair to study the pattern of stains on the acoustical tiled ceiling. Idly he wondered how many hours he'd spent in the same position doing the same thing in the two and a half years since he'd taken office. Ten? Twenty? A hundred? Did it matter? Probably not. The pattern of stains never changed and neither did his responsibility. He still had a murderer to catch, a murderer he would know personally.

He rotated his thumbs against his temples. His head felt like a balloon about to explode from the pressure of his own thoughts. He'd fled Dallas and the District Attorney's office there looking for peace, for black and white values, the good guys versus the bad guys. He thought he'd found all three in Crawford County.

On a sudden impulse he pushed Lindman's feet off the desk.

Lindman woke up with a vengeance. Or rather, a curse. "Damn it to hell, Matthews! Wake a man up like that. I might've shot your head off."

"A fellow officer is in trouble, and you're snoring like you don't have a care in the world."

Lindman rubbed his eyes and grinned. "Damn right, Matthews, because it ain't my county, and I'm gladder than you'll ever know."

Charles looked at the ceiling again. "Crawford County hadn't had a deliberate homicide in over eighty years, not since the turn of the century when an early pioneer woman poisoned her husband with arsenic. Until I took office, that is. I've investigated five homicides in less than three years. If you figured it per capita, that makes this county the murder capital of Texas. Maybe I'm a catalyst. Maybe my presence sets forces in motion that might not ordinarily erupt."

Lindman interrupted. "And maybe you're full of crap, Matthews."

Charles laughed and rubbed his chin. "I do sound crazy, don't I? Casting myself as some kind of instrument of fate? But God, Lindman, it's one way to avoid facing reality. The simple fact is that Rich Hansford was a bad guy. Until this morning his murderer was a good guy."

He sat up and uncapped his bottle of pills. "Society is in a hell of a mess when a Texas county sheriff needs a program to tell the good guys from the bad guys."

Lindman squinted at the bottle in Charles's hands. "I don't

know what's wrong with your gut, Matthews, but that junk isn't going to cure it."

"Butt out, Lindman."

"Sheriff." Raul stood in the doorway. "I need to talk to you."

Meenie shouldered his way in front of Raul and marched over to sit down by Lindman. "I told him there wasn't no use in talking to you, but he's being stubborn as a mule."

Charles shook out two antacid tablets as he eyed his deputies. "Raul, Meenie."

"Those pills are not good for your ulcer," said Raul.

Charles slammed the bottle on his desk. "Damn it, did Doc talk to you, too, or is everybody handing out unsolicited medical advice today? Before you say anything else, let me warn you that I'm not in the mood to discuss the state of my digestive tract."

Raul closed the door and walked to the center of the office. He removed his hat and stood looking at the map pinned on the wall behind Charles's desk. "No, it's something else."

"Damn foolishness is what it is," Meenie mumbled.

Lindman slid down on his chair and propped his feet on Charles's desk again. "He's sure come to the right place."

Charles felt his stomach tighten. Raul's face was stiff with a pinched look about the nostrils. "Don't keep me in suspense, Raul. I'm not in the mood for that either."

Raul drew a deep breath and spoke quickly, the lilt in his voice more noticeable than usual. "Sheriff, I wish to apologize for my behavior this morning. I violated my oath of office and my friendship with you. I was unprofessional and disloyal. If you want my resignation, I'll give it to you."

Charles chewed the two chalky-tasting pills as he contemplated his deputy. "In which law enforcement handbook did you read that little speech?" He took a sip of water. "Don't tell me. I don't want to know. And for God's sake, sit down. You look like you're facing a firing squad."

Raul fell into the last of the wooden chairs like a puppet whose strings had broken. Resting his elbows on his knees, he whirled his hat on one hand and looked at the floor. Finally he looked up. "I had no right to say what I did."

Charles wondered if his own eyes held as much regret and guilt as Raul's. Probably more, he decided. After all, he was the man in charge. Ultimately, the responsibility for covering up L. D. Lassiter's murder was his. "Everything you said was true."

"Then you're not mad?"

"I didn't say I wasn't mad. I am, but not because you reminded me of a choice I made that I wish I could forget. I'm mad because you and Meenie seem to want me to make that same choice again. And I can't. Not this time."

"Not even for justice?" asked Meenie.

"Goddamn it, I'm not Solomon!"

"Hold up there a minute!" shouted Lindman. "I don't know exactly what the three of you are talking about and my gut tells me I don't want to know, but all of you better swallow whatever is sticking in your craws and get on with the job. If you can't, then maybe all of you better turn in your badges and let Miss Poole run the sheriff's department. From what I've seen of that woman she could do it without working up a sweat." He folded his arms. "End of sermon."

Charles wiped his hand over his face, looked at Meenie and Raul, and grinned reluctantly. "I don't think Crawford County would appreciate Miss Poole as sheriff so I guess I better start acting like one. Frankly, I ought to fire you both for acting like top grade, U.S. prime horses' asses, not to mention obstructing a homicide investigation; but I'd have to fire myself, too. Besides, you happen to be just the horses' asses I need. You know Crawford County better than I do. You know who's feuding with whom, who plays poker together on Saturday night, who's drinking buddies with whom. I'm still trying to sort out who is kin to whom. The intermarriages and blood relationships in this county would give a trained genealogist fits, without trying to decipher interlocking friendships. So let's not have any more talk about resigning or about how Hansford deserved what he got. Maybe he did, but this time, we're not making that decision." He pointed a finger at Raul, then at Meenie. "If either of you pull a stunt like that one this morning, I promise you that God on Judgment Day will be more charitable than I."

"Yes, sir," said Raul. Meenie merely nodded.

"This is the first time I've ever seen anyone sit at attention, Raul. You make me feel like I'm back in the army. Relax and tell me if Doc Akin found anything else at the autopsy."

Raul sank against the chair and wiped his hand across his forehead. "Hansford may have been with a woman last night." A red flush darkened the skin over his cheeks.

Charles tightened his lips to keep from smiling. Another

deputy who was prudish about sex. "Doc is psychic maybe? How can he be sure?"

Raul turned even redder. "We found some hairs on the body that didn't match Hansford's. Long blonde hair."

Charles could feel Meenie and Lindman looking at him. "Hansford's wife is a blonde. Presumedly she might be close enough to, uh, shed on him."

"Not unless she saw him after he got dressed for hunting. We found three hairs twisted around a button on his shirt, two caught in the turquoise setting of a ring worn on his left hand, and five tangled in his watch band. Shorter blonde hairs were found on the nude body where"—Raul cleared his throat—"you'd expect to find them if Hansford had been, uh, intimate with a woman."

"I get the picture, Raul. No need to search for more Victorian euphemisms." He rubbed his temples again. His skin felt tight and hot, and he wished he could go home, apply an ice pack to his throbbing head, and forget Frederick Lee Hansford III. Better yet, he wished he could go to Angie's and let her apply the ice pack. While he was wishing, he might as well go all the way and wish he'd never been elected Crawford County sheriff.

"Guess we need to talk to that wife of his again, Sheriff," said Meenie.

Charles avoided looking at Meenie. "She has an alibi. According to her father-in-law, she never left the ranch."

Meenie grunted. "He sure was quick to give her one. And she was pretty quick this morning, too, for somebody that didn't like to get up early. That hired man of Hansford's didn't hardly have time to get to that guest house before she was steppin' through the living room door."

Charles shifted uneasily in his chair. "Maybe she was already up and dressed."

"Yeah, like she was expectin' us."

"Why are you on her case?" demanded Charles. "Haven't you read the statements yet? Nobody in the hunting party has an alibi worth a damn. And you're harping on the one person who does."

Meenie's shrewd blue eyes held an expression Charles didn't like. "Maybe I'm wondering why you're gettin' your back up defending her. Anybody else, you'd have them in here like a shot."

"Why would she meet him in the field? And why, if she did

shoot him, did she hang around the scene for an hour, then fake an accident? And how did she manage to get him out of that Suburban? She's a small woman and he was a big man, and you know as well as I do that a corpse is a dead weight in more ways than one." He shook his head, feeling almost lightheaded with relief as he considered his own words. "The scenario just doesn't work. Besides, she doesn't have a motive."

"And you ain't lookin' for one, Sheriff," said Meenie, folding his hands over his scrawny belly and staring at Charles.

Charles felt Meenie's accusation like an arrow sinking into his belly. He pressed his hand over his stomach hoping to ease the spasms of pain. "Are you accusing me of deliberately ignoring a logical suspect? Of obstructing an investigation for personal reasons?"

"I ain't saying that, but you're human like other folks. Like me and Raul, for instance. We don't want nobody we like to be guilty, and neither do you."

"I didn't say I liked Virginia. I just said I knew her."

"Judging from the way you turned white as a ghost and run out of her daddy-in-law's house a while ago, I'd say you was a sight closer to the lady than you let on."

"What's between Virginia and me is none of your business, Meenie, so back off."

"Stop it!" Raul shouted.

Lindman got to his feet, his eyes flickering from Charles to Meenie. "I think that's enough yelling from everybody."

"Madre de Dios!" continued Raul in a softer voice. "Rich Hansford is still making trouble. He has us fighting with each other like his ghost was putting words in our mouths."

Charles wiped his hand over his face. "Hansford was a lousy human being, but I don't think he has supernatural powers, Raul. As Meenie said, we're all human and we don't want to arrest someone we like for murder. But we're not paid to be human. We're paid to be cops."

"Ain't nothin' says we can't be both," said Meenie.

"We made that mistake once before, and once is all we can allow ourselves." Charles stood up, slipped off his jacket, and reached for his sheepherder's coat. "So let's go be cops."

Meenie rose and hitched up his pants. "And do what? Arrest Mrs. Hansford?"

Charles grabbed his hat off the filing cabinet and headed for the door. "Virginia Hansford isn't the only blonde involved in this case, Meenie. There's also the delectable Marta Turner."

"But she's Jess's alibi," protested Meenie.

"Is she now? Maybe it's the other way around."

CHAPTER 10

"DAMN IT! LOOK AT THOSE BEER TRUCKS!" Charles slammed on the brakes and fishtailed to a stop next to a white camper. A huge yellow and white striped tent stood like an inverted bowl in the middle of a pasture surrounded by cars, campers, pickups, station wagons, and even a motorcycle. The owners and passengers of said vehicles clustered around two refrigerated trucks whose drivers were busily dispensing free beer in plastic cups. It was a hunter's dream come true: free barbecue and beer. It was Charles's nightmare: liquor and guns.

Charles jerked open his door and scrambled out of the patrol car. "I'm stopping this right now."

Meenie burst out of the back seat and grabbed his arm. "Ain't nothing you can do, Sheriff. This here is Bill Adams's private property, and nobody's selling beer. It's free for the asking. You go in there acting like a crazy man, and Bill Adams'll have a right to call his lawyer. On the other hand, he probably won't have to. I think his lawyer's over there drinking beer. This here is the feed," he continued in a reverent tone of voice that made Charles grit his teeth. "It's mighty nearly as sacred as church. Nobody drinks too much. If they do, Bill sees to it they don't go huntin' again until they sober up. Take it easy. Remember what you came for; it wasn't bustin' up the feed."

"You got a bad attitude, Matthews," said Lindman, climbing out of the car and looking longingly at the beer truck. "How the hell did you ever get elected when you talk like a damn temperance leader? Meenie, you better watch him, or he sure won't get reelected."

"Get off my back, both of you. I promise I won't embarrass you. I'm just going to march in that tent and get the Turners."

Meenie licked his lips. "Sheriff, how about eating lunch here? Bill Adams cooks a real good calf fry."

"I haven't had any calf fries since the Fourth of July picnic," said Raul.

"Come on, Matthews. Let's have a plateful. I left Clayton at three-thirty this morning. I'm feeling peaked."

Charles swallowed rapidly at the thought of what calf fries—bull testicles sliced thin and deep-fat-fried until crisp, and served with french fries, slices of raw onion, canned peaches, and light bread—would do to his already burning stomach. "Just bring me a cup of coffee," he mumbled and ducked into the tent.

Inside was chaos. Hunters dressed in every imaginable garb from plain Levi's and red flannel shirts to army fatigues to tailored twills and quilted yellow vests milled around banquet tables borrowed from every church in town. Wearing a white apron over his hunting clothes, Bill Adams oversaw a small army of men slicing, cooking, and serving enough food to feed all of Crawford County. The smell of hot grease and cold beer, the odor of freshly sliced onions and raw potatoes, mixed with the sweet scent of peaches and the musk of sweating, unshaven men. It was masculinity in the raw. The few women present, mostly wives of Crawford County men, looked puzzled and uneasy, as if their husbands had metamorphosed into strangers.

Charles wove his way between the tables, nodding to the men he knew as he searched the crowd. He was deafened by the noise, choked by the rich mixture of odors, and coated by the dust kicked up by hundreds of pairs of feet, bruised by the back-slapping, arm-grabbing camaraderie of the locals. Before he was halfway across the expanse of seething humanity, he decided looking for two people in this Roman circus was not one of his better ideas. In fact, he decided every decision he'd made beginning with getting out of bed was ill-advised.

If he had not been between the Turners and the only exit, or if Jess had not been pulling Marta through the crowd, forcing it to part like the Red Sea, Charles might not have seen them. "Jess!" he roared, and began pushing his way through the wall of bodies.

Jess Turner threw Charles a desperate look and jerked on Marta's arm, pulling her toward the entrance, pushing and shoving at anyone in his way. Suddenly he made a ninety degree turn toward the wall of the tent.

Charles cursed under his breath as he watched Jess grip the bottom of the tent and jerk upward. Marta rolled under the tent wall, quickly followed by Jess.

"To hell with politeness," said Charles aloud, and elbowed his way through the crowd, hoping the various exclamations of pain by those in his path didn't indicate any real injury. He'd apologize later, he thought as he ducked through the exit and rounded the tent toward the spot he'd last seen the Turners. He leaped over guy wires, sidestepped a hunter leaning against the tent with a beer in his hand and a glazed look in his eye, barreled into another hunter who was carrying two plates of food balanced on glasses of beer. With one corner of his mind Charles acknowledged the hunter's legitimate complaint and the originality of expression with which he vocalized it. Even Lindman paled in comparison.

Glimpsing Marta's wheat gold hair, he quickly darted to his left, skirting a beer truck and bumping its driver as he was dispensing beer. "Excuse me," muttered Charles, running toward a row of parked cars.

"You dumb bastard!" screamed the driver. "You made me break the spigot. I'm gonna have beer all over the damn ground!"

"Sorry," said Charles, glancing back over his shoulder to see a fountain of foam spewing from the truck. Frantic hunters scattered as the beer sprayed bystanders. He made a mental note to try to bump the driver of the rival beer company's truck under similar circumstances. As Meenie would say, there was more than one way to skin a cat.

He ran between two parked cars and saw the Turners not more than a hundred feet away. "Jess! Stop!" he yelled, jumping a frozen rut cut by one of the hundreds of vehicles.

Jess looked back, desperation now twisting his features into a caricature of his usual placid expression. "No!" he screamed, and turned to run again, pulling Marta after him. One foot encased in its stiff work boot slipped on the edge of a rut, and he fell.

Charles heard the crack of breaking bone and Marta's scream almost simultaneously.

Charles shifted uncomfortably in the molded plastic chair and wished he were sitting anywhere but in the hall of Carroll

Memorial Hospital. He wished that he hadn't chased Jess and that Jess hadn't broken his leg. He wished that his eyes didn't burn from lack of sleep and that his belly didn't hurt.

"Have a cup of coffee," said Meenie, handing him a Styrofoam cup. "Tastes like mud somebody scraped off an eighteen-wheeler on Carroll Avenue. Nothing like it to take your mind off wishing."

Charles accepted the cup. "How did you know I was wishing?"

Meenie hitched up his pants with the automatic motion of somebody with no hips worthy of the description, and sat down beside him, tilting his chair back against the wall. "The look on your face, like you wished you were somewheres else besides Crawford County doing something besides being sheriff. You always get it when you're feeling guilty."

"Do you blame me?"

Meenie shifted his tobacco and contemplated his coffee. "I don't have to. You blame yourself for every dang thing that goes wrong whether it's your fault or not—and Jess Turner's busted leg ain't your fault. You never made him bolt out of that tent like a calf running from a coyote. Running from you was a dumb stunt. I'm surprised his wife went along with it. She always struck me as having a mite more between the ears than Jess."

Charles glanced down the hall at the closed emergency room doors and felt his belly twist with guilt. "She's got more than I do, too. I should have picked them up at their home. I made a bad judgment call."

"I might have known it wouldn't do no good to talk to you," said Meenie in disgust.

"Sheriff!" A tall gray-haired man in his early fifties slammed out of the emergency room and stalked down the hall, peeling off a white coat to reveal a red flannel shirt and Levi's tucked into hunting boots.

Charles sat his coffee cup underneath his chair and got up, feeling old and stiff and defensive. "Dr. Wallace."

The doctor stopped in front of Charles and glared at him. "I want to know what in the hell is going on. I'm drawing a bead on the biggest pheasant in Crawford County when my beeper goes off. Startled me so badly I jerked up my shotgun and blasted a hole right through one of Southwest Public Service's electric poles. I didn't exactly shoot it in two, but I wouldn't want to stand next to it in a strong wind. Damn utility company ought to bury their lines. Anyway, I drive like a madman to the hospital to find one of my best patients, which is you, Sheriff, standing guard over one of my other best patients, which is Jess Turner."

"A man was killed today—" Charles began.

"I know; I heard about it. Rich Hansford. He wasn't worth the powder it took to blow him to hell.

"How did you know about Rich Hansford? Did Jess Turner say anything to you?"

The doctor grinned. "I heard it over the police scanner. There must be a scanner for every two households in town. Helps us all keep up with the gossip. But what does that have to do with Jess Turner?"

Charles fought his rising temper. Everybody in Crawford County acted as if they were sitting on a jury and had a right to know every piece of evidence before anyone decided to cooperate. "Just tell me when I can see Jess Turner and you can go back to your blood sport, Doctor."

"I don't think so."

"You can't prevent my talking to him. I'll just assign a deputy to sit by the door until you release him from the hospital."

The doctor clasped Charles's shoulder. "If you'd stop getting irate and jumping to conclusions, your belly might not hurt so bad. I didn't mean you couldn't see Jess; I meant I wasn't going back out to hunt. To tell the truth, I was glad that beeper spoiled my aim. Saved me the trouble of missing my shot. I don't much like to hunt. I just do it because the farmers around here need the money so damn bad." He released Charles's shoulder and stepped back. "I'm trusting you not to tell anybody at the doughnut shop about that. Might ruin my macho image."

"You mean everyone doesn't already know? I didn't think there were any secrets in Crawford County."

The doctor shook his head. "I don't know where you got that idea. There are dozens of secrets, some that we talk about and some we don't."

"What's the difference?"

"Whether the secret hurts someone or not, Sheriff, like the one Jess Turner is keeping."

"Then he did tell you something."

"No, and I wouldn't tell you if he did. Your job is probing the dark places; mine is to make sure those dark places don't hurt my patients anymore than they can stand. Which brings me back to Jess Turner. He refused any painkillers."

"What!" exclaimed Charles, pressing his hand over his stomach to stop his own pain.

"No Demerol, no morphine, no codeine, not even a goddamn aspirin. I had to set that broken leg while he laid there with the sweat rolling off his face, chewing his lip until I stuck a wad of cotton between his teeth. He fainted a couple of times and I wished he'd stayed unconscious the whole time. That was a bad break. He was just damn lucky the bone didn't move because I don't know what in the hell I'd have done then."

Charles stuck his trembling hands in his pockets. "How soon can I see him?"

"Right now, damn it! He's not going to let me give him a shot for the pain until he talks to you. I told him I wouldn't let you talk to him if he was all doped up, but he didn't listen. He wants to get it over with, so get your butt in there and ask your questions. Then maybe I can fill him full of painkillers and send him home. But take it easy, Sheriff. I don't like to see a patient of mine suffer. Goes against my natural inclinations."

"Damn it, Doctor Wallace, I'm not going to torture him," said Charles.

The doctor tapped Charles on the chest. "You're my patient, too, Sheriff, and I've been watching you holding your belly. If you don't stop eating those antacid pills and get that prescription that I gave you filled, you're going to be hurting worse than Jess. I'll leave orders for Jess with the nurse, so I'd appreciate it if you'd tell her when you finish your questions. I'm going home. It just occurred to me that if all my patients think I'm out hunting, maybe I can eat an uninterrupted meal for the first time since I started practicing medicine twenty-five years ago. I want to see if my digestion can stand it."

The doctor hurried down the hall toward the nurses' station. Charles pushed open the emergency room door. Jess Turner lay on the examining table, his face as colorless as the sheets covering it. His hair was pasted to his head with sweat; his lower lip was swollen and bloody with unmistakable teeth marks. A heavy plaster cast covered his right leg from toes to hip with his ripped trousers draping it like a tattered skirt.

Charles squashed his impulse to send Jess home without questioning him. In spite of his appearance, Jess's sunken, red-rimmed eyes were alert—and wary. He would be no less wary tomorrow and Charles would be no less reluctant. "Jess, why did you run from me?"

"We weren't running from you, Sheriff," said Marta, sitting on a stool beside the examining table and holding Jess's hand. "We had another hunting party scheduled and we were late."

Charles shook his head. "No, Marta, you both saw me and you ran. Don't begin this interview by lying to me."

The Turners stared sullenly at him before Jess finally spoke. "We aren't answering any questions without a lawyer, Sheriff."

"You may call a lawyer. You may call ten lawyers. They will all tell you the same thing. Until you are the focus of this investigation or unless I arrest you, remaining silent is not one of your choices. You're not a suspect—yet. And I'm not arresting you. All I'm trying to do is clear up the discrepancies in your statements. Now let's try again. Where were you between four and six this morning, Marta?"

Jess reared up on one elbow. "She was asleep right next to me!"

"You told me this morning she was baking bread and fixing you steak and potatoes, Jess."

"I had my mornings mixed up. That was yesterday morning."

"You can't remember what you had for breakfast two hours after you ate it, Jess? Which was it, Marta? Were you asleep or baking bread?"

"I told you we were asleep! We slept until about five-thirty!" shouted Jess.

"If you were asleep, then you don't know if Marta was in bed with you or not, do you, Jess?"

"I thought you were a good man. When we visited with you at Angie's house, Sheriff," said Jess hoarsely. "But only a low-down bastard would keep after a woman the way you're doing."

A lowdown bastard or a sheriff, thought Charles silently. Right now he was both. "Is that why you shot Rich Hansford, Jess, because he kept after your wife?"

"I didn't shoot Rich Hansford!"

"We have evidence that there was a woman with the victim just prior to his death. Marta, did you meet Rich Hansford this morning between four and six? And did he sexually assault you?"

Jess tried to struggle to a sitting position. "Goddamn, Sheriff! You shut your filthy mouth and leave Marta out of this!"

"If he did, Jess, and you shot him, you better tell the sheriff now," said Meenie. "It ain't murder in this state if you kill a man for messing with your wife when she don't want to be messed with—as long as you catch him in the act, or at least don't give him time to do more than zip his pants. But you keep waiting around to admit it and the jury ain't gonna believe you didn't give it some thought first."

Meenie's interpretation of the legal defense of sudden passion was correct—as far as it went, thought Charles. Unfortunately, it didn't go far enough to cover Jess Turner. It was at least ten miles over mostly unpaved roads from the Turner farm to Bill Adams's field—a minimum of fifteen minutes driving time each way. Add another ten minutes or so for Marta to tell Jess what happened, and there was a time span of at least forty minutes from provocation to response. Too long. Sudden passion was very narrowly defined to be an immediate loss of control at the instant of provocation. Fifteen minutes of driving time turned sudden passion into cold calculation.

And why would Rich Hansford wait for forty minutes in the dark and freezing cold after he'd completed his assignation? And why would Jess Turner shoot him, then wait an hour to set up the fake accident? The scenario wouldn't play. Unless you changed the cast of characters.

"There's a way to leave Marta out of it, Jess," said Charles, breaking the brief silence that met Meenie's statement. "Let her voluntarily submit samples of her head and pubic hair for comparison with the hair found on the victim. If they don't match, then we've proved that Marta wasn't in that Suburban with Rich Hansford. Then I can look for another woman."

"You want to strip my wife and take hair from her privates? I'll kill you first!"

"I'm not taking the samples; Miss Poole will do that."

"Nobody's going to touch my wife! Nobody!"

"Hush, Jess," crooned Marta, putting her hands over his mouth. "We didn't kill Rich Hansford, Sheriff, and we're not fixing to say anything more."

In the Texas Panhandle, *fixing to*, was a future tense expression of intent. Charles knew that hell would freeze over before the Turners answered more questions. "Then I'll have to get a search warrant, Marta."

"Go to hell, Sheriff," said Marta Turner, her body so rigid that Charles knew touching her would be like touching flesh-colored stone. Or glass, he thought suddenly, because Marta Turner looked ready to shatter.

CHAPTER 11

"WHAT IN THE HELL IS GOING ON?" SHOUTED Charles, stalking through the door that separated the public reception area from the squad room.

The three people clustered around the dispatcher's desk looked up from their cards. "There's no need to shout. No one is hard of hearing. Sheriff Lindman suggested we pass the time waiting for you by playing this fascinating game of probabilities," said Miss Poole, fanning out her hand. "I believe he called it five-card draw."

"Lindman taught you to play poker?" asked Charles in disbelief.

"Learning new things keeps the mind active," replied Miss Poole. "I wish I had known this game when I was teaching sixth grade math. Probability is such a difficult concept for younger students to grasp. Playing poker might have helped. Mrs. Jenkins, it's your bet."

"I'll pass," said the plump J. P. "I'm having a terrible run of bad luck."

"Nonsense," said Miss Poole in a brisk tone of voice Charles was certain her former students would recognize, one that said to straighten up your mental attitude or else. "Luck has nothing to do with it. Winning is a matter of calculating the probability of my hand being higher than yours. Sheriff Lindman, I'll see your three and raise you two." She selected five toothpicks from a stack and added them to the pot in the center of the desk.

"What are the toothpicks worth?" asked Meenie, leaning over Miss Poole's shoulder to look at her hand.

Miss Poole's face looked blank for a split second while she assimilated his question and formulated her answer. Charles would bet the dispatcher's brain could process information faster than the average home computer. "You mean money, of course. Oh, we're not playing for money, although Sheriff Lindman did say it would make the game more interesting. But that would be gambling. I disapprove of gambling."

"It's a good thing, too," said Lindman as he stared gloomily at his hand. "If we'd been playing for a nickel a toothpick, I'd already be down forty-seven dollars. Miss Poole, I think I'm gonna have to—"

"Fold," said Charles, plucking the cards out of three different hands. "We have a murder investigation going on"—he grabbed the deck just as Miss Poole reached for it—"and this is no time to sit around playing poker. Get to work, damn it!"

"Since Mrs. Jenkins doesn't work for you, and Sheriff Lindman is here in a strictly advisory capacity, I presume you're talking to me," said Miss Poole. "I'll have you know that I'm not neglecting my duties. I have typed the statements, caught up with my filing, and answered all radio calls which have come in. Under the circumstances, it's been an exceptionally peaceful day. Mr. Hansford's murder seems to have had a sobering effect on the hunters, and we've only had four arrests—an altercation over whose shot brought down a particularly large pheasant. I dispensed Band Aids and aspirin to the participants, Mrs. Jenkins assessed each a small fine, and Sheriff Lindman delivered a splendid lecture on sportmanship. It was a very successful exercise in public relations."

"Let's try another exercise in public relations, Miss Poole, but this one won't be so pleasant," Charles said, dropping the card deck in a filing cabinet and locking it. "Draw up a search warrant, let me check it, then have Judge Waters sign it."

"I'll have to find him, Sheriff," said Miss Poole with a frown.

"Don't tell me; he's hunting."

"I believe so."

"I said don't tell me! Just find him."

"Being impatient isn't good for your ulcer," remarked Miss Poole.

"Must be nice to be an attorney as well as a sheriff so you can check over your own search warrants," said Lindman with a forlorn look at the locked filing cabinet holding the deck of cards. "I always have to settle for some shavetail assistant D.A. just out of law school doing mine. I sure don't want to violate somebody's civil rights."

"That's a very commendable attitude, Sheriff Lindman," said Miss Poole.

"No, it isn't," replied Lindman with a grin. "I don't want some piece of slime oozing out of going to prison just because I screwed up a search warrant."

"That's enough philosophy," snapped Charles, jotting notes on a blank incident report form. "Here are the particulars for the warrant, Miss Poole: name, probable cause, evidence I'm seeking."

Miss Poole looked at his notes and frowned. "Sheriff—"

"Charles!"

Charles whirled around at the sound of the melodious and familiar voice. "Angie, girl, what are you doing here?"

His tense muscles relaxed, and he felt a sense of homecoming. Maybe that feeling of belonging with another person was the real basis of love, he thought as he watched Angie Lassiter pull a stocking cap off her shoulder length auburn hair. She wasn't a beautiful woman—her nose was a little too short and her chin too square—but the wide-set hazel eyes, full mouth, and complexion that always reminded Charles of thick, rich cream, more than compensated for any irregularity of features. She warmed his soul and heated his blood, and he felt a sudden urge to carry her off to some exotic place where no one had ever heard of pheasant hunts or murder and do something crazy—like lap champagne from her navel.

In the meantime he'd perform the only socially acceptable action possible in polite company. He wrapped his arm around her shoulders and led her into the room. "Sheriff Lindman, may I introduce the woman I'm going to marry: Angie Lassiter."

Lindman held out his hand. "You're getting a good man, Mrs. Lassiter. He's a little contrary sometimes, but nothing you can't handle. Just hit between the eyes with a fence post when you need to get his attention."

Angie ignored Lindman's outstretched hand. "Charles, what are you doing to Marta and Jess?"

"Some days start bad and just get worse," said Meenie.

Charles's blood cooled down to the freezing point and visions of champagne and navels vanished. "What?"

"Marta called me from the hospital."

"She had no right to involve you."

"Of course she did, Charles. I'm her friend and this is Crawford County." Angie slipped away from his arm and stepped away.

"This is murder. It doesn't matter whether it happens in Crawford County or New York City."

Angie and Miss Poole glanced at each other, then Angie shook her head. "I think it does matter, Charles. In New York City everybody is a stranger. In Crawford County, the only stranger is you."

Charles felt as if the earth had split, creating a chasm that separated him from Angie and everyone else in the room. "I've lived here nearly four years, Angie. I've read the county history book; I've studied survey maps to learn the terrain; sometimes I even remember who's second cousin to whom—without asking Meenie—and that's not easy. I think three-fourths of you are interrelated."

"Actually, Sheriff, I believe only one-half of Crawford County families are related by blood," said Miss Poole. "Another one-fourth are related by marriage."

"And I suppose I'll be part of this big happy family when I marry Angie?"

"As I recollect, Sheriff, Miss Angie's only related to one other family in Crawford County, so you'll still be a mite short of cousins-in-law," said Meenie, scratching his head.

"That's not what I meant, damn it! How long before I'm accepted? Or will I always be a poor relation, Angie's weird husband, Charles, who can't even ride a horse?"

"Charles, you're being melodramatic," said Angie.

"And a trifle insecure," added Miss Poole.

"What I am is a *trifle* confused. I'm like the pheasant. I'm a transplanted exotic bird, welcomed, fed, and left totally alone most of the time—until there's a murder. Then everybody starts shooting at me."

"Charles, you *are* accepted," Angie argued. "No one thinks you're weird. Just different—and you can't help that."

"Thanks, Angie."

"It's just that when people are frightened, they notice that difference more, and suddenly you're a stranger again."

"And you know what I think, Angie? I think I'm like that pheasant in another way: I'm useful. I think I was elected sheriff at least partly because I *am* a stranger. I have no inborn loyalty to any one faction."

"Impartial, impersonal justice, Sheriff?" asked Mrs. Jenkins.

"Exactly."

Mrs. Jenkins rested her plump hands on her equally plump thighs and peered up at him. "If your words were solid instead of sounds and I saw them lying out in the pasture, I wouldn't step in them. There's no such thing as impartial, impersonal justice. If there's people involved, then justice is damn personal, and the smaller the town, the more personal it is. I think the voters elected you because they expected you to be impartial about personal justice. But we forgot that you don't know us. You don't know everybody's black spots. You don't know who's black spots are likely to grow until they smother out all the white, and whose aren't."

"And nobody is willing to trust me enough to tell me, either. Everybody's lying either by commission or omission."

"That's why I'm here, Charles," said Angie patiently. "I'm trying to tell you about the people involved. Jess Turner is a very gentle man. He could never kill anybody."

"That's true, Sheriff," said Miss Poole. "I remember his being a very conciliatory young boy."

Charles had no doubt that she did. Miss Poole had an infallible memory—and an interfering nature. "I'm not interested in Jess Turner as a boy; I'm interested in Jess Turner, the man."

"The child is father of the man, Sheriff," said Miss Poole.

"And the leopard doesn't change his spots," added Mrs. Jenkins.

Charles felt buffeted and bloodied by the three women, none of whom came up to his shoulder. "I said I didn't want to hear any more philosophy. I have to examine the evidence and follow where it leads."

"What evidence?" demanded Angie. "Show me one piece of evidence that points to Jess Turner ever hurting anyone."

"Damn it, Angie, you're interfering. I can't talk about a murder investigation with a civilian."

"I'm not a civilian, Sheriff," interrupted Miss Poole. "You can talk to me. Now about this search warrant. It will humiliate Marta Turner. She's always been sensitive about her extraordinary physical endowments. She was miserable as a student because she suffered a great deal of"—Miss Poole hesitated uncertainly—"unwanted masculine attention from her classmates."

Charles didn't doubt it. He was certain Marta Turner had inspired the most awesome testosterone rush ever experienced before or since by Carroll High School males. "That's why I need the search warrant, Miss Poole. To discover if Marta

Turner was the object of Rich Hansford's masculine attentions."

"No!" cried Angie.

"Very probably," said another voice that was also melodious and, unfortunately, very familiar.

Charles almost groaned aloud. The owner of that voice was a complication he didn't need. Not now, not here.

CHAPTER 12

"GINNY! WHAT ARE YOU DOING HERE?"

"May I come in, Charles?" asked Ginny Hansford, immaculate perfection from the top of her platinum blonde head to the tips of her fashionable high-heeled boots. She was beauty under glass, distant and untouchable, and Charles felt a wrenching sense of regret. Ginny had not always been encased in artifice.

"Certainly," said Charles, taking a step toward the door before he stopped, feeling like an awkward fool. That door had been permanently open since it was hung at a twenty-degree angle in 1933 by a carpenter on the second day of his three-day binge in celebration of the end of Prohibition. Fortunately, the rest of the courthouse had been completed before the repeal of the Volstead Act.

Ginny stepped through the door and glanced around the squad room at the battered desks, dented filing cabinets, scratched tile floor, and stained, peeling walls. "My God, Charles, they're right; you don't belong here."

Charles flushed. "I'll admit the sheriff's department is spartan, but the county commissioners are frugal with the taxpayers' money."

She dismissed his words with an elegant wave of her hand. "Don't apologize. I just wasn't prepared for the incongruity of seeing you in these surroundings, like a prince playing a not very convincing pauper."

Actually Charles felt more like a frog waiting for the magic kiss that would turn him into a prince, but Crawford County didn't seem to be in the mood to pucker up. "I may not be very convincing, but I'm committed for the run of the play."

"As the sheriff."

He nodded.

"Rich at least enjoyed your performance. He got his jollies from watching you try to fit in with the local hicks—his words, not mine. He was still very interested in you, Charles." Her eyes rested briefly on Angie, and Charles felt his stomach tighten. He was suddenly very glad Rich Hansford was dead.

"Mrs. Hansford, may I offer my condolences on the death of your husband," said Miss Poole, glancing curiously from Charles to Ginny.

"You're Miss Poole, aren't you?"

"I didn't know you two had met," said Charles.

"We haven't," replied Ginny. "But Rich described everyone in the sheriff's department in minute detail."

"I recognized her immediately," said Miss Poole. "I've seen her photograph in the Amarillo paper. I always read it from front to back."

Charles could believe that. Miss Poole probably even read the classified ads.

"I never read the society page," said Mrs. Jenkins. "I'm too busy reading the obituary column to see which folks from Crawford County died while suffering from foreclosure."

Ginny Hansford flinched and Charles stepped closer to her. "This is Mrs. Viola Jenkins, a justice of the peace. She's a little distraught from having to pronounce so many people dead lately, including your husband."

"You're Maggie Pace's aunt, aren't you?" asked Ginny. "Then I don't imagine it bothered you very much to see Rich Hansford dead."

Mrs. Jenkins bounced out of her chair. "It bothered me a lot, young woman, and not just because I don't much like inspecting cadavers. Rich Hansford alive was trouble enough, but dead he's going to bring grief to everybody in this town, man and woman, whether they deserve it or not. The sheriff's going to paw through every life your husband ever kicked dirt on."

"That's enough, Mrs. Jenkins," shouted Charles. "Ginny isn't responsible for what her husband did. And it's my job to ask about his business associates." He sensed the hostility in the room as if it were a low pressure area that heralded a thunderstorm, and knew at least some of it was directed at him. He and Ginny were the strangers here.

Ginny's laughter had an ugly sound. "Rich didn't have any business associates, Charles. His relationships were more like franchises. The minute a person signed on the dotted line, he discovered that he wasn't an equal partner after all. Rich always got his share first, the biggest share at that. He always collected his debts and he took payment in money or flesh. And he had plenty of offers of both."

"But not from Marta Turner," said Angie. "And if you think so, then you're wrong."

Ginny tilted her head to study Angie, assessing her unemotionally, as if to determine how important a part she might hold in the cast of characters. "You must be the fiancée. Rich mentioned that you were getting married, Charles. He clipped the engagement announcement with Mrs. Lassiter's picture from the newspaper and made a point of showing it to me. He had watched you constantly since we moved back to Amarillo two years ago and he learned you were sheriff. He even kept a scrapbook about you. Sometimes I think he became so involved with Carroll National Bank just so he would have an excuse to come to Crawford County. He needed a hunter's blind and the bank was it."

Charles felt a chill raise goose bumps along his spine. "But he stayed out of my way."

"'Of course he did. He was a hunter, Charles. He always studied his prey in its natural habitat—or unnatural in this case—looking for its vulnerable spots. He had decided that being sheriff was important to you, and he was willing to wait quietly in his hunter's blind—at least until the next election."

"What was he planning to do—finance someone else's campaign against Charles? It wouldn't have worked. No one would vote for a candidate supported by Rich Hansford," said Angie, studying Ginny in turn.

"The voters might not have known."

"They would've found out because *I* would've found out," said Angie. "Secrets are hard to keep in Crawford County."

"She's certainly nothing like Carin, is she, Charles?" asked Ginny. "But then I can understand why you would want someone completely different, and she does have a sort of wholesome appeal."

"Who's Carin?" asked Angie with a puzzled glance at Charles.

"Ginny—" began Charles.

"His wife. Didn't he tell you?"

"Ginny, let's go into my office. I have a few more questions about Rich's business deals," said Charles, feeling everyone in the room staring at him with expressions ranging from curiosity to shock.

"That's a good idea, Sheriff," said Meenie, shifting his tobacco from one cheek to the other. "I was wondering when you was going to get around to asking Mrs. Hansford why she interrupted her grieving to visit us. Other than to talk about what a horse's behind her husband was. We already knew that."

"You don't need to tell me my duties, Meenie," snapped Charles.

"Ain't telling you; I'm reminding you. Not the same thing at all."

"Mrs. Hansford, allow me to escort you into the sheriff's private office," said Lindman, rising and offering his arm to Ginny.

"Very subtle—Sheriff Lindman, isn't it?" asked Ginny, placing her slender hand on his arm.

"Yes, ma'am, and I got a reputation up in Union County, New Mexico, for being subtle. In fact, some folks accuse me of being downright sneaky."

"A reputation I'm sure you've earned."

"Charles, I've got that invitation list you wanted," said Brad Masters diffidently as he walked into the squad room. He was followed by Maggie Pace, a frail young woman who might have been attractive had her features not been a taut mask of months-old fatigue.

"Matthews, you couldn't be more popular if you were handing out free cigars and nickel beer," said Lindman.

"Mrs. Hansford," said Brad, walking toward Ginny with outstretched hand. "I'm sorry about Rich."

"I doubt that, Brad," replied Ginny. "I don't think anybody's sorry Rich is dead."

She glanced over the banker's shoulder at Maggie Pace. For a moment Maggie seemed to shrink away before her back straightened. "Isn't that right, Maggie, or do you agree with your aunt that Rich's murder will resurrect nasty secrets you'd rather not confront." Maggie Pace turned even paler, and she groped for Brad's arm.

"There's no need to speak to Maggie like that," protested Brad, wrapping his arms around Maggie and pulling her against his chest. "She hasn't done anything."

For a second Charles thought that he saw regret in Ginny's blue eyes, but he decided it was desperation instead.

"Hasn't she?" asked Ginny.

Viola Jenkins took a step toward Ginny. "No, she hasn't, and you hush up your insinuations. It's bad enough that Maggie's lost everything her family had and has to live with her uncle and me, without having the whole mess thrown in her face like she was the one who did something shameful. The sheriff already knows your husband foreclosed on her land, so that piece of dirty linen's already been hung out to dry. Being spiteful won't help the sheriff find the murderer any faster; in fact, it might slow him down. He's suspicious of enough people without your throwing names up in the air like wheat chaff just to see where the wind blows them."

Miss Poole grabbed the J.P.'s arm. "Mrs. Jenkins, see to your niece."

Ginny Hansford released Lindman's arm and clenched her fists. "I'll air dirty linen and repeat all the names I ever heard Rich mention if that's what it takes, Mrs. Jenkins. I'll expose the secrets you all are so busy trying to keep.,"

"Whether any of them are true or not?" demanded Angie. "Whether any of them will embarrass or humiliate or hurt someone who doesn't deserve it?"

Ginny shrugged her shoulders. "That's none of my concern. It's Charles's business to sort through the secrets until he finds the right one, and I'm staying in town to watch him do it—so all of you might as well get used to seeing me. Charles, I'll be in Room 243 of Carroll's Rest. Anything I forget today during our tête-à-tête, I can tell you later. I don't want to overlook anything—or anyone."

"My God," said Angie softly. "What kind of a woman are you?"

Ginny Hansford squeezed her hands together. "A desperate one."

"And I suppose you don't have any secrets," said Viola Jenkins, patting her niece's shoulder. "I suppose there's nobody on this earth you'd protect—except yourself, of course."

Ginny stiffened and whirled around to storm into Charles's office, slamming the door in Lindman's face.

Lindman scratched his chin and looked around the room. "I think I'll wait in your office with Mrs. Hansford, Sheriff. Crawford County ain't paying me enough to stay out here."

"Crawford County isn't paying you anything," snapped Charles.

"That's what I mean," said Lindman as he disappeared into Charles's office.

Meenie cleared his throat. "I think I'll go with him, Sheriff. I ain't very good at handling what's going on. Ever since this women's libber stuff started, I don't know whether to wrestle a woman back to a cell to calm her down like I would a man, or hand her a hanky." He darted through the door after Lindman, leaving Charles feeling surrounded.

"My God, what a vicious woman!" exclaimed Brad Masters. "I had no idea she was like that. She and Rich were a matched set."

"For God's sake, don't you people have any charitable feelings?" demanded Charles. "Can you blame her for striking back at you? Somebody murdered her husband this morning and then mutilated his body, and you expect her to feel kindly toward Crawford County? Maybe Rich Hansford was a worthless human being, but she's his widow, and she's still in shock and acting out of character."

"You ask me, she didn't act like much of a grieving widow," said Mrs. Jenkins. "And her knowing that we think you don't know enough about folks to ask the right question. Ask her how long she listened to what we had to say before she finally announced herself. Eavesdropping isn't very polite either."

"Maybe she was screwing up her courage," retorted Charles. "Maybe she was afraid of just what happened—that you would rip her apart."

"You can't expect people who were threatened by Rich Hansford to feel Christian charity toward his family, Sheriff," said Miss Poole. "It isn't human nature. Also, Mrs. Hansford appeared not to welcome any sympathy. In fact, she seemed almost antagonistic. Brad, help Maggie into this chair and get her a cup of coffee."

"She ought to write a thank-you note to whoever shot him," said Mrs. Jenkins. "It sounds like she led a dog's life living with him and knowing about his women."

"We have no way of knowing what goes on between two people behind the closed doors of a marriage, Mrs. Jenkins," said Miss Poole, holding a cup of coffee to Maggie Pace's pale lips. "Perhaps she loved him in spite of his not inconsiderable faults. Human nature again."

"Now that is a Christian statement, Miss Poole," replied the J.P.

The dispatcher shook her head. "Not really, Mrs. Jenkins.

I'm giving Mrs. Hansford the benefit of the doubt. However, Sheriff, if I were you, I wouldn't believe everything she tells you."

"Are you calling her a liar, Miss Poole, when you don't know anything about her?" asked Charles in exasperation.

"Certainly not, but I am saying that she might confuse rumor and gossip for truth. Since you apparently know her quite well, I assume you can sort the wheat from the chaff."

"I'm glad someone thinks I'm competent," said Charles.

"I never doubted it for a minute, Sheriff, but like most men you do have your blind spots, and Mrs. Hansford appears to be one of them. I hope that doesn't prevent your being suspicious of her motives."

"Are you implying that Ginny Hansford murdered her husband, Miss Poole?" asked Charles, feeling his last bit of control over his temper beginning to slip like worn brakes.

"I am suggesting that—in today's slang—Mrs. Hansford is sending mixed signals. She exhibits no outward sign of grief, describes her husband in terms that would slander Caligula, but still expects us to believe she's desperate to know who killed him. What does she hope to accomplish with her accusations, Sheriff? To identify a murderer or to sow strife?"

"Miss Poole," said Charles slowly, "don't ever give me the benefit of one of your doubts."

"I am just trying to be impartial and impersonal, Sheriff."

"Then type up that search warrant instead," he said, striding toward his office. "As impartially and impersonally as you can manage."

"But Sheriff—"

"Now, Miss Poole."

"Charles, I have to talk to you," said Angie, grasping his arm as he reached to open his door, her hazel eyes full of questions.

Charles swallowed. He couldn't answer any questions about Carin; he couldn't talk about Carin, period. Not here and not now. He'd bungle it just as badly as he'd bungled the last ten minutes—beginning when Ginny walked through the door trailing the past after her. Damn her for ever mentioning Carin's name; damn Rich Hansford for dying in Crawford County; and most of all, damn Sheriff Charles Timothy Matthews for being such a fool as to think he'd buried his past.

"Not now, Angie; soon, I promise," he said, brushing a kiss across her lips and escaping into his office.

But it wasn't really an escape. Another woman waited for him within.

CHAPTER 13

GINNY HANSFORD SAT BETWEEN MEENIE AND LINDman, her back stiff and her eyes looking straight ahead. Other than the staccato sound of her nails tapping on the arm of the wooden chair and the hiss of the radiator in the corner, the room was filled with the uncomfortable silence created by those who have nothing to say to one another.

Charles crossed to his desk and sank down in his chair. Taking a cassette recorder out of a drawer, he inserted a fresh tape, punched the record button, and sighed when he saw Meenie fumble to open his notebook. Charles had issued cassette recorders to everyone in the department, but he was the only person to actually use one. While it wasn't true that it was easier to enter the kingdom of heaven than to effect change in Crawford County, achieving salvation was considerably less wearing.

"Interview with Mrs. Virginia Hansford, December 7 at two-thirty P.M. Ginny—Mrs. Hansford, your statement will be transcribed, you may read over it before signing it, and it will become part of the official record of this investigation. Do you understand the procedure?"

Ginny's face was taut, as if her skin had shrunk against the bone. She almost looked her age. "Of course, I understand, Charles. I've done it before, or have you forgotten?"

No, he hadn't forgotten. Not the sympathy in the pathologist's eyes when he pulled back the sheet to reveal Carin's dead body lying on the gurney, not the sight of Ginny huddling on a couch after he told her, not the sound of the rain on the canvas canopy that protected the mourners at Carin's funeral.

He rubbed his eyes to block out the images, then folded his hands to hide their shaking. "I remember."

He caught Meenie and Lindman looking curiously at him, and concentrated all of his attention on Ginny. He'd worry later about what his two inquisitive observers thought.

"Ginny—Mrs. Hansford—"

"Please, Charles, call me Ginny. You sound so distant when you call me Mrs. Hansford."

"All right then—Ginny, you indicated when you arrived that you had knowledge of your husband's associates—"

"You mean his lovers, don't you, Charles?"

"Well, yes."

"Rich thought he was a great lover and graciously offered to prove it. Let's just say that if adultery is a race, my husband was in training for the Boston Marathon."

"Jesus," breathed Lindman.

Ginny smiled wryly.

"Did your husband ever mention Marta Turner?" asked Charles. He heard the spittoon ping as Meenie made a nonverbal comment.

Ginny tapped her nails on the chair arm. "Frequently and at length. Rich was forcing Brad Masters to foreclose on Jess Turner. His wife offered to exchange her body for a month's extension. Rich was pleased with his deal. I understand Marta Turner is very beautiful."

"Rich granted the extension?"

Ginny shook her head. "The foreclosure was set for Monday, as originally scheduled. Rich made the comment that no piece of ass was worth risking a good piece of property. He had done the same thing to another woman. It was nothing out of the ordinary for him."

"How did you find out about this?" asked Charles.

"Rich stopped keeping his affairs secret a long time ago. He had to have someone to brag to, and he certainly couldn't tell his board of directors, could he? I was safe. If I tried to warn any of the women, I was regarded as a jealous wife. If any of the women objected afterwards, they soon discovered that Rich knew how to cover his tracks. While it might be unwise for a banker to sleep with his female customers, it isn't illegal, and they had no proof of any kind of a sexual trade-off. Rich certainly didn't sign a contract or give them any little mementos. He thought he was enough of a gift. And he slept with enough other women to confuse the issue. Marta Turner was just one more."

"Why in the hell did you stay with the bastard?" asked Lindman. "Nobody swims in a cesspool if he has a choice."

"Lindman, as you pointed out, you're not on the payroll, so butt out," ordered Charles.

She squeezed her hands together and shrank back in her chair. "I know what my husband was, Sheriff Lindman. I didn't approve of what he did—I'm not as much of a bitch as those women out there think I am—but whether I left or stayed wouldn't have changed him. I had a reason for staying with Rich, and it has nothing to do with his murder."

Meenie twisted his body around in his chair to face her. "Excuse me, Mrs. Hansford, but we ain't got anybody's word for that but yours."

"Meenie, you butt out, too," ordered Charles.

"You wouldn't let that answer go by if it was coming from anybody else," protested Meenie.

"Ginny is not a suspect, remember? She's a witness, and the law doesn't give us a license to go fishing in every pond she owns just because we're curious about what's swimming in it."

Meenie scored another direct hit in the spittoon and wiped his mouth on a red bandanna. "Lindman and me ain't asking any questions the jury ain't gonna be asking themselves if Mrs. Hansford has to testify in a murder trial. As a witness for the prosecution, she's just what the defense ordered in the way of reasonable doubt. That jury's gonna wonder why she didn't kill him herself, then they're gonna wonder if maybe she did."

"I didn't kill Rich!" cried Ginny, covering her face with her hands.

Charles sprang out of his chair and leaned over the desk. "That's enough, Meenie. Do you think Fred Hansford would alibi Ginny if he thought she murdered his son? Not a chance. So Ginny's reason for staying with Rich isn't any of your business, or my business, or the jury's business. You just back off and let me ask the questions."

Meenie pushed his hat back to reveal a narrow band of untanned skin below his sparse hair. "Then before you come over the top of that desk and wrap your hands around my scrawny neck like it looks like you're fixing to, you might ask Mrs. Hansford about those folks on your short list."

Charles sat back down. "How did you know I had a short list?"

"I ain't stupid, Sheriff. Unless we got one of them serial killers who just happened to be prowling in old man Adams's stubble field about the time Hansford drove up, then we got to figure that whoever met him wasn't out there 'cause he didn't have nothing better to do. Since there ain't no highway markers or street signs on them dirt roads—and it was black as sin and cold as hell this morning besides—I don't figure a stranger could've ever found the right field even with a map. I reckon that means a Crawford County boy with a real strong grudge. All the local hunters in Bill Adams's field this morning had a grudge against Hansford over sex or money or both. We heard Mrs. Hansford talk a lot about sex"—Meenie's leathery face turned pink—"but we ain't heard much about money. Losing in the bedroom makes a man testy, might even make him kill, but losing in the pocketbook makes a man a damn sight madder for a damn sight longer."

"Not a very romantic view, Meenie," said Charles.

"I ain't ever been called no Casanova," said the grizzled deputy.

"Ginny, did Rich ever mention any particular Crawford County men whose property he was planning to foreclose on besides Jess Turner?"

"Bill Adams, but then Rich's father told you about him this morning. Jess Turner, of course. Rich was pushing him the hardest. And then there's Brad Masters."

"What about Brad?" asked Charles.

"Carroll National Bank was behind on its payments on the accommodation loans owed to Rich's bank in Amarillo. Even foreclosing on the mortgages used to secure the loans wasn't enough."

"Because the fair market value of the properties used as security didn't equal the amount of the loan," Charles finished for her. "Most of those loans must have been made when high inflation artificially raised real estate values. But why didn't Brad ask Rich to allow restructuring of the loans to lower the interest rates and extend the payments? Allow these men at least a chance to survive?"

"Brad did ask—about six months ago—but Rich refused," answered Ginny.

"Why the hell did he do that?" asked Meenie. "Why force good farmers off their land? Bill Adams and Jess Turner are hard workers. Cut them some slack and they'll tighten their belts and make them payments if they have to go barefoot to do it."

"I don't know why. Maybe he just wanted the land, or

maybe the farmers made him mad. It doesn't matter; either way Rich won."

"He must have been mad at Brad Masters, too," remarked Charles.

"Brad Masters?" asked Meenie incredulously. "I didn't know he could make anybody mad. He's got the least mean streak of any banker I ever heard of. I even heard he'll turn down a loan application, then turn around and loan the money out of his own pocket. Why do you say Hansford was mad at him?"

"Because Rich Hansford was ruining Brad Masters along with the farmers," said Charles. "By demanding payment in full on any note used to secure an accommodation loan if even one payment was missed, Rich Hansford was forcing Carroll National and Brad into insolvency. The most Brad was allowed by banking law to demand when he auctioned off a foreclosed property was full market value. If that didn't equal the loan, then Carroll National had to make up the difference. It doesn't take many foreclosures like that before a small bank finds itself in trouble, and since Brad owned the majority of the stock, it meant he would be destitute along with Bill Adams and Jess Turner."

"And Rich Hansford was gonna buy their land when Brad auctioned it off?" asked Meenie. "And his bank, Lone Star National, got the money, and Brad and Crawford County got nothing?"

Ginny nodded her head. "He always bought agricultural land. He said that as long as people have to eat, then farm land is a good investment."

"That son of a bitch had a motto for every occasion," remarked Lindman. "Did he needlepoint them and hang them on his walls?"

"The idea of a man like Rich Hansford controlling any part of what I eat gives me heartburn," said Meenie.

"Know what, Matthews?" asked Lindman, propping his feet on the corner of Charles's desk. "I hope that when you arrest somebody, the grand jury will vote to hand down a good citizenship award instead of an indictment."

"How come you know so much about Rich's business all of a sudden?" asked Meenie. "You told the sheriff this morning that Rich didn't talk to you about who hated him."

"He didn't, but the reverse wasn't true. Rich always talked, raved really, about anybody *he* hated."

"Did Rich tell you about an oil company leasing a piece of property after he foreclosed on it?"

"No, but it sounds like something he would do. I'm presuming the landowner knew nothing about any oil leases."

"Did Rich ever mention Ick Johnson?" asked Charles.

Ginny tapped her fingers on the chair arm and tilted her head. "I don't believe so. No."

"He never mentioned deliberately foreclosing on Ick's hardware store?"

She laughed. "What would Rich want with a hardware store? There wouldn't be enough profit in it for him. I'm not saying that Rich wasn't planning to foreclose, but it was probably a purely business decision. He didn't have ulterior motives for every foreclosure, Charles. Usually people were just names on a mortgage to him—unless they made him mad."

"Ick was well known among the independent drillers, and Rich didn't want him to start an oil well service company to compete with his own."

"I didn't know Rich owned such a company. I don't think his father did either."

"Rich recently bought an interest in a local company."

"Oh? Which one of Crawford County's businessmen was about to find out that Rich Hansford was never a minor shareholder in anything?"

Charles hesitated only for a moment. Presumably Ginny would find the contract among Rich's papers anyway. "Mayor Culpepper."

"Culpepper?" Ginny leaned her head against the back of the chair and laughed. "Charles, you've been conned by someone. Rich thought the man was a clown; he wouldn't have hired him to sweep the floor at the bank. If he bought into Culpepper's company, within a month the mayor would have found himself sleeping on one of his own park benches."

"Matthews, sounds like you ought to have another powwow with his honor, the mayor," remarked Lindman.

"I intend to," said Charles, wondering if Rich Hansford had underestimated the mayor as badly as he had. On the other hand, the mayor didn't have long blond hair, and neither did the mayor's wife. Regardless of what Meenie thought, Charles knew sex was as powerful a motive for murder as money. Put the two together as in the case of the Turners, and the combination was as deadly as gasoline fumes and a lighted match, more so than an oil well service company.

"When did you see your husband last?" Meenie asked Ginny suddenly, startling Charles out of his brooding assessment of his case.

Ginny hunched her shoulders defensively before letting them slump, as if she were a long distance runner who'd crossed the finish line only to find that she had another lap to go. Charles started to intervene, but decided against it. Meenie's question was legitimate, one he should have asked himself. He nodded at Ginny to answer.

"I saw him at seven o'clock yesterday morning before he left for the bank. He was planning to drive straight to Carroll National after work—some kind of pre-hunt party. I went to a cocktail party at the Amarillo Country Club—names of witnesses available upon request, Deputy—then drove to the ranch. I often do that when Rich is gone. I don't like staying alone in Amarillo. Rich's dad doesn't think much of me, but I'm better than nothing and he's a lonely sick old man."

Charles imagined them sitting in the drab old-fashioned living room, two lonely people with nothing in common but a man who loved neither of them. He felt his throat knot up in sympathy. "When did Rich get there, Ginny?"

Her head jerked up in surprise. "He didn't, Charles. He stayed at Carroll's Rest. That's really why I came to see you. I wanted to get his personal belongings—and the manager won't let me in the room."

"Damn it!" exclaimed Charles, turning off the cassette recorder. "I assumed Rich stayed at his father's last night. A motel manager is a better cop than I am. He at least knows better than to let anybody in a murder victim's room."

"That's not why, Charles," said Ginny. "He said Rich left instructions that nobody was to enter his room. I told him I was Mrs. Hansford and that Rich was dead, but it didn't make any difference. Even dead, Rich inspires fear."

"I hope so. I hope that manager followed his instructions to the letter and didn't even let the maid in. Not that I have much hope of that. The room's probably been vacuumed, polished, and the walls washed."

"What difference does it make?" asked Meenie. "He wasn't murdered there. We ain't gonna find any bloodstained fingerprints."

"We don't know that until we look, do we? Where in the hell is Raul? I want photographs of everything in that room."

"He said he was going back out to help that young deputy

search the field," said Lindman. "Sounded like a good idea to me. That kid didn't look any too perky the last time I saw him."

"Go tell Miss Poole to call him on the radio. Have him meet us at Carroll's Rest."

"In the honeymoon suite," said Ginny.

"How do you know that?" asked Meenie. "You said the manager wouldn't let you in Hansford's room."

"He didn't have to; I knew which one it was. Rich always stayed in the honeymoon suite. It's the best room at Carroll's Rest, and Rich always wanted the best."

Lindman lumbered toward the door. "If anybody in Union County, New Mexico, ever hears that I spent the weekend running errands for a Texas sheriff instead of hunting pheasant, I'll never live it down. Probably lose the next election."

"Lindman?"

"Yeah, Matthews?"

"The honeymoon suite."

Lindman slammed the door on the tail end of a curse.

"Meenie, go tell Miss Poole to draw up a material witness warrant for Marta Turner as well as the search warrant," said Charles. "I don't want her running away again until we get a match on the hair samples."

"I don't like it, Sheriff," said Meenie, his face one large expression of disapproval.

"It's not on my list of things I want most to do either, Meenie, and if it turns out that I have to arrest her or Jess, I'm hiring a defense attorney for them. As you pointed out, I've got a hell of a lot of money, so I ought to be able to buy the best. Ginny, you can tell Fred Hansford what I'm planning. It's my job to find his son's murderer, but it doesn't mean I have to like it."

He frowned at Meenie. "What are waiting for? Go tell Miss Poole."

Meenie hitched up his pants. "I'm going—but it don't mean I have to like it." The door slammed behind him.

Charles pushed his chair back and stood up. "We'll have to continue this interview tomorrow, Ginny. I still have a few more questions."

Ginny gripped the chair arms, a panicked expression on her face. "No, Charles! Please let's finish it now. Maybe if I spew out all the rotten things Rich did so I won't have to think about them, I can start remembering the good things about him. Don't let it be like it was with Carin. I can't stand it this time. You questioning me again and again, day after day, until I couldn't eat, couldn't sleep."

Charles sat back down and turned the recorder back on. "I'm sorry, Ginny, but it was my job."

"It wasn't your job! You weren't a homicide detective; you were an assistant district attorney and no one had been charged yet. You had no right to badger me. You were obsessed, Charles, and I can't live through another one of your obsessions."

Charles slammed his fist on the desk. "It wasn't an obsession!"

"Rich never murdered your wife, Charles!"

"Carin was murdered by someone she knew. A neighbor saw her at her apartment at seven o'clock that night. She was found the next morning in an alley six blocks away, bludgeoned to death. The time of death was between eight-thirty and ten o'clock. Remember that night, Ginny?"

"God, Charles, you never let me forget it."

Charles felt the sweat run down his face and drip off his chin, felt his heart pound until he wondered why it didn't burst through his chest. His vision narrowed until he only saw Ginny's face, saw the shared memories reflected there, and knew they were both locked in a time and place far away from his drab office in Crawford County.

"It was dark by eight-thirty and there was a thunderstorm. Carin was pathologically afraid of the dark and thunderstorms terrified her. She would never have walked six blocks by herself in the dark and the rain. And she never drove because her car was still parked in front of her apartment."

"She was a drunk and a drug addict, Charles. Maybe it was a drug deal that went bad."

He shook his head. "There were enough drugs and alcohol in her apartment to send half of Dallas on a three-day high. She had no friends, no job. She wouldn't have gone out in the dark even in a car unless it was with someone she knew, someone she was so obsessed with that she ignored her fear. The only person with that kind of power over her was her lover—your husband! No matter how many alibis you gave him, Rich Hansford murdered Carin, and I shouldn't ever have left Dallas until I proved it."

"Ain't no wonder you got a bellyache all the time," said

Meenie, leaning against the door with his arms folded. "Something like that stuck in your craw."

Charles jerked around. "How long have you been standing there?"

Meenie ambled over to Charles's desk. "Long enough. I started to interrupt, but decided I might just as well hear the whole story instead of half. Like they say, be hung for a sheep as a lamb. You wasn't gonna be no madder one way or the other."

"You were eavesdropping on a private conversation," said Charles, feeling exposed, as if he'd been caught nude in public.

"I'm nigh onto sixty years old, Sheriff. I've heard a lot of private conversations in that many years, but I don't go around repeating them." He leaned over, turned off the cassette recorder, and dropped it in Charles's pocket. "Better not leave that laying around on your desk. Never know who might listen. Now, let's go see that motel room."

CHAPTER 14

CARROLL'S REST WASN'T THE TALLEST ESTABLISHMENT of its kind in Crawford County—that distinction was still reserved for the four-story hotel downtown, even though its top two stories had been boarded up since 1962 in order to ensure its owner a reliable tax loss. Nor was Carroll's Rest the newest facility—that accolade was claimed by the Stop 'N' Rest, a motel reputedly built of reinforced cardboard and owned by a local conglomerate consisting of a lawyer, a chiropractor, and a plumber whose income equaled that of both his partners. To Carroll's Rest, however, went the honor (and income) of being the most popular motel in town.

As an outside observer, Charles judged that its popularity rested less on its clean rooms, adequate soundproofing, decent restaurant, and indoor swimming pool than on its vegetation. Built in the form of a giant rectangle with its rooms forming the outside walls, Carroll's Rest's entire interior was a jungle of exotic ferns, grasses, vines, flowering shrubs, palms with real coconuts, and the only honest-to-god banana trees in Crawford County—or anywhere else in the Panhandle, so far as Charles knew. In a region where trees are on the endangered species list, all that greenery seemed a Garden of Eden without the disadvantage of a talking serpent.

But Charles knew there was never a Garden of Eden without its serpent—and the honeymoon suite had been its lair.

"He wasn't very neat, was he?" remarked Lindman, as he and Charles stood in the doorway of Rich Hansford's room. "Looks like my teenage son's room—and I expect the health department to condemn that any day."

Charles stepped inside. "Raul, get a couple of pictures. Meenie, lift the fingerprints off that chair that's on its side.

Lindman, I've never seen your son's room, but unless he has prize fights in it, it doesn't look like this one. Broken whiskey bottle, a chair turned over, papers scattered on the floor, the spread half off the bed. Somebody had a hell of a fight in here."

Lindman nodded. "I guess you're right. My mind's a little fuzzy; comes from getting up at three-thirty in the morning to drive to Crawford County."

"You should have slept in. Then you would have missed all this."

Lindman lifted his Stetson, smoothed his hair, and grinned as he replaced his hat. "Hell, Matthews, I'm enjoying myself. Somebody else has got his feet to the fire instead of me. That doesn't happen very often. So who do you suppose Hansford was wrestling with?"

"A woman."

"How come you're so sure?"

"There's been a fight, but it was an unequal fight. We have some papers on that table in the corner and others scattered on the floor on either side of it. The overturned chair is in a direct line with the door." He knelt down and pointed to the broken whiskey bottle. "The seal's still intact, and there are glasses on this table by the door, all still with their plastic wrappers on." He stood up and dusted his hands. "I think Hansford was looking over some paperwork at the table—"

"Probably deciding which widow and orphan he was going to foreclose on next," muttered Lindman.

"—someone knocked at the door and he lets her in. He's so unconcerned about who it is that he goes back to the table. She follows him and sweeps some of his papers off the table to get his attention. He gets up and hits her or threatens her—no way to tell from the evidence—and she runs for the door, pushing a chair in his way. He shoves it aside and catches her. She grabs the unopened bottle and hits him. Raul, did you find any stains on Hansford's clothes?"

The deputy snapped a picture of the bed and nodded. "On his left sleeve, and there was a bruise on his arm. It's in my notes. I didn't tell you because I was—well, I was worried about something else."

"I know. You were too busy worrying about resigning. It doesn't matter. I've been so thick today, I probably would have misinterpreted the information if you had remembered to tell me. Anyway, to continue. I think Hansford dragged the woman over to the bed and threw her on it." He hesitated, suddenly sick at where his mental images were leading him.

"He did a lot more than throw her, Matthews," said Lindman. "Look at that bedding. It's all over the place. He held a struggling woman on that bed, and from what I've heard about Hansford's libido, he did more than talk. He raped that woman!"

"Why didn't she scream?" demanded Meenie. "This is Crawford County. Ain't nobody gonna turn their backs on a screaming woman."

"You answered your own question, Meenie. Marta Turner wouldn't want the whole county knowing Rich Hansford raped her."

Lindman turned around. "I'm going outside a minute. I think I may puke."

"What's wrong, Lindman. Don't you have rape up in Union County?" asked Charles, wishing he could go outside, too. But vomiting couldn't cleanse his mind.

Lindman took a deep breath. "Yeah, we got rape. We even got rape and murder together, but goddamn it, Matthews, they're hotblooded. This is cold, so cold, I think this bastard had ice water in his veins instead of blood, and you know why?"

Charles nodded. "The pillow. It's lying on top of the sheets with the imprint of a head on it. I think Rich Hansford took a nap after he committed rape. That's why he didn't bother picking up any of the mess before he drove out to that field. He was asleep."

"This is just terrible, Sheriff," said Robert Beauregard Picket Davis Jones, son of an unreconstructed Southerner who had married one of the local girls at the behest of her father's shotgun. There was a rumor to the effect that his father-in-law's shotgun also had something to do with his decision to seek friendlier surroundings after the baptism of his son, but it remained unsubstantiated. The county had promptly nicknamed the offspring Johnny Reb for obvious reasons.

"That's sure as hell a matter of opinion," said Lindman, leaning on the front desk of Carroll's Rest next to Charles.

"Johnny Reb, did anybody ask for Hansford's room number?" asked Charles.

"We never give out our guests' room numbers," said the

manager, polishing his thick glasses with a handkerchief and blinking at Charles.

"Very commendable, but did anybody ask?"

"No."

"What about Mrs. Hansford?"

Johnny Reb replaced his glasses and peered at Charles like the shortsighted owl he somewhat resembled. "She didn't ask for his room number. She asked me to unlock the door. I didn't do it, of course. Mr. Hansford said nobody was to go in his room, and Mr. Hansford had a terrible temper."

"But the man was dead!" said Lindman. "Mrs. Hansford told you that."

Johnny Reb blinked and pursed his thin lips before speaking. "It wasn't that I disbelieved Mrs. Hansford—one does expect a wife to keep up with whether or not her husband is alive—but *I* hadn't seen Mr. Hansford dead, and he was a very unpredictable gentleman. Besides, I wasn't certain Mrs. Hansford *was* Mrs. Hansford, if you get my meaning. She didn't sound at all like the lady who called him early this morning."

"How early this morning?" asked Charles.

"Three-thirty or so. I hesitated to ring his room—it was so early—but I did. Mr. Hansford always got phone calls from women when he stayed with us. I often wondered if his room number was written on the wall of a ladies' room, but his relationships with members of the opposite sex was none of my business—as long as he behaved discreetly in my motel."

"Would you recognize the woman's voice if you heard it again?" asked Charles quickly.

"It was a Crawford County voice—I recognized the accent—but otherwise it was muffled, as if the lady were speaking through a hanky. But Mr. Hansford must have been pleased. When he dropped by the desk to instruct me not to let anyone in his room, he was quite excited. I even joked with him, and he wasn't the kind of man who enjoyed jokes. I told him the pheasants were still asleep at four in the morning. He winked at me and said there were other things to hunt besides pheasant."

"So he left here at four," murmured Lindman to Charles.

"It's thirty minutes or so to Mr. Adams's field, add a few more for an argument, and the pathologist was nearly right on the money. Hansford must have died between four-forty and five o'clock." Charles looked back at Johnny Reb. "Do you have a record of that phone number?"

The manager shook his head, looking like a peeved owl. "Really, Sheriff; it was an incoming call. And I don't have the number Mr. Hansford called just after eleven when he returned to the motel either. It was a local call. He dialed an outside line. Our switchboard automatically charges a fee to his bill, but it doesn't record the number."

"That cuts it down some, Matthews," said Lindman. "Probably only a couple thousand phones in this county."

"I took the liberty of making up Mr. Hansford's bill, Sheriff. Do you think it would be crass of me to include it with Mrs. Hansford's bill when she checks out, or should I remit it to his estate?"

Charles suddenly understood why Carroll's Rest was the only profitable motel in town—and the jungle in the courtyard was just part of the reason. "Whatever you think best, Johnny Reb."

"The estate, I think. I've found recent widows totally unreliable. I remember one who refused to pay her husband's bill at all. I had to be quite firm. Of course, I did sympathize with her position that if the young lady who was sharing his room when he had his fatal coronary claimed to be his wife, then she could pay the bill."

"Johnny Reb," interrupted Charles before the manager delivered another chapter of motel memoirs. "Did you see anybody walk up the stairs or take the elevator to Hansford's room?"

"Sheriff, this is hunt weekend! The motel was full! I had people coming in all night. Some of them had trouble finding the stairs, and one man wound up in the broom closet because he thought it was the elevator."

"So much for your theory about the screams, Matthews," said Lindman.

"Screams? We didn't have any screaming guests. Most of them went to sleep immediately when they got to their rooms. I did have two that didn't make it as far as their rooms. One passed out in the lobby—just walked in the door and folded up on the floor—and my clerk and I found the other one asleep behind the potted palm in the interior courtyard." He giggled. "I thought it was a suitable place—potted palm, potted guest—but of course I didn't leave him there. But there were no screams. Believe me, I would have heard them."

"Did you see any *women*?" asked Charles desperately. "Any blonde women?"

Johnny Reb looked disapproving. "I don't encourage my

guests to take unregistered women to their rooms. I don't rent beds by the hour, Sheriff; at least, not knowingly. This is a family motel most of the time. The people in Carroll eat dinner here after church on Sunday. I can't have loose women wandering around."

Charles wondered why tight men were more respectable than loose women, but was afraid to ask. Johnny Reb would probably tell him. "I know you don't encourage prostitution, Johnny Reb, but did you see any unregistered women in the motel last night?"

The manager shook his head. "Absolutely not, Sheriff." He fidgeted with his glasses for a moment, then leaned across the desk. "I have to be absolutely honest, Sheriff. There is a back door and two side doors to this building and they're never locked. There is a possibility that someone could have slipped past me."

"In other words, you're not certain."

"I'm afraid not, Sheriff."

CHAPTER 15

"DID YOU GET ANY GOOD PRINTS, MEENIE?" ASKED Charles as he and Lindman walked into the honeymoon suite again.

Meenie squatted on the floor dusting Hansford's briefcase. "Yeah, some real good ones, but not very damn many. I don't know who Johnny Reb hires as maids, but they sure don't slop through their jobs. This room was cleaner than any motel room I ever stayed in. 'Course I don't stay in the best places either."

Charles frowned at his deputy.

"Anyhow, except for a smeared set of prints on a light bulb, I ain't found but prints from two people—or I think two people, judging from the fact that I got arches and whorls. Only about five percent of the population have arched fingerprints, so I don't reckon more than one person left those prints. Only about thirty percent got whorls so I'm on a little thinner ice when I say the same person left all the whorls. When I get back to the courthouse, I'll compare the arches I lifted off the aftershave and other stinkum in the bathroom and from the table and headboard with Hansford's prints that Raul took at the autopsy. I ain't done nothing with these papers. We just don't have what we need here in Crawford County to lift prints off paper. Takes iodine fumes or ninhydrin spray or God knows what else. My fingerprint textbook's about five years old. No telling what them big time experts have come up with that I don't know about. I'm just gonna slip them all in a bag and send them over to Amarillo. Let the big boys loose with them."

Charles was striving to keep his impatience in check. "Have you looked at the papers?" he asked urgently.

Meenie glanced away and shifted his tobacco from one

cheek to the other. "Best I could without touching them. They're all banking stuff, mortgages and such. You'd probably understand them better than me, but I did find a letter from an oil company to Rich Hansford talking about leasing such and such a property."

"Whose property?"

"Don't know; they don't call it by name. They describe it—you know—north corner of the west section or whatever. Have to get a county plat map."

"I've got one," said Charles. "Hanging behind my desk. Remember? Don't send those papers to Amarillo yet. Bring them to the office. We'll put them between plastic to protect the fingerprints, but I want to read them."

"If you say so," said Meenie.

"I say so. Now what about the other fingerprints?"

Meenie rose to his feet and dusted his hands. "I found the whorls on that chair, the table, the door and the wall next to it, and on the neck of that broken whiskey bottle. Right where you'd expect to find prints if you was right about what happened here, Sheriff."

"You can compare them to Marta's prints, Meenie. I asked for them in the search warrant."

"You're pushing that search warrant awful hard," cautioned Meenie.

"I haven't pushed it over the edge yet, so relax," snapped Charles. "Raul, have you found anything?"

The Hispanic detective held up several evidence bags. "More blonde hair, Sheriff. I found it on the bed and over by the door."

"Does it look the same as what you found on Hansford's body?"

Raul shrugged. "It's blonde and it's long. That's all I can say."

"When you finish collecting hair and fiber and whatever, Raul, call in one of the other deputies to run it over to Amarillo and air freight it to Dallas. I don't want you out of pocket any more."

"Speaking of out of pocket," said Meenie. "You're running up a bill for yourself. The sheriff's department dang sure don't have that kind of money, and the county commissioners might all wake up at the same time if you ask them to pay it."

"It's my treat," said Charles. "I just want fast answers. I'm going to be on the county's collective shit list when I arrest somebody anyway, so I want to get it over with as fast as possible. Give people time to cool down. I don't want everyone boycotting my wedding and hurting Angie's feelings just because they're mad at the groom."

"I'd be more worried about the bride if I was you," replied Meenie. "Appeared to me that she was a mite peeved at you when we left the courthouse. I'd take out a little time and explain some things. She's got a right to know about your first wife."

"You're not me, and I'd appreciate it if you'd mind your own business. I told Angie I'd been married before."

"Must have been a real short conversation. Miss Angie didn't even know your wife's name. You know, Sheriff, burying Rich Hansford ain't gonna bury what's eating up your gut."

"Shut up, Meenie!" shouted Charles.

"I think you should do what the sheriff says, Meenie," said Raul, stepping between the two men and grasping the deputy's shoulder. "Things aren't as bad as they look. It is a test of faith."

Meenie stood looking at Raul, an expression on his face that Charles couldn't interpret. "I got as much faith as anybody, Raul."

"What are you two talking about now?" demanded Charles.

"Nothing," said Meenie. "Just worried about you putting all your eggs in one basket and pushing so hard on the Turners."

"You let me worry about where I put my eggs," said Charles, then told his deputies about the phone calls. "So you see, Meenie, Hansford could have called Marta at eleven, they argued, and he ended up raping her. She goes home, tells Jess, then calls Hansford at three-thirty to set up a meeting in the field—except Jess shows up instead of Marta and murders Hansford."

"Why did he wait an hour to go back and move the body, Sheriff?" asked Raul.

"As Meenie pointed out to me, Jess isn't as bright as his wife. I think faking the hunting accident was Marta's idea."

"Then why didn't she tell Jess to do it the same time as he killed Hansford—if he killed Hansford?" asked Meenie.

Charles caught himself gritting his teeth again from irritation and relaxed his jaw. "Maybe she didn't know he planned to kill Hansford. Everybody is so damn anxious to tell me what a softie he is. Maybe Marta thought he'd just punch out Hansford."

"I got a real problem with that," said Meenie stubbornly. "Mrs. Turner's too bright to think old Jess is taking his twenty-two just for the hell of it. If she called Hansford to set the whole thing up, then she knew what was gonna happen and she'd have told Jess what to do. Your idea has got more holes in it than a sieve."

Charles paused to consider Meenie's objections. As usual, the deputy had a point, several of them in fact—and they were all sticking holes in his reconstruction. "You won't get any argument from me. Apparently my first scenario was the right one."

"What scenario? That Hansford raped Mrs. Turner in the Suburban and Jess went out and shot him? 'Less he raped her twice, that idea don't hold water anymore either."

"Actually, Meenie, I've thought all along that Marta shot Hansford and Jess tried to cover it up by faking the accident. It fits the facts even better now that we know the rape occurred here."

"What facts?" demanded Meenie, thrusting his chin forward belligerently. "You ain't got no facts; just a bunch of guesses. We don't know yet whose hair decorated Hansford's buttons, and we don't know whose fingerprints are on that broken bottle. You're hell bent on it being the Turners."

"Because the Turners are lying, damn it, and besides—" He stopped abruptly, appalled at the implications of what he'd nearly said: that the Turners had a good chance of winning suspended sentences, if not outright acquittal. Was he pursuing them because he thought they were guilty, or because they made the best scapegoats and he didn't want anybody serving jail time for killing Rich Hansford? He didn't trust his own motives anymore.

"Besides what?" prompted Meenie.

"Never mind. You just worry about getting your butt back to the courthouse as soon as you finish here, and let me worry about everything else." He turned and left.

"At least my butt ain't in a crack like yours is," Meenie called after him.

Charles heard the gentle shuffling of cards and the low mutter of voices placing bets before he saw the three women seated around the dispatcher's desk. "Miss Poole!" he shouted.

"What in hell are you doing? Did you serve those warrants? Where's Marta Turner?"

Miss Poole laid down her cards, a long-suffering expression on her face. "I told you before that you needn't shout. I'm not hard of hearing. Of course, I've observed that men often shout when they're frustrated, so I don't suppose you can help it. As for what I'm doing, it's obvious. I'm waiting for you."

"You're playing poker! I thought I locked up the cards."

"A game of probability occupies an idle mind," said Miss Poole in a voice almost as prim as her starched blouse and slacks. "And the locks on our filing cabinets respond to a hair pin. Now, if you'd stop interrupting, I'll answer your other questions. I served the warrants, but I'll warn you now that I'll resign before I ever submit another woman to such a humiliating experience. Marta Turner was more than distraught; she was a shivering wreck. Absolutely frozen. You should be ashamed of yourself."

"Damn it, Miss Poole, I didn't order it to be cruel. I had to know if she and Hansford had been intimate."

Miss Poole blanched. "Dear God, what a horrible case this is."

He squeezed her shoulder. "I know, Miss Poole. Believe me, I know better than anyone. But go on. Where's Marta Turner?"

Miss Poole swallowed. "She's gone, released on bail."

"Bail?"

"A judge can order bail on a material witness bond, Sheriff, and Judge Waters so ordered—fifty dollars, just so you'll know. He was disturbed by Marta's mental condition, too. Had you forgotten that the judge is Marta's mother's cousin's husband?"

Charles blindly sat down on the desk and uttered a four letter word.

"I've observed men also often curse when they're frustrated," Miss Poole said, peering around Charles at Viola Jenkins.

"Like sailors," agreed the justice of the peace.

> "There once was a woman from Clives
> Who had a bad case of the hives . . ."

"What in the hell?" began Charles as a chorus of voices rose to a crescendo.

"... She frowned as she itched
And quietly bitched
About fleas on the men of St. Ives."

He jerked his head toward the heavy iron door that led to the Crawford County jail. "What's that?"

"I believe it is supposed to be a limerick," replied Miss Poole.

"I know it's a damn limerick!"

"Although it's a very poor example of one," continued Miss Poole. "I'm not certain that a flea bite would necessarily result in hives."

"Miss Poole," asked Charles, rubbing his face. "Can you tell me who the hell is making all that racket in my jail?"

"Another case of frustration, I'm afraid. Several, actually. One of the deputies brought in seven hunters whose anguish at not shooting a single pheasant today resulted in their seeking compensation in Scotch. Judging from their condition, more than one bottle. According to Mrs. Jenkins, who has more experience than I, it was a very inferior brand of Scotch."

"Rotgut," said Mrs. Jenkins.

"Drunk? I have drunken hunters in my jail? Drunken hunters singing dirty limericks?"

"I didn't know there was any other kind," observed Lindman, cocking his head to listen to another poetical composition.

"There once was a gal from Texas
Who couldn't keep track of her exes—"

"Damn it to hell!" roared Charles, springing out of his chair and fumbling for his key ring.

"What are you planning to do, Matthews?" asked Lindman.

"Shut them up!"

"You can't mistreat prisoners, even if they do sing like they all have ruptured hernias."

"Sheriff, I've already asked them to please not sing," said Miss Poole. "One of them, a lawyer, told me they had the right to freedom of expression."

Charles unlocked the jail door and swung it open. "Miss Poole, you obviously didn't ask in the right way." He smiled, looking forward to the confrontation. Shouting had its limitations at relieving frustration.

The Crawford County jail had twelve cells, six on either side of an aisle so narrow that it was possible for a prisoner to reach through the bars and grab whoever walked down it. After several incidents between prisoners and deputies, culminating in Slim being tied to the bars with his own belt, Charles had forbidden entering the jail without a backup.

But he didn't need backup in a confrontation with drunken hunters. He strolled down the aisle and back again, studying the seven unshaven bleary-eyed slack-mouthed hunters who smelled of sweat-soaked flannel and cheap Scotch.

"Hey Sheriff, when you gonna let us out?" shouted one, staggering off his bunk to cling to the bars of his cell.

Another hunter leaned against his cell wall. "I'm suing for false imprisonment on behalf of myself and these other hunters." His threat might have been more effective if he hadn't slurred *suing* into *shoeing*.

Charles tilted his head and studied the swaying figure. "If it isn't my friend, Roy the lawyer."

"That's right, Sheriff, and I'll personally see that you serve time in prison for these violations of our civil rights! You and all your deputies!"

Charles glanced down the row at the other six hunters. "Is that the way you all feel?"

There were nods from those of the hunters sober enough to move their heads without tipping over.

"I see," said Charles, resting his hands on his hips and smiling. "You certainly couldn't choose a better spokesman—"

Roy the lawyer preened. "Innocent citizens can't allow you redneck sheriffs in these backwoods counties to abuse your authority."

"—to get the lot of you in more trouble than a mere charge of drunk and disorderly." Mumbling and head-scratching ensued among the other hunters. "Tell me, Roy my friend, did you happen to notice that one of the deputies is a woman?"

Roy leered. "You mean that scrawny old broad in your office?"

Charles shook his head sorrowfully. "Such language, Roy. It's almost as offensive and sexist as the lyrics you and your fellow choirboys were singing. I'm certain Miss Poole will include it in her suit for sexual harassment she plans to file Monday morning against the seven of you."

Roy the lawyer's mouth gaped open momentarily. "What?

That's ridiculous! Don't listen to him, boys. No federal judge in his right mind would accept such a lawsuit."

Charles examined his nails. "The judge in whose jurisdiction you're standing isn't a man, Roy, and Her Honor doesn't care for sexual harassment. But it really doesn't matter whether Miss Poole actually wins her lawsuit or not because you gentlemen, and I use the word lightly, will be adequately punished."

"What do you mean, Sheriff?" asked another hunter, one clearly a little more sober than the others, since he was standing straight rather than at an angle.

"With the exception of Roy, you're all bankers. Perhaps you'd better do a mental count of how many female depositors you have now, and how many you'll have *after* Miss Poole gives a press conference detailing how you acted in the best tradition of male chauvinism."

"My God!" said one, looking suddenly more sober. "My bank will be out of business."

Roy the lawyer, inspired by either the justice of his cause or the fear that he might lose six legal fees, jumped into the discussion. "He's bluffing! Don't listen to him. I intend to go ahead with our lawsuit."

"Shut the fuck up, Roy!" shouted one hunter, his face gray and sweaty, whether from bad Scotch or the thought of a female boycott of his bank, Charles couldn't decide. "And count me out of your scheme. I'm not suing the sheriff. Hell, we were drunk as skunks—still are—and on your goddamn whiskey!" He wiped his face on his sleeve and looked at Charles. "Tell your lady deputy I apologize for the dirty songs."

"Any other apologies?" asked Charles, running his eyes along the row of cells. The other hunters nodded, shuffling their feet and glaring as best they could at Roy the lawyer. "Then I'll try my best to persuade Miss Poole not to include your names in her lawsuit, but you have to understand that she's a very determined lady. I might not be successful." He hesitated, watching several more hunters turn gray and sweaty. Definitely the effect of a possible boycott, he decided. "Perhaps if you gentlemen were very quiet and polite, or sang a few old-fashioned ballads, she might—might—believe that you've reformed. Miss Poole is an advocate of self-improvement."

"Yes, sir, we'll do that, Sheriff," said one, and the others nodded.

"Fine—and I'll talk to Miss Poole." He walked out and locked the jail door behind him, turning to face Lindman and the lady poker players. He spread his hands and shrugged. "It's all a matter of using the right weapons."

Miss Poole's face was a study in disapproval. "I knew when I accepted a job with the sheriff's department that I might be exposed to crude and uncivilized behavior, Sheriff. I have no intention of filing a suit for harassment. I believe that if you can't stand the heat, get out of the kitchen. I certainly don't appreciate your implying to those men that I can't take it."

"Miss Poole, I was only trying to prevent those drunken sots from embarrassing you and Mrs. Jenkins!"

"Don't bother about me," said Mrs. Jenkins. "I've heard dirtier songs than those. Matter of fact, I've *sung* dirtier songs."

Charles hoped his legs would hold him up long enough to get to his office and close the door. He needed a time-out before he strangled Miss Poole, Mrs. Jenkins, and whoever else was handy.

"Sheriff?"

The voice was soft, hesitant, and only vaguely familiar. Charles swung around to focus on the third card player. "Miss Pace, what are you doing here? Do you have an idle mind, too?"

"You never looked at the invitation list, Sheriff. In fact, what with everything going on, Brad never even gave it to you." She reached into a voluminous handbag and handed Charles a neatly typed sheet of paper. "Here it is. I stayed to answer any questions you might have. Brad had to go back out to Mr. Adams's place to hunt. He feels like he should, since so many of the hunters are guests of the bank."

Charles took the list. "Thank you, Miss Pace." He hesitated a minute, studying her pale face. She looked better, stronger, but if she drank much of Miss Poole's coffee, her improved appearance was more likely a caffeine rush than the result of rest and relaxation. "Miss Pace, I apologize for Mrs. Hansford's comments. I'm sure she'll apologize herself when she's had a chance to consider it."

Maggie Pace smiled bitterly. "I doubt it, Sheriff. She acts just like her husband, and he never apologized for anything. Did she slander me again when you talked to her? Did she tell you that I slapped him when he showed up to bid on my farm when it was auctioned off? Did she tell you how much I hated him? Oh, God, what did she tell you? I've been sitting here wishing I was dead, so afraid she'd say I must have killed him."

Mrs. Jenkins patted her niece's hand. "Now, Maggie, you're working yourself into a state again. If the sheriff questioned everybody who ever called Hansford a nasty name, he'd have to haul in everybody in the city directory. I slandered him myself that day, too, if you remember. You just have to stop dwelling on it, that's all. You just have to be tough. Like me. Have another drink of that coffee. No, on second thought, don't. You're already twitchy enough." She looked up at Charles. "Tell this girl that you're not going to use a rubber hose on her, Sheriff."

Charles rubbed his eyes, then blinked at Maggie. God, but he was tired of being characterized as an ogre. "Miss Pace, Mrs. Hansford never mentioned your name while she was in my office. When I speak to her again, I'll remember what your aunt said, but you should realize that Mrs. Hansford isn't being deliberately malicious. She's merely mentioning everybody who ever had any dealings with her husband."

He looked at all three women, their expressions ranging from dubious to frightened. "For God's sake! You people have to trust me." No one looked convinced, and he stalked toward his office. "Since I'm obviously about as popular as a boil, I'll take my unwelcome presence into my office and concoct my next dastardly exploits. Miss Poole, send Meenie and Raul in when they come back from the motel. Lindman! Come on! I want company in my misery."

"You have company," said Miss Poole in what Charles thought might be a malicious tone—except that he'd never known Miss Poole to be malicious. "Angie's waiting for you."

"Can I sit in for a hand or two?" asked Lindman, hastily pulling up a chair next to Miss Poole. "Three's a crowd, and I never liked misery much anyway."

"Coward," muttered Charles, opening his door.

"You or me?" asked Lindman, shuffling the cards.

Charles closed his door, flung his hat in the direction of his file cabinet, and shrugged out of his coat, all the while watching the slender, silent figure in the bulky red sweater and jeans who stood staring out his third-story window.

He cleared his throat. Lacking a clever overture, he opted for the truth. "Angie, I know I promised we'd discuss Carin, and I know I sound as if I'm evading the problem, but this isn't the time. Or the place. This is my office, for God's sake. It's where I lead my professional life. Carin is personal. I know it hurt you to have Ginny—Mrs. Hansford—throw her name in your face. I know you felt like a fool, but right now I can't delve into my own past, my own problems. I feel besieged by Hansford's murder—and not a single goddamn person in this whole county is on my side. I'm even beginning to doubt myself. So be mad at me, throw something at me, but please no more questions."

Sitting down, he pulled open the center drawer of his desk and fumbled for his antacid pills. He watched Angie turn to walk across the room toward him.

Angie walked around his desk and squeezed in front of him, forcing him to roll his chair back. "Charles, you're right about this being your office, so I'm saving my opinions about how damn little you know me until we're alone in a private place. Then I intend to beat you bloody, but that's personal, and this is professional."

"What's professional? Carin?"

Angie slapped her hand over his mouth—none too gently—and leaned over until their faces were level with one another. "Charles, don't talk. It's my turn, and you're going to listen. You're not walking out of here until I finish, and I don't care if there's mass murder at the doughnut shop or blood washes down Carroll Avenue. Don't look toward the door either. Miss Poole has orders to keep everyone out."

Charles pushed her hand away. "Miss Poole is a sheriff's deputy and she doesn't take orders from anyone but me. Angie, damn it, you're interfering again."

"Miss Poole loves you just like I love you and Meenie loves you, and your whole damn department loves you, and none of us intend to stand by and let you flail around making any more mistakes. This is Crawford County, Charles. We take care of our own even when our own don't want us to."

"Angie—"

"Shut up, Charles, and listen. Or rather answer. What did your Mrs. Hansford tell you about Marta? I wouldn't ask, but you didn't leave any notes for Miss Poole and me to read. And please don't say anything about my being a civilian. This is too important. So get off your high horse and tell me."

"She's not *my* Mrs. Hansford—"

"That's personal, too, and we'll argue about it later," interrupted Angie. "I just want to know if she told you that Marta Turner was having an affair with Rich Hansford."

"Yes! And I'm telling you that much because you can infer that much from what she said earlier in the squad room."

"She's lying, then. Marta would never have an affair for any reason."

Her lower lip jerked. Charles felt her hand trembling. He sensed his line between professional and personal lives wavering and wondered why he ever thought it would hold. Or why it should for that matter. In this town of shared secrets he'd have to trust Angie to know which ones would hurt. She probably knew better than he anyway.

He lowered his head and kissed her palm. "Angie, honey," he said softly, "Marta had a good reason." He watched her face as he told her, expecting every reaction but the one he got: pity.

Angie shook her head. "Charles, where women are concerned, you must be the last hopeless romantic in America. You really believe Marta would make such a sacrifice for love."

"It's better than doing it for money," he retorted, wondering how being called a hopeless romantic could make him feel like such a fool.

Angie leaned her hips against his desk, crossed over the other, and folded her arms. "Love has nothing to do with it. Most women are more practical than men, Charles. Marta is too practical to believe that being Hansford's lover would stop him from foreclosing or even delaying foreclosure."

He reached for her left hand and rubbed the scars only half-hidden by the engagement ring he had given her. "All this talk of being practical from a woman who slammed her hand against her first husband's headstone, then buried her wedding rings on his grave when she realized what a louse and a liar and a cheat he'd been. I'd call that a romantic gesture."

Angie pulled her hand back and turned her head, a faint red tint of color staining her cheeks. "About those rings, Charles."

"Yes?"

She met his eyes, a defiant expression in hers. "I went back the next week with a metal detector and dug them up. L. D. had already taken all our money—in cash—without spending a minute wondering how the girls and I would live without taking charity from my father. When he burned to death in that plane crash, every last dollar burned with him. I decided that

I'd be damned before I'd let that cold murdering bastard have the only thing of value he didn't steal before he tried to escape. I sold those wedding rings and bought a CD for the girls' education."

"My God, Angie," Charles breathed, so astonished he couldn't think of anything else to say.

"You presume I'm soft and helpless, Charles. I'm not like that on the inside. I'm fierce sometimes. And the same is true of Marta. She may look like your idea of an easy lay, but she's not that at all."

"Angie! I never thought she was—but women have been trading sexual favors for gain of whatever kind since man climbed out of the primeval swamp. And I'm not standing in moral judgment of Marta Turner or any other woman who is desperate enough, or hungry enough, or frightened enough, for plain survival, to trade her body to some bastard in exchange for hope. It happens. And it evidently happened with Marta Turner. Unfortunately, it ended in murder."

Angie took a breath and clenched her fists. "I'm not saying that there aren't women who would do exactly what she accused Marta of doing, because my gender has its share of impractical airheads just as your gender has its share of romantic idiots, but Marta Turner isn't one of them. But you don't know that because you don't know Marta. I'm going to tell you a secret, Charles, one I hope to God you never have to repeat—"

"Because it's one of the secrets that hurt?" he asked.

Her eyes widened in surprise. "You make me feel like such a shrew, Charles. You're wiser about Crawford County than I thought."

"No, I'm not. Dr. Wallace is. He told me how to distinguish between secrets. Go on, Angie love, we romantics never hurt anybody if we can help it. Especially women."

She leaned over and kissed him, then leaned back before he could return the favor. "We women do love you romantics, but sometimes you exasperate us." She smiled at him, then turned somber. "Charles, did you ever wonder why Marta married Jess when she could've had any man in the county—or the state for that matter?"

Charles shifted uncomfortably. "Love, I suppose."

She nodded. "That's true, but only partly. She married Jess because he is a very gentle man—and she wasn't afraid of him."

"Afraid?" asked Charles, trying to numb the intuitive feeling that he knew what Marta's secret was, and that it was going to make him feel ashamed.

"She was sexually afraid of most men, Charles. A legacy from an *un*romantic man who thought brutally raping a sixteen-year-old girl was macho. It was never reported, and the only people who knew about it were Dr. Wallace, Miss Poole, Jess, and me."

"Oh God, and I had Miss Poole execute that search warrant. Why didn't you tell me sooner, damn it?"

"Because I hadn't planned to tell you at all. I thought you suspected Jess. That's what Marta told me when she called from the hospital. She wanted me to tell you that Jess couldn't kill even to defend himself. I'm not even certain he'd kill to defend Marta."

"Then what was he doing pheasant hunting, Angie?"

"Jess? Pheasant hunting? He's never shot a pheasant in his life. He goes to the pre-hunt party at the bank and allows hunters in his fields, but he doesn't hunt. Marta says it makes him sick."

"He was in Bill Adams's field this morning—with a shotgun."

"Oh, God, Charles, I don't know why he was there, but I know he couldn't have killed Hansford." She stopped and sucked in a breath—and Charles knew instantly what his face had revealed. "You think Marta killed him, don't you, Charles? You think she slept with him, then shot him when he refused to delay the foreclosure."

"No, Angie. I think she went to his motel room to argue with him and he raped her. She called him at three-thirty to ask him to meet him in the field and she shot him. Jess faked the accident, then went pheasant hunting with Bill Adams so he'd be on the scene to see if I bought the accident. If it didn't happen that way, why did they lie? What are they hiding?"

"I made your case stronger by telling you about Jess, didn't I, Charles?"

He nodded and watched her close her eyes briefly before facing him again. "I'm sorry, Angie. I'm sorry about Marta and Jess. I wish there was something I could do differently, but I can't."

"It doesn't matter, because you're wrong. Those hair samples won't match. They couldn't. Marta Turner would never have gone to Rich Hansford's motel room and she would never have gotten in that car alone with him. She was terrified of Rich Hansford. He was the one who raped her."

CHAPTER 16

"CAN I COME IN?"

Charles looked up and motioned toward a chair. "Did Miss Poole win all your toothpicks at poker?"

Lindman sat down and propped his feet on the corner of Charles's desk. "If she didn't have religious convictions about playing for money, I'd bankroll her in Las Vegas." He studied Charles's slumped figure. "I've seen roadkill that looked healthier than you. Did your girl give you a bad time?"

"Bad enough," admitted Charles. "Lindman, let me pose a hypothetical question. If all the evidence points to a certain suspect, if motive and opportunity are present, and alibi is lacking, yet there is a persuasive argument that the suspect is psychologically incapable of committing the crime, what would you do?"

Lindman stroked his chin, his fingers rubbing over the whisker stubble with a raspy sound. "That must have been some talk you and your intended had. Which one of the Turners is psychologically incapable?"

Charles opened his bottle of antacid and popped two of the tablets in his mouth. "According to Angie, both of them."

"I'd ask you what your gut says, but the way you been eating those pills, I don't think it's too reliable; so I'll give you my views of psychology. It's what a cop always asks himself about a suspect: what's in it for him. The answer is always one of the five P's of murder: passion, profit, psychosis, protection, and panic. There's nobody that one of those P's doesn't cover."

"So you believe anybody can kill?"

Lindman laced his fingers together and tapped his chin. "Yeah, I do. Let's take your suspects for example. You got ordinary law-abiding folks who earn a living, do good works in the community, mind their own business, and let other people mind theirs. They got a conscience and they got self-control, and those two things are the best safeguards against murder. But they're still brothers under the skin with Hansford. Crowd good people hard enough—like Hansford did—and they'll kill. It just takes more provocation, because they have to overcome their consciences and their self-control."

"So the suspect with the highest number of P's is the one I'd better look at the closest?" asked Charles, intrigued with Lindman's theory.

"Nine times out of ten, particularly if that suspect doesn't have an alibi worth a damn and the evidence is against him," replied Lindman. "It's the tenth time that drives cops crazy because that's the time that the suspect with three P's didn't commit the murder; the suspect with only one P did. But it was the right one. That's the trouble with this psychology business. It's not how many reasons a suspect has; it's which reason to kill is the right one. That's why cops and prosecutors and juries love evidence. Takes the damn guesswork out of murder."

Charles wished he were in Lindman's place, sitting on the other side of the desk, uninvolved, relaxed, and able to give fatherly advice to the new kid on the block. "Then I hope my evidence holds up, because otherwise I'll drown in an alphabet soup of your five P's. I don't trust my guesswork anymore."

"Just what exactly did your young lady say, Matthews?"

"It's one of those secrets that hurts."

Lindman nodded. "We got those in Union County, too. Makes it damn hard on a man to know what to do."

"I almost wish I didn't have any evidence, Lindman," Charles burst out. "Because I hated Hansford as much as anyone. Whoever killed him did me a favor, too."

"I figured that from what Mrs. Hansford was saying, and I also figured that's why you're pushing so hard to find the killer. If you let the case peter out, then it would be like you killed him yourself—psychologically speaking. Must be hard, though, having to hunt down somebody you're indebted to. It's no wonder your gut is torn up."

"Thank you, Dr. Lindman, for that cogent analysis."

"Us jake leg psychologists aim to please," said Lindman modestly. "It's all we can do for what ails you."

"And that is?"

"Duty." Lindman tipped his hat down over his eyes and let

his head sag forward. Before Charles could think of a rejoinder, the New Mexican was snoring.

"Damn it, Lindman," said Charles softly to the sleeping man. "I wish it were that easy."

Raul knocked and entered without an invitation. His expression caused another spasm in Charles's belly and a grunt from Lindman as the closing door woke him up. "Here are those papers from the motel, Sheriff, and I found out whose property Hansford was leasing to the oil company." He spilled the plastic-encased papers onto Charles's desk and separated them. "I matched the property description in the letter to the property descriptions on the mortgages in Hansford's briefcase. It's Jess Turner's property."

Lindman's feet hit the floor. "I'll be damned. That just goes to show you how far off base psychology will take you, Matthews. You figured Marta Turner killed Hansford out of passion because he reneged on their deal, and for protection because he threatened to throw Jess off his land, when all along it was another P. It was profit. Hansford was going to cheat them out of a possible fortune."

Charles checked the two papers Raul had shown him, then carefully stacked all of them and placed them in his bottom drawer. He braced his elbows on his desk and rubbed his temples. "Where's Meenie? Why the hell isn't he finished with those fingerprints?"

"He's right behind me, Sheriff. He just wanted to check the gun."

"What gun?"

"Slim's back. He found a gun and the floor mat from the Suburban in a Waterman hydrant."

"A what?"

"It's a pipe that connects to the water line that runs around a field. It serves as a sort of faucet for the irrigation system. The top screws off, and the gun and floor mat were inside." Raul hesitated, as if suddenly surprised by an unexpected notion. "Slim did a good job, Sheriff, because those pipes generally run straight down for about five feet and are full of water. A lot of deputies wouldn't have thought to look there. Or be as thorough when they did."

"I always knew that kid would make a good deputy. You and Meenie always underestimated him," said Charles, ignoring the fact that until this morning he hadn't trusted Slim to do more than count paper clips. "He's not such a screw-up."

"Guess again, Sheriff. He'll need a new antenna on his patrol car. He made a hook out of his old one to fish the gun out of the pipe."

"Sheriff!"

Meenie stood in the office doorway, his Adam's apple bobbing up and down as he chewed his wad of tobacco. "Sheriff, I got to talk to you."

Charles looked thoughtfully at his deputy's masticating jaws. He tried to remember if he'd ever seen Meenie actually chewing his tobacco and decided he hadn't. Meenie always tucked it neatly in one cheek or the other, like a squirrel carrying a walnut. Seeing him do otherwise made Charles uneasy.

"I suggest you come in first. You look like a harbinger of doom standing in the doorway."

"I just might be," said Meenie. Charles's unease increased. Ordinarily his deputy wouldn't admit to understanding what a harbinger of doom was. Meenie never admitted understanding any words of more than two syllables.

"Did you tell him yet, Meenie? What are we going to do now, Sheriff?" Like a curious puppy, Slim followed Meenie through the open door.

"Tell me what?"

"Dang it, Slim!" snapped Meenie. "Quit sneaking up on me."

"Tell me what?" repeated Charles.

"I didn't sneak. I just followed you."

"I got a shadow that follows me. I don't need no wet-behind-the-ears deputy doin' it, too. And quit fiddlin' with your beard. If you start to molt, I'll tell you."

"At least I can grow a beard," retorted Slim, then looked as if he wished he'd swallowed his words before they'd escaped his mouth.

Meenie fingered the scraggly stubble on his chin, the only visible results of six weeks' effort. "You insulting me, son?"

Charles eyed the two with disfavor. The beard craze had hit the sheriff's department with the virulence of a flu epidemic. Every deputy sprouted facial hair of every color, texture, and degree of luxuriousness. Ordinarily he was amused. Ordinarily he chuckled at the sight of grown men combing their beards and arguing over the best brand of mustache wax. But this wasn't an ordinary time. He wasn't amused and he damn sure didn't feel like chuckling.

Charles catapulted out of his chair. "That's enough! From

both of you," he added in a lower voice. "It's pheasant season and instead of eight thousand hunters, I've got seven thousand, nine hundred and ninety-nine. Instead of an ugly squint-eyed bad guy as a suspect, I've got one beautiful terrified traumatized woman. And instead of professional, enthusiastic deputies, I've got bickering feet-dragging second-guessing goof-offs. Now Meenie, get to the point."

"Them fingerprints ain't Marta Turner's. They ain't even in the same neighborhood. And if the fingerprints ain't hers, then I figure the hair ain't either."

"Charles!" Ginny Hansford exclaimed, her eyes darting from him to the three men behind him. "And you brought your whole department with you."

"Ginny," he said, taking her hands and turning them palm up. "Ginny, you lied to me."

Ginny jerked out of his grasp. "This is history repeating itself, Charles. You accused me of lying when Carin died, too."

"And you're doing it again—to protect the same man. He's dead, Ginny. He can't hurt you anymore. But *you* can hurt people. You deliberately encouraged me to suspect Marta Turner."

"I wasn't lying about her! Rich was obsessed with Marta Turner. He was the one who offered to delay foreclosing on Jess Turner if Marta would sleep with him. And she was going to do it, Charles! I saw the Turners once when they came to the bank in Amarillo. She and Rich were like a rabbit and a snake. He fascinated her. She acted as if she didn't have a will of her own, just sat in that chair in front of his desk like a rag doll and twisted her purse strap. I was so repulsed that I finally dragged her out into the lobby for a cup of coffee, and it was like leading a sleepwalker. Rich loved to dominate people."

Charles was repulsed, too. Marta hadn't been fascinated; she'd been too terrified to run. "Is that what he did to you early this morning in the honeymoon suite, Ginny? Did he try to dominate you?"

Ginny's face blanched and she momentarily sagged. "I—I don't know what you're talking about, Charles. I never saw Rich this morning."

Charles walked over to a couch and sat down. He couldn't stand over her, using his height to intimidate her. Even if she was lying, she was one of the walking wounded, another fragile woman broken by Rich Hansford. "Fingerprints, Ginny. And blonde hair on Rich's body and in his room. There are two blondes in the case—you and Marta Turner. But Marta Turner's fingerprints aren't swirls and yours are. I looked at them when I held your hands just now." He took his recorder out of his pocket, set it on an end table, and turned it on. "Do you want to revise your statement, Ginny, and tell me the truth?"

Ginny sank to the floor. "Oh, God."

If she noticed Charles leaping off the couch or Raul lifting her up and sitting her on a chair, she didn't acknowledge either action. Instead she stared at her hands as though they had betrayed her.

"Ginny, I'm sorry," said Charles.

She finally looked up at him with thousand-year-old eyes. "I thought he'd pick up the room so you wouldn't know there had been a fight. Rich hates messes. I knew you'd find the fingerprints, but I wasn't worried because mine aren't on file anywhere—and you had no reason to demand them. I never thought about the hair."

"What happened, Ginny?"

"I drove to Carroll after I left Amarillo and went to Rich's room. I knew he'd leave the party fairly early after he subtly tortured everybody he was planning to foreclose on, and why stay after that? It wasn't as if he had any friends anxious to talk to him. Crawford County people didn't like him and wouldn't pretend they did. So he was already in his room when I got there."

"What time was that, Ginny?"

"Time?" She frowned. "I don't know. Midnight maybe. Anyway, he was already dressed in his hunting clothes reading over some papers—mortgages—and gloating. I tried reasoning with him—tried to persuade him to let those poor people alone. If you don't believe anything else, Charles, please believe that. I tried to save Jess Turner and Bill Adams and Brad. He laughed."

She swallowed and pressed her hands over her stomach as if she hurt inside. "Then I scattered his papers and told him I wanted a divorce. He hit me between my breasts with his fist and knocked me against a chair. I ran for the door, but he caught me and swung me around by my hair. I smashed a bottle against his arm, and that's when he . . ." She kept swallowing as if her next words were bile. "That's when he raped me."

She hunched her shoulders and looked down at the floor,

and Charles saw the same embarrassed horror on the other men's faces as he knew his own reflected. "I'm sorry, Ginny."

She looked up, a grimace on her face. "He never raised his voice, Charles—even when he said there would be no divorce, even while he was raping me—he never raised his voice. And when it was all over, I felt so guilty. He violated me, and I was the one who felt guilty!"

Charles never remembered moving off the couch, but he never forgot the faint scent of magnolias that clung to the silvery hair that he stroked as he knelt by her chair. He heard feet shuffling and throats being cleared as the other three men tried to think of something to say, and finally settled for awkwardly patting her shoulder in turn.

Finally Ginny raised her head. "Charles, may I speak to you alone?"

He nodded and motioned the others outside. "What is it, Ginny?"

Her face looked red and swollen, as if it might be sore to the touch. She licked lips that Charles noticed were chapped, as if all the moisture in her body had been drained away in tears. "I'm sorry I tried to cause trouble between you and your fiancée. I was jealous that you'd finally put Dallas behind you, that you'd found another life, and I was still trapped in the one I had. Do you suppose I can still find a life, too? That I can finally forget?"

He stroked her cheek. "Let's both put it behind us, Ginny. Tell me the truth now that they're both dead. Did Rich murder Carin? Did you lie for him?"

Ginny pushed him away and huddled in her chair. "Rich had another lover—your boss's wife. That's why he pulled you off the case, why he fired you. I told him Rich was prepared to give a statement that he was with her until nine o'clock that night. He came home a little before ten."

Charles rocked back on his heels. "Why, Ginny? For God's sake, why? Rich could have murdered her between nine and ten. If you'd told the truth, the police could've gotten search warrants. They might have found something in his car, blood on his clothes—something! This was murder, damn it! What's a sex scandal compared to that?"

"I had to do it, Charles! You were out of control, raging around like a madman. You even knocked your boss unconscious when he fired you. That made it even worse."

"Goddamn it, if I'd known why that bastard knuckled under,

I'd have killed him! I should never have stopped pushing. I should never have given up and left Dallas."

"There were forty witnesses to your assaulting the District Attorney. Everybody in the Adolphus Hotel lobby saw you. You didn't have a choice; you had to leave. It was the only way the D.A. wouldn't press charges."

He pushed himself up and paced the room, feeling choked again just remembering the frustrated anger, the hopelessness, the self-disgust, that had sent him fleeing Dallas to a self-imposed exile in the Texas Panhandle. "I had a choice, Ginny. I could have gone to prison rather than let my wife's murderer walk, but I felt incapable of making that kind of a noble gesture. I think I've hated myself ever since."

He stopped and looked at her. "Why did you do it, Ginny? Why did you protect that bastard?"

"I wasn't protecting him! I was protecting you!"

"What?"

"I swore to the police that Carin and Rich were with me from seven-thirty until ten that night because I was protecting you! You were the one without an alibi, Charles. You were the one the police kept asking about. *You* were the one they suspected."

CHAPTER 17

CHARLES SLID INTO HIS CAR AND SLAMMED THE door.

"What did she want to tell you, Sheriff?" asked Meenie.

"A personal matter," said Charles, rubbing his taut face. When he realized that his hands were shaking, he wrapped them around the steering wheel.

"You okay, Sheriff?" asked Raul.

"I'm fine," he snapped, and immediately felt guilty. Meenie and Raul were curious—and concerned. Natural reactions, he supposed, if he looked as pathetic as he felt.

"You want me to arrest her, Sheriff?" asked Meenie.

"Who?" asked Charles, feeling hollowed out, as if all he thought he was had been crudely exorcised. He, who hated guns, who had eschewed violence since stepping off the plane from Vietnam, had been a murder suspect. Perhaps still was. Unsolved murder cases were never closed—only filed away—time bombs ticking away. Any decent defense attorney digging into Hansford's background would find a former Dallas assistant district attorney, and Charles's past would become part of Crawford County folklore: the sheriff who might have murdered his own ex-wife.

Damn whoever murdered Rich Hansford because Sheriff Charles Timothy Matthews might become his second victim.

"Mrs. Hansford," answered Meenie.

Charles could feel Meenie's blue eyes squinting at him and wished the deputy would find someone else to examine under his psychic microscope. "Ginny? Are you crazy? She didn't do it. She's got an alibi."

"Alibis been broken before."

"Do you think she knew where he'd be at five o'clock this

morning? Then there's the gun. Do you think Ginny Hansford ever heard of a Waterman hydrant, much less knew what one looked like?"

"She's got a motive," said Meenie stubbornly.

"So she's got a motive—one of your famous P's, Lindman—so what? Everybody in the county's got a motive. What time is it, Raul?"

"Seven o'clock. Why, Sheriff?"

"Because we're going to rattle some cages, and I think we can catch our first suspect home in his."

"Who's that, Sheriff?" asked Meenie.

"Bill Adams. Hit the siren, Lindman. I'm tired of being jerked around. I want some answers."

No one said anything until Charles stopped in front of the old white frame farm house. He pounded on Bill Adams's front door, ignoring the threatening growls of a half-dozen dogs of varying sizes and breeds. Farm dogs seldom actually attacked visitors; that was left to the farmer and his shotgun. The dogs were four-legged burglar alarms.

Adams opened the door and stepped back. "Figured it was you when I heard the siren. See you brought everybody. I didn't know I was so dangerous."

"Saves explaining things more than once" said Charles, stepping into the square living room crammed with furniture that dated from the Fifties.

"Come on back to the kitchen, Sheriff. We might as well be comfortable. I got a pot of coffee on and there's pie."

"I've got some questions," said Charles.

"Figured you did," said Adams, leading them back to a spotlessly clean if old-fashioned kitchen and pointing to a round oak table covered with faded oil cloth. "Sit down. How many for coffee and pie?"

"I'd like a—" began Lindman.

"No takers," interrupted Charles. "This isn't a friendly visit, Mr. Adams. I don't think breaking bread with you is appropriate."

"Suit yourself," said Adams, cutting himself a wedge of pie.

Charles reached in his pocket for his cassette recorder and found only lint. He pinched the bridge of his nose and silently mouthed a curse. He'd left the damn thing on the end table in Ginny Hansford's motel room, forgotten in his shocked haste to escape the impact of her confession.

"Raul, take notes. I can decipher your spelling better than I can Meenie's." He blocked out the sound of Meenie's muttered protestations and focused his attention on Bill Adams. "Rich Hansford was planning on foreclosing on your farm, is that correct?"

Adams shrugged. "He was forcing Brad to, so it amounted to the same thing."

"Where were you between four-thirty and five o'clock this morning, Mr. Adams?"

"Sound asleep."

"Do you have any witnesses who'll swear to that?"

"Nope. It's just me and the dogs since the wife died."

"Do you own a twenty-two pistol?"

Adams put down his fork. "What would I need with a pistol? If it's a four-legged varmint, I got my rifle. If it's a two-legged varmint, I got my shotgun. What do you want to know for?"

"Where were you between five-thirty and six o'clock?"

"Driving to the bank. What do you want to know where I was at two different times for? Did somebody shoot Hansford twice to make sure he stayed down?" He pushed his pie away, his faded blue eyes focused on Charles. "That's it, ain't it? I wondered this morning how somebody managed to keep him still long enough to shoot his face off from that angle."

"Did you kill Rich Hansford, Mr. Adams?" asked Charles.

Bill Adams pushed his chair back and stood up. "No, I didn't, Sheriff. I'll admit the idea crossed my mind—and maybe if I wasn't having such a good pheasant season and if somebody hadn't beaten me to it, I might've done it. Look out the back window, Sheriff. What do you see?"

Charles went to the window and pushed back the curtains. "A barn and tool shed and a cellar."

"That ain't no cellar, Sheriff. That's the dugout my grandfolks lived in when they first came to the Panhandle. My daddy was born in it 'cause this house wasn't built until the First World War. I was born in the front bedroom. I lived through depression and drought on this land—and ain't no two-bit city banker who never stepped in cow shit was gonna run me off now." He sat down and picked up his fork. "I didn't kill Rich Hansford. Don't much care who did."

"Mr. Adams, the road that runs by the front of this house

leads to the field where Hansford was killed. There's no other way to get there. Did you hear any cars or trucks drive by your house last night?"

Bill Adams chewed his pie and washed it down with a sip of coffee. "I'm a real sound sleeper, Sheriff. I never heard a peep until my alarm went off about five-fifteen."

"You're lying, Mr. Adams. You've got a yard full of dogs. Don't tell me they didn't bark last night every time a car went by. Don't tell me you slept through it."

"I ain't telling you anything, Sheriff."

"Matthews, I think that old man will stay clammed up till hell freezes over," said Lindman, buttoning up his coat to his chin. "Meenie, turn up the heater."

"Where to now, Sheriff?" asked Meenie, rolling down the window to let in a rush of frigid air.

"Goddamn it, Meenie!" exclaimed Lindman. "Roll up the window! I can see my breath."

"A man's got to spit," replied Meenie. "Besides, it keeps the windshield from fogging up from all the hot air inside."

"We aren't going to have to worry about that," said Lindman grimly. "The damn thing will ice over first from the sleet blowing in that window. Don't you people in Crawford County have anything between you and the North Pole, Matthews?"

"Five states and Canada," replied Charles.

"Car thirty-two, come in."

If there was one thing guaranteed to send Charles over the edge into a screaming fit of hysteria, it was having to talk to Mabel. "Answer that, Meenie, while I concentrate on unlocking my jaw muscles."

"Don't know that I'm up to it on an empty belly. That woman's voice makes my gut knot up."

"This department only has room for one man with a delicate stomach, and that's me. Answer the damn call."

The radio emitted a high-pitched squeal that would have shattered crystal. As it was, Charles would swear he saw the thick windshield shimmy under the blast of sound.

"Goddamn it, Matthews! Does that woman do that on purpose?" asked Lindman, clapping his gloved hands over his ears.

Meenie grabbed the radio receiver. "Car thirty-two. Yeah, Mabel?"

"I need to speak to the sheriff."

"He ain't available right now," replied Meenie, glancing at Charles.

"What am I supposed to do with those hunters he put in jail? Some of them keep singing the same song over and over again. I don't know how I can concentrate on keeping the radio operating when my nerves are so jangled from listening to "Red River Valley" twenty-seven times. I counted."

Meenie thrust the receiver at Charles. "Here. I ain't any good at talking to women with jangled nerves."

Charles pressed the send button. "Mabel, this is the sheriff. Tell those hunters to sing a different song."

"What about the one who wants to sue me?"

Charles counted to ten. "Why does he want to sue, Mabel?"

"He said"—there was an audible sniff over the air—"that I was trying to poison him when all I did was give him a cup of coffee."

"Miss Poole's coffee?"

"I believe so."

Charles sighed. "Mabel, don't—I repeat *don't*—feed the hunters any more of Miss Poole's coffee. We don't want to violate anybody's civil rights."

There was an indignant sniff, followed by another squeal. "It was never like this during pheasant season when I worked for Sheriff Johnson."

"Over and out, Mabel," said Charles. "Damn hunters!" He pulled out the invitation list to the bank party from his pocket and turned on the dome light. "Meenie, who did Hansford talk to at the bank party?"

Meenie spat out the window and cleared his throat. "I didn't keep my eye on him the whole time, Sheriff. Could've jawed with a hundred people."

"Let me rephrase that question: whom did you see Hansford talking to? Does that make it any easier?"

Meenie picked at a loose button on his coat. "I guess I saw him talking to our four suspects."

"You didn't think I might want to know?" asked Charles.

"I been meaning to mention that, but things kept happening and I lost track."

Charles uttered a profanity and saw Meenie look at him in

shocked disapproval. "What else have you been meaning to mention? I want it all this time. No holding back. Otherwise, get the hell out of this car, walk back to the courthouse, and clean out your desk!"

The words reverberated in the enclosed space. Charles felt a sense of loss overwhelm his feelings of isolation. The chasm between himself and the rest of Crawford County was widening. Now Meenie was standing on the other side.

"Don't go jumping in a mesquite thicket until you know what's in there, Sheriff. All the suspects left right after they talked to Hansford, but that don't mean nothing. According to you, they ain't got no alibis anyhow." Meenie plucked at his loose button again. "Except maybe Brad Masters."

Charles seized his deputy's shoulder. "What alibi? Brad never claimed an alibi."

Meenie shuffled his feet. "That's why I never said nothing. I figured that if Brad was acting like a fool, it was his business, and if he was telling the truth, I didn't have no business gossiping when I don't know nothing for sure."

"Tell me!" demanded Charles. "I love gossip."

Charles watched the flush creeping up Meenie's neck. It turned the deputy's face red before he finished his story.

Brad Masters looked disheveled, but no more so than his guest. Without shoes, without lipstick, and awkwardly attempting to restore order to her mane of black hair, Maggie Pace appeared both startled and guilty. She bit her lip and looked wildly at Brad. Like a knight of old, the banker rode—or stumbled, since he tripped over one of Maggie's sling pumps—to the rescue of his lady. "Maggie and I were just talking, Sheriff. About the, uh, wedding."

Maggie Pace clutched Brad's arm. "Did Aunt Viola send you after me, Sheriff?"

"Why should she do that, Miss Pace?" asked Charles.

Her tense body relaxed. "I thought Aunt Viola needed her car. I forgot to tell her I was stopping by here on my way home. She hates to drive my uncle's pickup. She says she's too short to climb in it without a ladder. I was getting ready to leave anyway."

In spite of his depression, Charles almost grinned. Obviously, Mrs. Viola Jenkins's niece did not want news of her behavior to reach her aunt's ears. Grown or not, engaged or not,

Maggie Pace clearly expected her aunt to disapprove of any intimacies before marriage, an attitude shared by most Crawford County parents and honored more in the breach than in the observance by their children.

"Not yet, Miss Pace. I have a question or two," said Charles, removing his hat and perching on the arm of a chair.

"Look here, Sheriff," said Brad, looking belligerent. "What's this all about?"

"What time did you leave the bank party, Miss Pace?"

"Sheriff—Charles," interrupted Brad. "The pre-hunt party is a stag affair."

"For God's sake, quit lying to me, Brad," said Charles, looking at the banker. "There were a hundred or more people there. Do you expect them all to lie? Or was Maggie wearing a cloak that turned her invisible." He turned back to Maggie. "When did you leave?"

"She left early," answered Brad. "She had to get home."

Without turning from Maggie, Charles spoke to Meenie. "Take Brad into the bedroom and stay with him. Miss Pace doesn't need a ventriloquist."

Maggie looked desperate for a second, then she glanced up at Brad. "You didn't tell him, did you, Brad?"

Brad's face lost its florid color. "Maggie, I—"

She turned back to Charles, her face hard, as if she'd made a decision and intended to carry it through. The sheriff thought Mrs. Jenkins could stop worrying about her niece: Maggie Pace showed every indication of toughening up. "We left the party right after Rich Hansford showed up. I was upset. Brad knew I couldn't stand to be in the same room with that man, so we left. I spent last night here—with Brad—until five-thirty, when I woke him up and then went to the bank to start the coffee and set out the doughnuts. Aunt Viola is purply pissed at me. That's why I thought she might have called you when I didn't follow her home tonight."

"Why didn't you tell me this morning, Brad?" asked Charles.

Brad wiped his face on his sleeve, his flush deepening. "I didn't want everybody in town talking about Maggie. Viola Jenkins would kill me. She's ready to anyway after last night."

Charles studied the two. Brad shifted his weight from foot to foot and avoided looking at him, while Maggie sat obstinate and quiet, a calculating expression in her eyes. "If you were so worried about her reputation, Brad, why didn't you take her home, let Viola take care of her?" he finally asked. "Why did you bring her here?"

Brad jerked his head up to stare at Charles, his eyes blank. "I didn't think of it. Maggie—Maggie was upset."

"That's interesting. As your secretary, it seems to me that Maggie had to suffer Rich Hansford's presence frequently at the bank. Why was last night any different?"

Brad's eyes evaded Charles's. "It just was."

"Was it the first time that you and Maggie slept together?"

"That's none of your damn business!" exclaimed Brad, glaring at Charles.

"Why last night, Brad? Between hosting a party for out-of-town bankers and businessmen whose good will you need very badly, and a five-thirty wake-up call, it doesn't seem the best choice for first-time lovers."

Brad's forehead was glistening with sweat. His skin had turned a dusty red. "I don't have to answer that question. I never thought you'd be like this, Charles, prying into a man's personal life and making filthy comments."

Charles flinched. "This is murder, and your so-called personal life is your alibi. That gives me the right to ask about it."

"You've asked, and we've told you," said Brad. "Now you can get out."

Charles shook his head. "You are the worst liar on the planet, Brad. You had another reason for leaving the bank and bringing Maggie here. What was it? Did you decide to take advantage of her condition? Lure her into bed while she was too upset to say no?"

"Goddamn you, Matthews! Do you think I'd take advantage of Maggie, or any other woman?" He lunged for Charles. Lindman caught the banker's wildly swinging fist, swung him around, and sent him staggering toward Raul and Meenie, who grimly hung on to both his arms.

Charles swallowed, nauseated by the results of his own questions. "I don't want to, Brad, but it beats the hell out of the alternative explanation. You murdered Rich Hansford and set Maggie up as an alibi."

"You're crazy, Matthews!" shouted Brad.

"What are you—fifteen, sixteen years older than Maggie?" asked Charles, glancing at the stone-faced young woman huddled on the couch. "Enough older to be an authority figure—maybe a father substitute. You're the prosperous banker who gave her back her pride by giving her a job after Hansford foreclosed on her land. You're the man who is going to marry her. I imagine she'd swear to almost anything if it would help you."

Brad struggled to escape the deputies' grip. "I didn't kill Hansford! I didn't have a reason."

"You said Rich Hansford ran a one-man show at Lone Star National, but he had a board of directors. What was his board's position on your accommodation loans? With Rich Hansford dead, will his board restructure those loans?"

Brad's face turned even more crimson and he stared at Charles like a hypnotized rabbit, then slumped until he appeared to be standing upright only because Meenie and Raul held his arms. "Yes, the board will reconsider all the loans."

"So you have a strong motive, don't you, Brad?" asked Charles slowly, looking at Maggie Pace. "And your only alibi is not exactly unprejudiced."

Tears glistened in Brad's eyes. "You shouldn't have said anything, Maggie. I'd rather go to jail than have you involved."

Maggie rose and straightened her shoulders as if she were a condemned prisoner facing the firing squad. Charles felt a tug of sympathy. "You have everything backward. I wasn't upset last night. Brad was. Hansford told him he was calling in the accommodation loans. I had to get him out of there and calm him down before he had a stroke or a heart attack. Brad has dangerously high blood pressure. That bastard could've killed him, and you're not any better."

Charles noted Brad's brick-red color and felt alarmed. "I didn't know."

"No one does," said Maggie grimly. "Brad was afraid the bank would lose depositors if anyone knew its president and major stockholder was sick. I brought him home, gave him his medication and stayed with him. He didn't kill Rich Hansford because he was dead drunk. If you don't believe me, Sheriff, ask Dr. Wallace. Ask the doctor how sober Brad would be after mixing his antianxiety pill with four beers."

Charles nodded. "I will, Miss Pace, but Dr. Wallace can't

guarantee that Brad actually took the medication last night, can he?"

The youth and color drained from her face, leaving it aged and sallow. "Go to hell, Sheriff."

CHAPTER 18

"KINDA HARD ON THEM, WEREN'T YOU, SHERIFF?" asked Meenie.

"No!" said Charles, fishtailing down Brad Masters's gravel road toward the highway. "He shouldn't have lied to me this morning."

"At least he has an alibi now," said Raul, sitting in the corner of the back seat furthest from Meenie's open window.

"He has nothing but the strongest motive of any of the suspects! He *knew* that if Hansford were dead, his and everyone else's hides were saved. P for profit, Lindman," he said to the other sheriff.

"You got to admit, Matthews, that his story sounds like it might hold water," said Lindman.

"So does a bucket! He and Maggie have had all day to concoct their story. I can't prove anything one way or another. Brad lives out here on the edge of town. The nearest neighbor is a half mile away and doesn't even share the same gravel road with Brad, so I don't have a damn witness. Brad could've shot Hansford and driven back to town in time to make it to the bank by six o'clock. Maggie could be lying for him."

"Then who moved the body?" asked Lindman.

"How the hell do I know?" retorted Charles savagely. "Meenie, where does Ick Johnson live? And no lectures on how I should know every damn inhabitant of every damn house in town right down to the dogs and cats. I'm not in the mood for more criticism from anybody. And roll up that damn window!"

"Ain't no need to get testy, Sheriff," said the deputy, rolling up the window an infinitesimal degree. "And Ick lives over on Oak in that big square house with them queer wrought-iron shutters. Don't know what good they are in this country. Don't keep the dust or the cold out."

Charles could have informed Meenie that those shutters with their delicate flowers laid over the grillwork were as artistic as pieces of sculpture, but he didn't bother. His deputy wouldn't see wrought-iron flowers as art.

The inside of Ick Johnson's house was as surprising and unexpected as the exterior. Free standing walls separated one enormous room into different functional areas. Poster-sized photographs of oil rigs in both black and white and color dominated every wall, and starkly modern couches and chairs in brilliant primary colors nestled on a deep pile white carpet.

It was an amazing room, stamped with the many-faceted personality of its owner—a personality Charles suspected was as little known to the rest of Crawford County as it was to him. The contrast between the hardware store owner behind his counter and the Ick Johnson sitting comfortably in a leather chair in front of the white brick fireplace and sipping a Mexican beer was more than shocking; it was almost dumbfounding. Ick Johnson was a man who knew how to keep secrets—and his biggest secret was himself.

"Sit down and take a load off, Sheriff. You might as well be comfortable. I'd offer you a beer, but I don't want you thinking you're welcome. I don't confuse an interrogation with a social call."

Charles leisurely circled the room before stopping beside Johnson's chair. "At least you're honest. And"—he surveyed the room—"not at all like the rest of Crawford County."

Johnson laughed, his dark brown eyes crinkling at the corners. With his face relaxed, his blunt features were almost handsome. "Neither are you, Sheriff. Not that it bothers folks most of the time. Gives them something to talk about. Except, of course, *I'm* the local boy who left home and returned a little different, and *you're* the outsider who almost fits, but doesn't quite."

"Now that we agree that we're both misfits, why don't you tell me where you were between four-thirty and six?"

Johnson held his beer up to the light and squinted at it. "Is that what time he was killed?"

"This is *my* interrogation, remember?"

"I was asleep."

"Until when?"

"Until I woke up and drove to the bank. I got there about six like everybody else."

"Is there anyone who can corroborate your statement?"

Johnson took a long swallow of beer. "I don't need a witness. You don't have a goddamn shred of evidence that ties me to little Rich's murder, so you can fuck off, Sheriff."

"There is the matter of the mortgage on your hardware store, Ick."

Johnson set the empty beer bottle beside his chair and stretched out his legs, crossing them at the ankles. "There is that, but I'm hardly alone, am I, Sheriff? If you lined up the people Rich Hansford screwed or planned to screw, they'd stretch from one end of this county to the other. I'm not unique. And I do have other skills. I know my way around the oil and gas business."

"Not a healthy industry at the moment, is it, Ick? Not much drilling, and not a lot of opportunities—particularly if Rich Hansford deliberately bankrolled a potential competitor's oil well service company just to keep you out." Charles watched him closely.

Ick Johnson's hands curled around the arms of his chair and he pushed himself to his feet in a graceful motion. "You're way off base if you believe I'm paranoid enough to think Hansford had it in for me—enough to foreclose on my store *and* shut off future sources of income. Why would he? I didn't kiss his ass, but I didn't go out of my way to antagonize him, either."

"That ain't what it looked like last night," said Meenie.

Johnson's impassive face didn't change. "I forgot you were there, Meenie. You witnessed my temper tantrum." He shrugged suppliantly. "I admit it. But it doesn't matter. It's a long way from a broken whiskey glass to a shotgun blast."

"Do you own a twenty-two pistol, Ick?"

"I sell guns at my store, in case you'd forgotten, Sheriff. So somebody popped him off and made a mess of covering it up. That ought to tell you it wasn't me—"

"Because you would have strangled him," Charles interrupted. "That's what you said this morning, Ick."

"Because I wouldn't have screwed it up." Johnson smiled as he corrected Charles.

"Why are you sounding so mellow tonight? What—or who—changed your mind?"

"I think you're the one who's paranoid, Sheriff. I didn't like

Hansford—he was a prick—but I'm not lamebrained enough to kill him because I couldn't make my mortgage payments." He stretched and yawned. "I think we've covered the subject, Sheriff. Good night, gentlemen. I believe you can find your own way out."

Charles could feel Ick's eyes watching until the door closed behind them.

"That's one tough son of a bitch," observed Lindman as Charles drove off.

"He rattled on, but he didn't tell us a dang thing more than Bill Adams did," said Meenie, rolling down the window and spitting.

"On the contrary," said Charles. "He told us more than he intended."

"You must have heard a different conversation than I did, Matthews," said Lindman, blowing on his hands. "All I heard was him talking out of the other side of his mouth from this morning."

"But it's the same mouth, Lindman," said Charles. "This morning he was doing everything but standing on his head to make sure I knew he hated Hansford—and that Hansford's financial stranglehold was enough reason to kill him. Tonight he tells us that he still hates Hansford, but the foreclosure was nothing personal and he wouldn't kill a man over money. He's changed his tactics but not his strategy. He's still talking about motive. Why?"

Meenie spat out the window again. "Maybe he figured that if you thought his motive wasn't no motive at all, you'd leave him alone."

"Then why didn't he think of that tactic this morning, Meenie? Everyone else did, and Ick's not stupid."

"It still don't mean he's protecting somebody. It might just be his own behind he's looking out for."

Charles shook his head. "In that case he left half of it hanging out, because he didn't ask me who Hansford was bankrolling."

"According to Mrs. Hansford, your Mayor Culpepper was lying, Matthews," said Lindman.

"Ginny—Mrs. Hansford—didn't offer any evidence to support that, Lindman, except to say that Rich thought Culpepper was a boob. But even boobs need a reason to lie, and Culpepper doesn't have one."

"That you know of," said Lindman.

"That I know of," agreed Charles, wishing the other sheriff was a little more optimistic. "But even if Culpepper is lying about the loan, don't you think Ick would still be curious enough to ask his identity, if for no other reason than to argue me out of believing our illustrious mayor? Instead, he says that Hansford has no reason to feel vindictive. That's like saying the fox has no reason to steal chickens. Hansford didn't need a reason. He was a bastard because it was his nature to be a bastard. Culpepper's story rings true. Ick's doesn't. If Ick hadn't made that one mistake, I'd be taking his motive apart with a pair of tweezers and examining it under a microscope."

"What the hell you talking about, Matthews?" asked Lindman, pushing his nose against the metal screen that separated the back seat from the front, his bright blue eyes glittering in the light from the dashboard.

Charles stopped the patrol car in front of the courthouse. "Ick has no alibi and unlimited access to guns, yet he nearly conned me into concentrating on his motive, first by waving it under my nose, then by denying he even had one. A variation on the carrot and the stick. I may not be a bloodhound, but I know about following a false scent."

"So where are you going to sniff instead?" asked Lindman.

"Guns," answered Charles. "Raul, get a search warrant for Ick's files on the guns he sells. Compare his invoices and his sales slips against his inventory. Find out if there's a twenty-two missing and if its serial number matches the gun Slim found."

"That ain't gonna prove Ick Johnson's guilty," said Meenie.

"What are you—his defense attorney?" snapped Charles.

"You're getting testy again. I'm just pointing out that you got a few chuckholes in your case."

"And if I'm lucky, Ick Johnson will step in one," said Charles, sliding out of the car to open the rear door for Raul, since department vehicles had no inside door handles for passengers riding in the back seat, a sensible precaution considering most passengers weren't voluntary guests. "Take off, Raul. I want some answers. And tell Mabel to let those hunters out as soon as they sober up. Preferably before they all develop laryngitis."

Raul climbed out. "Where will you be, Sheriff?"

"Filling in another chuckhole. I'm going to try to disprove Ick's alibi."

"But he doesn't have an alibi," protested Raul.

Charles arched one eyebrow. "Of course, he does. He was asleep."

CHAPTER 19

CHARLES STOPPED A HALF-BLOCK FROM ICK JOHNSON's house and gripped the steering wheel as if it were the only stable object in the universe. Regardless of outside events, it remained an amalgamate of plastic firmly anchored onto a metal column. It was solid, functional, and a symbol of control. No one who saw it would ever mistake it for something else.

He wished to hell he could say the same about himself. Unfortunately, he couldn't. The only solid thing about Charles Timothy Matthews recently was the space between his ears. He only nominally functioned; he controlled nothing, certainly not outside events; and he was firmly anchored in the quicksand of guesswork psychology and his own gut instinct. And as Lindman had so succinctly pointed out, his gut wasn't very reliable.

"You gonna hang onto that steering wheel all night, or are we getting out?" asked Meenie.

Charles released the wheel and opened the door. "We're getting out."

"And doing what?" asked his deputy. "You ain't exactly been boiling over with conversation since we let Raul out."

"An exercise in group dynamics, Meenie. I'm going to approach Ick Johnson's neighbors and collect the latest gossip about our odd storekeeper. My instincts tell me that Crawford County is too curious for Ick's own good."

Meenie spat at a tumbleweed rolling down the middle of the street and hit it dead center from a distance of ten feet, a feat of marksmanship that Charles was certain demonstrated mastery of both higher mathematics and the physics of velocity. "Sometimes, Sheriff, you act like you got good sense."

"Thank you, Mr. Higgins," remarked Charles dryly.

"You've had kind of a bad day what with being wrong so many times. I figured you needed a pat on the back."

Charles didn't reply. He knew when he was beaten.

If Charles felt beaten, Ick Johnson's next door neighbor, Eddie Joe Ferris, looked it. A gash pulled together with black stitches slashed across his forehead, bordered above and below by livid, puffy flesh. Swollen eyes surrounded by sooty-colored bruises looked as if they might fall out of his head at the slightest motion. Charles decided that if Eddie Joe were a foot taller and possessed a knob on each side of his neck, he could pass for Frankenstein's monster.

"I appreciate your not saying anything about how I look, Sheriff," said Eddie Joe in a nasal tone Charles thought might be the result of a nose swollen twice its normal size. "I been catching it from the guys at work today. They think it's funny when they call me Frankenstein. But then they ain't real original."

Charles coughed. "How did it happen, Eddie Joe?"

Eddie Joe sighed and propped his size thirteen feet on the coffee table. "I work at the packing plant, and last night I zigged when I should've zagged. Don't want to do that, Sheriff, when you're slicing up sides of beef and everybody on the line's got one son of a bitching sharp knife. Jesus, I thought I'd been scalped."

"What happened to your eyes?" asked Meenie. "Did the side of beef give you them shiners?"

Eddie Joe frowned, then grimaced as his stitches pulled. "No. That happened when I was coming home. I had to go to the hospital—stitches, tetanus, the whole nine yards—and I was feeling woozy driving home. It was so damn early this morning even the roosters were still asleep, and I didn't figure I had to worry about traffic. In a way it was as much my fault as my neighbor's. I didn't have my seat belt on and I wasn't operating on all cylinders like I said. I was kind of slumped down in the seat peering through the windshield when he backed his pickup out of his driveway, and the two of them took off like a bat out of hell. I slammed on my brakes and bounced my skull right off the steering wheel. Hit myself square across the bridge of my nose and blacked both my eyes."

Charles saw Lindman and Meenie straighten up as if they

were puppets and someone had jerked on their strings. "What time was this, Eddie Joe?"

Eddie Joe scratched his head. "Well, I was working overtime at the plant when I had my accident—figured on taking home a little extra pay to help out at Christmas—so it must have been around two-thirty. Drove back to town to the hospital and Doc Wallace worked on me, cussing me all the time for not being careful. Then he stuck me full of tetanus—acted like he enjoyed it, too—gave me a horse pill, and sent me home."

Charles clenched his jaw. Ordinarily he enjoyed the way Crawford County people answered questions by layering mundane replies with meticulous details until every answer became a mini-story. Tonight it irritated the hell out of him. "Eddie Joe, what time did you see the pickup?"

Eddie Joe looked perplexed by Charles's tone. "I was getting there, Sheriff. I was about to say, I turned the corner, looked at the clock in my pickup, and thought Lordy, but I wasn't gonna get more than three hours sleep before I had to go back to the plant. Don't want to take sick leave when I don't need it. Working in a packing plant, a man never knows when he might get hurt bad and need every hour of sick leave he's got. Anyway, it was about four-forty—right on the button."

"Who was the neighbor, Eddie Joe?" asked Charles, and held his breath waiting for the answer.

"The guy next door—Ick Johnson."

Charles leaned forward. "Who was with him?"

Eddie Joe looked surprised. "How the hell would I know, Sheriff? I lost interest when I cracked my nose on the steering wheel."

Lindman slapped Charles's shoulder. "By God, Matthews, when you sniff out a trail, you catch your man with his pants down taking a morning crap. What's next? You going to offer Ick Johnson a roll of Charmin and tell him to come clean?"

Charles crossed the street, hunching his shoulders against the wind that whistled down its narrow length. "Not yet. I want to know who the other person is."

"You figure you're going to find two people who were awake at four-thirty?" asked Lindman, as he and Meenie followed Charles up the sidewalk to a house directly across the street from Ick Johnson's. "You ain't asking for much, are you, Matthews?"

"Just a little more luck," answered Charles, jerking his hand back just short of the doorbell as he read a note fastened with bobby pins to the middle of a ripped screen door: *Please knock—sleeping baby.*

Charles tapped on the door. He removed his hat when the door was opened by a weary young woman with a toddler wrapped around one leg and an infant slung over her shoulder. "Ma'am, I'm Sheriff Charles Matthews and these gentlemen are Deputies Higgins and Lindman." He ignored the other sheriff's expression of outrage. "We need to ask you a few questions."

"Are you here about the child support?"

"Uh, no."

"Come in anyway. You're the first people I've seen in a week who don't wear diapers and who speak English. Besides, I want to know what you people are going to do about my child support. That worthless bum hasn't paid any in two months. Is the law going to let him get by with starving his children?"

"No, ma'am. You file a complaint on your ex-husband for failure to pay child support, and I'll arrest him—personally."

"Will you put him in the worst cell you've got?" she asked, dragging her toddler-clad leg as she led the law officers into a toy-cluttered living room barely large enough to hold a vintage playpen, a worn couch, and two mismatched easy chairs.

"I guarantee it," said Charles grimly as he glimpsed a half-filled plate of beans and cornbread sitting on a dilapidated table in the adjacent kitchen.

"And will you put him next to somebody who snores real loud?" she asked as she popped the infant into the playpen, where it immediately began investigating the day's flavors in thumbs. "Lance can't sleep if somebody snores."

"I guess I could manage that," replied Charles, puzzled when the young mother smiled broadly, then clapped her hands.

"Good. The baby has colic and I haven't had a whole night's sleep in five months. I want that bastard to know what it's like. His name is Lance Wayne Hammond. I call him the jerk. I'm Joella Hammond." She peeled her toddler off her leg and handed him a stuffed animal of some indeterminate species. "Hang on to that awhile, Bobby. Mama's leg's going numb." She looked back at Charles. "You said you had some questions, Sheriff? It's nothing I've done, is it? I haven't hardly had time to get into trouble the last few months."

If Mrs. Hammond's precarious existence didn't qualify as trouble, Charles couldn't imagine what would. "Do you know Ick Johnson, Mrs. Hammond?" he asked.

Joella Hammond smiled and her gray-green eyes took on the wistful expression of a child who knows that however much she wants the doll in the toy store window, it will never be hers. "Isn't he nice, Sheriff? And his house! It's so beautiful—and white. I was only in it once, but I held Bobby the whole time, just scared to death he'd touch something. Ick said not to worry, that there wasn't anything in his house that couldn't be washed, but kids Bobby's age are always so gummy—like they have some kind of sticky film all over them. I was afraid he'd sit on that white carpet and stick to it like a wad of Double Bubble." She leaned down and patted her son on his head.

Charles tried to imagine blunt-featured ex-roughneck Ick Johnson as the man who loved children and decided his suspect had more sides than a hexagon. "So you're a friend of his?"

Joella looked wistful again. "No, I'm just a neighbor he feels sorry for." She gestured at her clothes: a frayed blouse and jeans whose faded color Charles suspected owed more to frequent laundering than to fashion. "Even if I was cleaned up nice, I'd fit in that house about like a jelly jar with the nice china."

Meenie cleared his throat. "You ain't giving yourself enough credit, ma'am."

Joella's smile lit up her face. "You're just fooling with me, but thanks anyway. I don't hear many pretty things." She turned back to Charles and her smile faded, leaving her tired, worn, and plain. "I think you better explain why you're so curious about Ick. He's been nice to me in a kind of offhand way, and I'm not fixing to say anything against him."

Charles suppressed a shudder as he heard her say the deadly words: *not fixing to*. He wished he could question just one person who didn't preface his remarks with that expression. "Ick is involved in a case I'm investigating and—"

"What kind of case?"

"A murder case."

She shook her head vehemently. "Ick didn't kill anybody, and if he did, it wasn't murder."

Charles held onto his temper only because Joella Hammond

was frail and courageous and put upon by her lousy ex-husband. She didn't need another man verbally assaulting her. Still, he was getting damn tired of everyone in the county making a distinction between murder and killing. "I'm not accusing Ick of committing murder, Mrs. Hammond." *Yet,* he added silently, "I said he was involved. He had the means and the motive. We're trying to discover if he had the opportunity. In other words, I'm checking on his alibi. I need to know if you were up with your baby last night—"

"I'm up with the baby every night."

"And if you happened to look out your window and if you happened to see Ick Johnson."

Joella stared at him, an obstinate expression in her eyes. "I look out my window sometimes."

Charles wiped his forehead. "Mrs. Hammond, I have a dead man, a murdered man. Frankly, he wasn't a decent human being, but that fact doesn't grant immunity to the murderer. No one has the right to decide that lack of decency is a good enough reason to take a life. That is not our prerogative, and it is not your prerogative to protect Ick Johnson from the consequences of his actions, whatever they were. I won't lie to you. Ick's in trouble and he may stay in trouble if I don't learn the truth. I have to know where he was last night and early this morning. This is a test of faith for you. If you're certain Ick Johnson would never commit murder, then the truth can't hurt him. If you lie, and I never discover the murderer, whatever faith you have will erode away because you'll always wonder if Ick is truly innocent or if your lie saved a guilty man. Doubt is the most corrosive emotion there is, Mrs. Hammond. It will burn away trust and dreams and even love. You'll have nothing left of the nice man you know."

He ran out of words and sank down on the couch, almost too tired to care if Joella Hammond spoke or kept silent. Either way he'd keep pushing, because he had to find Rich Hansford's killer; otherwise, the bastard would never really be dead. He would always be an unanswered question hovering at the edge of Charles's mind and haunting Ginny's life. If ever the dead could walk, Rich Hansford would be the first to do it.

"Sheriff?" Joella's face looked older and with a melancholy expression that bruised Charles's heart. Even if Ick was innocent, Charles knew he'd destroyed a hero for a girl who had so few. Maybe only one.

"Sheriff, I don't like to mess in anyone else's life, and I hate people who gossip about personal things. I mean, we don't always know everything there is to know, do we? Sometimes what we think is wrong might be right for someone else." She stopped and drew a deep breath. "But it's never right to be a coward when stepping forward will save somebody else from trouble. A man has to stand up and be counted, my daddy always said, and I guess it goes for a woman, too."

"I never thought you were a coward, Mrs. Hammond."

"I'm not talking about me! I'm talking about that woman who was with Ick last night. Why didn't she tell you where he was?"

"I'll be damned," said Lindman quietly.

"What woman?" demanded Charles.

"I don't know who she is. I've only seen her late at night sneaking into Ick's house with him."

"What do you mean, with him?" asked Charles.

"Just what I said. Ick brings her to his house late at night, maybe twelve or one o'clock, then takes her home at five or so. It's happened maybe two or three weekends a month for the last three months or so that I know of. I don't think she's respectable, Sheriff. I mean, I think she's married because there wouldn't be any reason for her to act so . . ."

"Furtive?" suggested Charles.

"Yes! Furtive." She caressed the word with her voice, rolling it around her mouth as if it were a piece of candy. "That's how she acted: furtive—like her seeing Ick was a secret, and that means she's married because Ick's a bachelor and nobody cares if he has overnight company. Oh, I guess the neighbors would talk, but a man can get by with a lot more. Let me do something like that, and people would be all over me like flies on a cow patty."

"Maybe Ick is being a gentleman and trying to protect a lady's reputation," said Lindman.

Joella chewed on a fingernail and frowned. "That's exactly what he is. He's being a damn gentleman and protecting her reputation because she's married. Well, I'm not putting up with that and I don't care if he gets mad about it. A man shouldn't go to jail because he's being a gentleman. Discourages the rest of the men in town, and God knows some of them don't need another excuse to be horses' asses."

Having delivered her opinion on the fine art of being a gentleman in Crawford County, she returned to her original topic. "Another reason I know she's married is because he always brings her to his house. Why don't they stay at her house unless it's because there's somebody already there?"

"Seems to me a man might notice his wife sneaking out every night," said Meenie. "Seems to me he might at least ask where she's going."

Joella laughed bitterly. "Maybe some men, but if he's like Lance Wayne, he'd figure she was in the bathroom, or seeing to the kids, or something. At any rate, he wouldn't bother waking up enough to really notice because he might have to help. Lance Wayne could sleep through a tornado if it meant he didn't have to help close the windows. Besides, if everything was right, why didn't he go around with her in the daytime? Why didn't he ever take her to lunch out at Carroll's Rest? Why didn't Crawford County know about her unless there was something wrong?"

"When did you see this woman last night, Mrs. Hammond?" asked Charles.

"Ick drove up with her about one-thirty and they sneaked into his house like they were robbers come to steal the silver. I finally got the baby to sleep and just died sitting right there in the rocker. If I'd gone back to bed, I probably wouldn't have seen them leave. My bedroom is in back, but the baby's room is in the front of the house. I heard a door slam and I woke up. When you're a single parent you get that way—real sensitive to noise. You have to be. There's nobody else to watch out for your kids. Of course, even when I was married, there still wasn't anybody else. Lance Wayne was kind of worthless. Anyway, I looked out the window and saw them getting in the truck, and that's the first time I ever really got a look at her. The pickup's interior light came on and I saw it shining on her blonde hair. That was a little after four-thirty—earlier than when he usually took her home."

Charles leaned forward, bracing his elbows on his thighs and clasping his hand together. "Did you recognize the woman, Mrs. Hammond?"

"No, I didn't get that good a look, just at her hair, and about every third woman in this county has got blonde hair of some shade, either natural or by request. County was settled mostly by Germans and Polish and English who came up from south Texas looking for cheap farmland."

Charles knew Joella Hammond was a native by the way she reeled off the county history without taking a breath. Mothers must feed their children local history along with their formula. "Did you notice anything else about her?"

"No, because she ducked down real fast. Just like a coward, Sheriff, because that's what she is. If she were any kind of a woman, she'd speak up for Ick no matter how much trouble she got into."

Charles smiled at her indignation and decided that for all her problems, Joella Hammond hadn't lost her youthful idealism. "Mrs. Hammond, in Crawford County it's more respectable to be suspected of murder than of adultery."

CHAPTER 20

"NOW WE KNOW WHERE MARTA TURNER WAS THIS morning," said Charles grimly as he turned on the ignition.

"Ain't you jumping awful fast again?" asked Meenie. "Could be another blonde. Like Mrs. Hammond said, blondes are pretty thick on the ground."

Charles turned his head to glare at his deputy. "I've had about enough of you and Lindman automatically assuming there's some other explanation for every fact we uncover. Look at it logically. Ick Johnson has to be protecting Marta Turner. Otherwise why was he so damn intent on drawing my fire this morning? Why deliberately provoke me? The only logical explanation is to keep me from looking too closely at the other suspects, and remember, as a bank director, he was in a position to know whom Hansford was screwing over."

"There ain't nothing to say that Ick wasn't protecting Bill Adams or Brad," said Meenie.

"Do you see Ick Johnson, the man Mrs. Hammond called a gentleman, sticking his neck out for another man? I don't. He'd let them defend themselves. And if he were protecting an uninvolved blonde, he'd have still lied about his alibi, but he wouldn't have called attention to himself. He would have used tonight's tactic this morning. He'd have dismissed his motives as economic bad luck and taken a chance that I believed him, at least enough not to dig too deep.

"That don't make sense either, Matthews," objected Lindman from the back seat. "He must have known that we'd find somebody who knew he was sharing a midnight snack with a blonde. In a town this size, that's kind of hard to hide."

Charles shrugged. "It was an acceptable risk as long as I

didn't suspect the woman was Marta. If Jess Turner hadn't tripped up by telling such an elaborate lie, I wouldn't have."

Cheek bulging with tobacco and eyes narrowed, Meenie looked like a lopsided, disgruntled chipmunk with a squint as he stared at Charles. "Sounds farfetched to me, Sheriff. What does Ick do, drop Mrs. Turner off at her doorstep and kiss her goodnight?"

Charles felt irritation turn his face hot. Meenie had a way of making him sound like a fool, but even fools were sometimes right, and this was one of those times. "You're forgetting the dogs, Meenie."

"What's dogs got to do with the price of peas?" asked Lindman, leaning forward to peer through the metal screen.

"Ick can't drive up to the Turners' because the Turners' dogs would bark," explained Charles. "Marta must meet him somewhere else in her own vehicle."

"I ain't never thought Jess Turner is the brightest man in Crawford County, but it appears to me that he keeps a little better track of his wife than that. Unless you're fixing to tell me that he knows and don't care," said Meenie. "And I ain't buying that at all."

"You don't have to, Meenie. Did you know Jess Turner hated to hunt—refused to do it, according to Angie? But he was in Bill Adams's field with a shotgun."

Meenie squinted his eyes again. "And if you're right about his wife, you don't figure Jess was there to shoot a pheasant."

"I think he was there to bag Ick Johnson," said Charles. "But Hansford's body turned up, I started asking questions, and Jess panicked—and lied. Ick realized immediately how vulnerable Marta was and metaphorically leapt between me and her. He knew he didn't kill Hansford, so he felt reasonably safe as my chief suspect."

"Wait a minute, Matthews, how do we know that he didn't murder Hansford? Maybe he stopped by that field on the way to Marta's house and sent Hansford to a better world. Or at least a warmer one." Lindman added, folding his arms across his chest and sticking his gloved hands under his armpits.

"Then stopped on the way back and set up the accident scene?" asked Charles. "The only part of Ick Johnson's act tonight that I bought was when he said that if he'd killed Rich

Hansford, he wouldn't have screwed it up. Although that's not the only reason why I think he's innocent."

"You think he's innocent?" asked Meenie, spitting out the car window without marking a target first, an act so out of character that Charles knew he'd finally succeeded in shocking his deputy. "Since when, 'cause you sure ain't been acting like it up to now. You been on his trail like a coyote after a newborn calf."

"Because he lied to me!" exclaimed Charles. "Just like everyone's been doing. Subconsciously, I think I've known since this morning that this murder didn't have Ick Johnson's fingerprints on it, but I damn well had to push him. Because I can't trust anybody! But now that I know about Marta, now that I'm unraveling some of these relationships that are so tangled up with the murder, I'm more objective about certain things—like the gun."

"What about it?" asked Lindman.

"Ick Johnson has been selling guns for years. He knows they leave a paper trail—serial numbers, manufacturing records, shipping invoices, sales slips. He would never have left that gun at the murder scene. He would never have risked its being traced—and I should've realized it sooner."

Charles pulled away from the curb, felt the rear wheels skid on the sleet encrusted street, and fought to control the car. The county commissioners might—*might*—view a passenger door full of buckshot as an Act of God and caution him against inconveniencing the hunters again by parking between them and the pheasant, but those same men would consider a traffic accident caused by three inches of ice on an asphalt street to be pure ineptitude.

And they might be right, he thought, since he skidded because he pulled away from the curb too fast, for no better reason than that he was angry at himself. If he hadn't been so preoccupied with the emotional factors involved in Hansford's death, including his own history, he would have considered the physical evidence much more objectively much sooner. The gun, the time lapse between the murder and the mutilation, Hansford's papers—all needed to be examined rationally. It was time for Charles Matthews, the left-brained sheriff, to take charge of the investigation and exile the right-brained Matthews, whose creative leaps in deduction had landed him unerringly in all the wrong mud puddles.

"Sheriff," said Meenie. "I want you to listen to what I got to say without getting mad."

Charles clenched his teeth and consciously controlled his urge to stomp the accelerator all the way to the floor, viciously jerk the steering wheel, and send his deputy hurling out that damn open window, seat belt and all. His intuition told him that Meenie Higgins was about to rain on his hypothesis, and he didn't want to hear it.

"I won't get mad."

Meenie looked dubious, but settled his tobacco securely in one cheek and cleared his throat. "You explained all about Ick and Mrs. Turner and Jess, and it all sounded real good. Everything fit together like one of them jigsaw puzzles, but the picture just ain't right. I don't believe Mrs. Turner is a hussy."

Charles pondered Meenie's word choice and felt his throat tighten and burn with sympathy for Marta Turner. If what he suspected was true, Marta Turner would be called worse than that. "She's not a hussy, Meenie. Sex has nothing to do with her relationship with Ick Johnson. Psychologically, she's incapable of having an affair with a man as strong-willed and tough as Ick even if she was morally capable of it, which I doubt. But she needed a friend, somebody to talk to, a role model to give her courage, a man who didn't cower when Rich Hansford threatened him."

"So she sneaks out of the house at night to see a friend?" asked Lindman. "Come on, Matthews, tell me a story I'll believe."

Charles struggled for an answer that made sense of Marta Turner's complex personality. "What was she supposed to do? Have lunch or dinner with him? In Crawford County? Where everyone would gossip about it? She would have destroyed her marriage, and that's the one thing I don't think she wants to do. Unlikely as it may seem to the rest of us, I think she loves the gentle man she married, loves him enough to want to protect him. I think that's what this case is all about: protection. Rich Hansford was murdered to protect someone. Sex and money—your passion and profit, Lindman—are red herrings. Marta Turner murdered Rich Hansford to protect Jess."

"Jesus Christ, Matthews! How do you figure that when you just got through saying that she was with Ick Johnson?" demanded Lindman.

"She was last seen between four-thirty and four-forty. If Ick dropped her off at her own vehicle, I think she had time to drive by that field on her way home and shoot Rich Hansford. Besides, there's always the psychological aspect to her alibi and Jess's."

"I hate to ask, but what psychological aspect?" asked Lindman.

"Jess gave Marta an alibi beginning before four-thirty—when he awoke and realized she was gone. Marta's alibi for herself begins at around five-thirty—when she must have gotten home."

"So who moved the body in this scenario?" asked Lindman.

"Marta," answered Charles. "After Jess left, she realized she'd better cover her tracks a little better—including getting rid of the gun. She's a tall woman, and strong enough to pull Hansford out of that Suburban. She also knows what a Waterman hydrant is, and how unlikely it was that anyone would find the gun until she had a chance to dispose of it permanently. She was unlucky enough to catch Slim on a good day. That might not happen again for a hundred years."

"So Marta Turner's guilty after all," mused Lindman.

Charles shrugged. "Maybe. Probably. It seems likely."

"Matthews, you'd drive the pope into sin. Which is it? Guilty or not?"

"At this point, it doesn't matter which."

"Meaning you aren't going to arrest her?"

Charles laughed. "On what grounds? The mishmash of guesswork and the statements of eyewitnesses who have identified nobody? On physical evidence linked to no one? I've got a better case against Santa Claus for breaking and entering than I have against Marta Turner—or anybody else, for that matter. I've alienated everybody in the county with my inquiry, Lindman, and I can't arrest a single damn individual. Unless Raul traces that gun, somebody—maybe Marta—is going to get away with murder, and there's nothing I can do about it. That ought to make Crawford County happy."

"Car thirty-two, come in."

Charles grabbed the radio receiver. "What the hell is wrong now, Mabel?"

She sniffed, and Charles thought about force-feeding her antihistamines. "About those hunters."

"Didn't Raul tell you to let them out when they sobered up?"

"Yes, and I did, but we lost one."

"One of the hunters died?" exclaimed Charles.

"Of course not, Sheriff. I would've said so. One of them wouldn't leave. He said the rest of the hunters would beat him up."

Charles pinched the bridge of his nose. "Let me guess. Roy the lawyer?"

"I think he's a lawyer."

"So how did we lose him, Mabel?"

There was another sniff. "We didn't lose *all* of him. Slim still has one of his legs."

Charles choked back the urge to scream hysterically. "What in the hell are you talking about, Mabel? Did that idiot Slim dismember a hunter?"

"I'm trying to tell you, Sheriff, but you keep interrupting. Sheriff Johnson never interrupted me."

"If you don't tell me what's happening in five seconds, Mabel, *I'm* going to dismember *you*!"

There were two sniffs. "The lawyer wanted to leave the jail by the back door."

"The jail doesn't have a back door!"

"Shut up, Matthews!" growled Lindman. "I gotta hear this."

"That's what Slim told him, so he crawled out the window instead."

"The window at the end of the aisle between the cells—the one I wanted to put bars on, but the county commissioners voted to cover with a wire mesh screen instead?"

"That's the only window in the jail, Sheriff."

"Goddamn it, Mabel! The jail's on the third floor!"

"So is the window, Sheriff, and three-fourths of the lawyer is hanging out of it. Slim wants you to hurry before he loses his grip and drops the other one-fourth."

Charles hit the siren, but he could still hear Lindman's hysterical laughter.

Slim had braced his feet against the wall below the window and had Roy the lawyer's left leg in a death grip. "I didn't do it, Sheriff. He tore the screen off the window before I could stop him. I barely grabbed his leg in time. I don't think he's real sober yet."

"Don't drop me! Don't drop me!" screamed the lawyer over and over, waving his arms.

Charles leaned out the window and grabbed the lawyer's

other leg. He braced himself against the windowsill. "Pull," he grunted to Slim.

Roy the lawyer reentered the jail hind end first, bumping his chin and nose on the windowsill in the process. "I'll sue for damages," he said, lying belly-down on the concrete floor where Charles and Slim had dropped him, and gingerly wiping his nose on his sleeve. "I've been harassed, threatened, nearly poisoned, and physically injured. My left leg is definitely sprained."

"I should've dropped him," muttered Slim.

Charles hauled the lawyer up by his belt and collar and marched him down the aisle and out of the jail. "I'll make a deal with you, Roy, my friend. If you walk out the front door of the courthouse, turn left, and keep walking for fourteen blocks, you'll be out of the Carroll city limits. Twelve miles further south, and you'll be out of Crawford County. If you do both before sunrise tomorrow, I won't file on you for sexual harassment of a female deputy, disturbing the peace, destruction of public property, and attempted murder."

Roy the lawyer's bleary eyes widened. "Attempted murder?"

Charles nodded and clapped Slim on the back. "You attempted to pull my deputy through that window and to his death. Isn't that the way you saw it, Slim?"

"Damn straight!" exclaimed Slim, nodding vigorously. "I'm lucky to be alive."

"That's ridiculous!" shouted the lawyer.

"Maybe it is," agreed Charles, "but you know how us rednecks are. Now get the hell out of my county before I change my mind and file charges on you."

The lawyer scuttled out the door, and Charles sank down on a chair. "What else do you think can happen today, Lindman?"

"Mabel, patch me through to the sheriff." Raul's lilt was more conspicuous than usual.

Meenie flipped a switch on the radio. "Something's got Raul's blood up. He sounds dang near like he's got an accent."

Mabel's voice, on the other hand, had no accent unless one defined a nasal screech as having an ethnic origin. "Don't touch my radio set!"

Charles sighed as he rose and crossed the room to the old-fashioned communication system. "Calm down, Mabel." He leaned over the set. "I'm here, Raul. Have you got a problem?"

"You might say so, Sheriff. I'm at Benny's hardware store with Ick Johnson. We need you at the scene."

Benny's Hardware sold more than nuts and bolts, hammers and saws, nails and screws. It was an anachronism, a frontier general store existing out of its proper historical era. Benny's shelves held bolts of gingham, stacks of Levi's and insulated work clothes, felt and straw hats, work boots and cowboy boots, Western shirts and suits, dusters, leather belts, woolen socks, and what townspeople claimed was the largest stock of union suits—or long johns—in the entire Panhandle.

In addition to supplying Crawford County with working clothes, Benny's also stocked rope—both nylon and the hemp variety, or grass rope as the cowboys called it—bridles, saddle blankets, saddle bags, canning supplies, a few churns, frying pans of all sizes, Dutch ovens, small appliances such as toasters and mixers, glassware and dishes, knives both for the table and for hunting, plumbing supplies, batteries, plows, harrows, kerosene lanterns, camping tents, and light bulbs of every conceivable size and wattage. Rumor said that Benny's basement held such outdated items as buggy whips and high-button shoes purchased in 1910 by the store's former proprietor. That gentleman had suffered from a love of bargains, the mistaken dismissal of the automobile as a smelly passing fancy, and the heartfelt belief that a lady's virtue was somehow endangered by an unclad ankle. Ick Johnson denied the rumor, but it clung tenaciously to life like the tumbleweed clings to the fence row. Charles always believed the rumor in much the same way he believed other Crawford County folklore: if it wasn't true, it ought to be.

But one thing was true: Benny's Hardware sold guns. Shotguns, rifles, revolvers, automatics, in all sizes and calibers, were displayed in securely locked cabinets behind the counter. Anyone wanting to examine a gun could—but only under Ick's supervision and only after showing proof of age. Ick never sold guns to anyone under twenty-one, and he never sold to strangers unless a local resident attested to their character and intent. It wasn't that Ick held moral scruples against hunting or self-defense—Charles knew Ick had little patience for animal rights activists or the anti-gun lobby—but he objected to anybody equating a gun with manhood.

Ick traced the heavily engraved grip of a special issue Colt revolver. "I got no use for some impotent bastard that sees a gun as some kind of substitute for a hard-on, Sheriff, and I don't sell weapons to anybody I even think might confuse the two."

Charles looked around the store at the undisturbed shelves and piles and bins and tables of goods, then at the locked gun cabinets. "But it's not the guns we have to worry about, is it, Ick? Whoever cut your alarm and jimmied open the back door already has a gun—or had one. Damn it, Ick, why did you keep all your records at the store?"

Ick Johnson laid the revolver back in the display case and locked it. "Where the hell else am I supposed to keep business records, Sheriff? I didn't expect anybody to break in here and steal all my sales slips and invoices for the last six months."

"Which means you sold someone the murder weapon in the last six months," said Charles.

"Maybe or maybe not," said Ick calmly. "I might have sold it last year."

"Then why didn't the thief steal last year's slips?" demanded Charles.

Ick grinned. "Because he couldn't find them. I only keep six months' worth of sales slips in my office. After six months I enter all the information on computer and store the paper in my vault for at least ten years—if the paper pertains to guns. If not, I keep it for five years."

Charles stared at him incredulously. "You don't have a computer! You're famous all over town as the last businessman who still keeps books in pen and ink."

Ick nodded his head toward a steel door. "I don't keep buggy whips and high-button shoes in the basement, Sheriff; I keep a computer. My store may look like a holdover from Dodge City because that image brings in a lot of business, but my bookkeeping practices are of the twentieth century. Crawford County just confused image with reality."

"And you didn't discourage it?" asked Charles, wondering if anyone in town really knew Ick Johnson.

Ick shook his head. "I'm a private person, Sheriff; I don't live my life in front of an open window, and in this case, you ought to be thankful. I can check your weapon's serial number against my records and tell you whether or not I ever carried that gun in inventory."

"If you didn't purchase it in the last six months?"

"There is that restriction."

"This burglary was convenient for someone, wasn't it, Ick?"

The proprietor nodded.

"Did you steal your own records?"

Ick Johnson smiled, an expression of genuine amusement so far as Charles could determine—which wasn't very far, given Ick's talent for hiding reality behind image. "Would I call attention to myself, Sheriff, when it would be safer and easier to simply erase my computer record and destroy a single invoice?"

"Why not?" asked Charles. "When you've been doing it all along. Would you care to identify the woman who left your house this morning?"

All expression disappeared from Ick Johnson's face as if he'd flipped an internal switch. "When hell freezes over. She didn't kill Hansford, and I'm not having you drag her through the filth like you've been doing to everybody else. You're about as popular as a boil on the butt right now, Sheriff. Nobody can figure out why you're so damn set on arresting somebody for blowing away that son of a bitch."

"Didn't you ever hear of justice, Ick?" asked Charles.

Ick Johnson rubbed his square jaw as he studied Charles. "Justice has already been done. Somebody got pushed too far and struck back in self-defense because they couldn't figure out what else to do. It's not like killing's going to become a habit with these people."

"What people?"

Ick smiled, this time without amusement. "I can figure out who the suspects are without a printed program, Sheriff, but knowing who you're chasing doesn't explain why you're riding them so hard. I know you don't like killing, or violence, or guns, and I know you've pushed hard in the past whenever somebody got murdered, but this is different. This is more than just doing your job. You're acting like you've got a personal stake in finding Hansford's killer, and everybody is beginning to wonder why."

"Do you remember selling a twenty-two pistol to Marta or Jess Turner, Brad Masters, or Bill Adams in the last six months?" Charles forced the words past numb lips.

"No."

"No, you didn't sell any?"

"No, I don't remember," said Ick Johnson. "I got a real poor memory."

CHAPTER 21

CHARLES PROPPED HIS FEET ON ONE OF HIS DINING room chairs and watched the underbellies of the clouds flame red as the rising sun touched them. His dining room faced south, but its bay window curved to provide a view of the horizon from southeast to southwest. Built a mile south of Carroll on the edge of the Canadian breaks, where the terrain gradually changed from flat to rugged as it descended toward the Canadian River, the house was larger and more sprawling than anyone in Crawford County realized, since only its western side was visible from the highway, and that only from a distance. It was also much more expensive, filled as it was with a mixture of custom-made furniture and valuable antiques. Charles supposed no one would mistake it for anything but the home of a very wealthy man—if anyone were ever invited in, but his guest list was as restricted as Ick Johnson's.

He didn't like living his private life in front of an open window either—but for different reasons.

"When you get married, you better forget about propping your feet on the furniture," observed Lindman, sitting on the other side of the table with his boots resting comfortably on another chair. "Wives don't like it."

"I guess I'll have to change a lot of habits."

"You might start by teaching that dog of yours not to sleep on the bed—at least not in your guest room. I woke up last night to go take a leak, and that animal was sleeping on the pillow right next to me. Damn near scared the crap out of me."

"He doesn't like to sleep alone."

"I don't much like it either, but I'd prefer my bedmate not to have long, floppy ears. Besides, the son of a bitch snores." Lindman cocked his head and studied Charles. "You know,

Matthews, the guest of honor at the last autopsy I went to looked more alive than you do. What time did you stop staring at that fireplace of yours and go to bed?"

"About two, I guess."

Lindman looked at his watch. "Little after seven. A man can live on less than five hours sleep—but he can't live very long. I hope you wind this case up before I have to go to your funeral instead of your wedding." He took another drink of coffee. "So what did you decide? I saw all those yellow legal pads spread all over your den. You must have made enough notes to write a book, but did you decide on the end to the story?"

Charles idly traced the rim of his coffee cup. "Yes, I did. I decided the case is just like this cup: it goes around and around. Everyone is protecting everyone else, and unless a crack suddenly appears in the rim, there won't be an ending." He picked up the cup, drained it, and threw it against the opposite wall. "Goddamn it, Lindman! I can't leave it like that!"

Lindman stared at the wet spot on the wallpaper. "I don't know about breaking cases, but I'd sure break the habit of throwing dishes. Wives don't like that either."

Charles rubbed his face to hide the flush of embarrassment he felt heating his skin. "I don't usually throw things."

Lindman dropped his feet to the floor and turned his chair to face Charles across the table. Cynicism, resignation, and patience coexisted in the bright blue eyes that were so incongruent with his olive skin. "Son, my experience teaches me that every man will lie for a good cause—the best cause being to save his own hide. You're assuming everybody's motive is altruistic. That's bullshit. All your suspects are lying, but one of them is lying to save himself. Instead of throwing cups at the wall, maybe you ought to turn everybody's story inside out. Take a look at things in reverse: black for white. You've got nothing to lose."

"And if I determine who is lying to save himself, then what?" asked Charles, already mentally toying with Lindman's suggestion.

Lindman poured himself another cup of coffee. "Maybe not a damn thing. Maybe you just have to have a little patience. Murder's like an unstable solution. Wait for something to explode."

When the phone rang, Charles sat motionless, knowing his own eyes reflected what he saw in Lindman's. No one called a sheriff at seven-thirty on a Sunday morning without a very good reason, and that reason was often violent. As he reached for the receiver, he saw the other man briefly close his eyes and cross himself.

"Sheriff Matthews."

"Sheriff, this is Johnny Reb—at Carroll's Rest. I called your office, but Mabel said you were still at home. She wanted to know what was wrong, but my grandfather always said to go directly to the top, and really, that woman is such a gossip, and this is a delicate situation for the motel. I'd appreciate it if you'd be as unobtrusive as possible—given the circumstances, of course." He stopped and Charles heard him take a deep breath.

"Johnny Reb, what are you talking about?"

There was a squawk, and then the hysterical sounds of a woman alternately sobbing and screaming in Spanish too rapidly for Charles to translate. He heard Johnny Reb calling deprecations down upon the heads of all members of the female sex, particularly those female employees who made emotional scenes at the front desk of such a respectable business establishment as Carroll's Rest. After a minute or two, when the sobbing turned into an occasional hiccup, Johnny Reb's breathless voice took up his story in mid-sentence.

"—just terrible, Sheriff. I can't imagine why things like this happen. I wish I'd never rented a room to Rich Hansford and brought this down on my head. It was greed, that's all. The honeymoon suite isn't rented all that often, and he never objected to the price I asked—which I have to be honest was a wee bit more than what I charged real honeymooners. But, my God, I never dreamed"—his voice quivered and broke with what Charles swore was a sob—"it would end like this, and it wouldn't have if I'd told him there was no room at the inn the very first time. Then she would never have stayed here, don't you see? Come at once, Sheriff. Oh, that poor woman."

Charles felt his chest freeze inside his skin. "What woman?"

"Mrs. Hansford, Sheriff. She's dead."

"Sheriff?"

Charles looked up at Meenie with the sense that it wasn't the first time the deputy had called his name. He saw Raul and Lindman and a nervous looking Slim hovering behind Meenie while Viola Jenkins, looking older and curiously shrunken, leaned against a wall in Ginny Hansford's motel room. He wet his lips, but found he couldn't force any words through his constricted throat. He didn't remember crying, certainly not as much as the man who knelt on the other side of Ginny's body, staring fixedly at the blood-encrusted blonde hair that only partially hid the woman's misshapened skull.

Charles didn't need to look. He'd seen it all before.

Blunt force trauma—a fancy way of saying that someone had bludgeoned Ginny Hansford to death. A single blow to the right of her skull just above the mastoid, where the bone was thin and translucent. The circle had closed. Carin had died of a similar blow. There was no weapon left behind then, and none now. Other than the means of death, the women shared one other thing in common: Rich Hansford. The only real difference between the two victims was the time and place of their death. And the suspects, of course.

"Sheriff, the Parker brothers are ready to take the body. Doc Akin's waiting for her."

"Raul," began Charles, and stopped, as images of Carin on a pathologist's gurney superimposed themselves over that of Ginny. He blinked and swallowed convulsively as grief and guilt threatened to choke him. Of those who played a part in the tragedy in Dallas, only Charles Timothy Matthews survived—if living with ghosts could be called survival.

"I'll go with the body, Sheriff," said Raul quickly.

Charles nodded, grateful that Ginny would have company on this trip at least. Her last ride, the one to the cemetery, she'd travel alone.

He climbed to his feet, waving back Lindman's outstretched hand. He had to stand up by his own efforts, if only to prove to himself that he could, that his own sense of failure hadn't crushed him. He was still sheriff of Crawford County, still responsible for the investigation. Guilt was an old friend; it would gladly wait for another time.

"Ick, Ginny was the woman at your house this morning, wasn't she?" he asked, as the Parker brothers lifted the body onto a stretcher.

Ick's eyes followed the two morticians as they carried Ginny Hansford's body out, leaving only a bloody smear on the carpet to mark her passing. He turned his head slowly back toward Charles. "Yes. We'd been lovers the past four months. I used to drive out to old man Hansford's place and wait for her to meet me. That guest cottage is only a quarter of a mile or so from the road. I couldn't go to her there even when Rich

Hansford wasn't there—which was most of the time—because of the goddamn dogs barking. Besides, that cottage wasn't empty; he was always there even when he wasn't. It was like the son of a bitch haunted her. So I'd bring her back to my house and take her home real early. She didn't want her father-in-law knowing, for reasons even you can understand. And besides, I think she liked the old man and didn't want to hurt him."

"And when you saw Hansford's body in the field, you made a suspect of yourself because you were afraid Ginny had shot him?" asked Charles.

Ick nodded. "Yeah. I didn't see how she knew where he was, couldn't figure out how she did it, but I couldn't take a chance. I didn't want you suspecting her; she had too much motive. I made sure you knew I hated Hansford and had a motive to kill him."

"So you weren't protecting Marta Turner?"

His head jerked up and he stared at Charles. "Marta! Marta's got Jess. He's no ball of fire, but he can at least take care of his own wife."

"And last night, when you tried to persuade me that you didn't have a motive after all, you were following Ginny's lead, weren't you? You talked to her yesterday, got your stories coordinated? She told me Culpepper was lying, that Hansford's foreclosing on your business wasn't a personal thing, and you had to back her up. You didn't change tactics to convince me to pay attention to your motive instead of your alibi. You did it to convince me not to take your motive too seriously. I had everything in reverse. The real danger was my investigating your motive and maybe discovering Ginny. Once I discovered her, then you'd move up to the number one spot on my suspect list. Ginny lied about Culpepper, but she lied about something else, too, didn't she? Hansford's foreclosure on you was very personal, wasn't it? He knew about you."

Ick gave Charles back his level stare. "Ginny went to his room last night to persuade him to lay off me, that we'd just disappear into small-town life and he could forget us. That's when he raped her. I didn't know what she was going to do—not until after she'd done it. I don't send a woman to do my begging. Hell, I don't beg, period. I'll be honest with you, Sheriff, I was going to stage a little hunting accident of my own, but somebody beat me to it. They screwed it up, too, or we wouldn't be having this conversation, and Ginny wouldn't be dead." His blunt features twisted, and tears rolled down his rough cheeks. Whatever else Ick Johnson was, he wasn't a man afraid to cry.

"Slim, take Ick back to the office. Meenie, call in another deputy to help with the crime scene. Lindman, come with me."

The former roughneck allowed Slim to help him to his feet, then suddenly shook off the deputy's grip and staggered over to Charles, his red-streaked eyes burning with grief and anger. He grabbed Charles's lapels, twisting them in his work-scarred hands. "You catch the son of a bitch who killed her, or I will, Sheriff."

Charles jerked his coat out of Ick's hands. "Get him out of here, Slim. And take the maid I can hear screaming in the hall with you. I'll talk to both of them later."

He watched as Slim escorted Ick out of the room, his throat burning with the words he hadn't said. If Ick had told the truth about his involvement with Ginny, maybe she wouldn't be dead. Or maybe she would be—because he hadn't a clue as to why she'd had to die.

"Sheriff, I'm heading back to your office, too," said Viola Jenkins. "The way people are dying in this county, there's no sense in my being out of pocket in some damn stubble field. Besides, I'm not much interested any longer in hunting pheasant, but I think you ought to be."

Charles nearly gagged at the thought of any more killing. "What are you talking about?"

"Somebody's sure hunkered down in the stubble like a pheasant. If he doesn't move, you're going to overlook him, and I think you ought to be ready for that. Not all the pheasant are bagged, Sheriff, and it's no reflection on the hunter."

"Not this time, Mrs. Jenkins. There's no limit on my hunting season. I'll walk down every row and kick every dried milo stalk if that's what I have to do."

"You're liable to kick a few quail that aren't part of your hunt—like you did to Marta Turner yesterday, when all the time you should have been looking at Mrs. Hansford."

Charles flinched from her accusation, but part of him accepted it stoically. "Then the quail had better sit up and identify themselves and quit lying."

"Maybe they figure you'd kick them anyway."

"Maybe I would, Mrs. Jenkins."

The J.P. looked away for a moment, as if deciding how to respond, and Charles felt a sense of loss. He liked Viola Jenkins, liked her forthrightness, her grit—for want of a better word. He'd miss her approval.

"I'm sorry about Mrs. Hansford, Sheriff. I didn't like what I knew of her, but I guess you knew her better—you and Ick. That's what's bad about a small town; there's no way to keep from knowing how bad we hurt each other." She straightened her shoulders and pulled on her orange stocking cap. "I'll leave you to it now. There's nothing more I can do here. This county can't relive yesterday, and I'm not so sure that Rich Hansford would if the Lord gave him the opportunity. As much as that man liked to hurt people, he must be laughing in hell at how many people his murder's already hurt. Watch your backside, Sheriff. I don't want you to be the next one."

"I'll be all right, Mrs. Jenkins. I don't trust anybody enough to turn my back on them."

"Johnny Reb, let me see your guest registrations," said Charles.

The motel manager pushed his glasses further up his pug nose, and Charles noted again how much he resembled an owl. A stubborn owl in this instance, as he clutched his old-fashioned register to his narrow chest. Every other establishment in the United States and several foreign countries might depend on computer-generated registration forms, but at Carroll's Rest, guests still signed a book in addition to a more prosaic credit slip. Johnny Reb had strong feelings of tradition. "Sheriff, I'm not certain of my legal position. I mean, I'm not certain if I should require a search warrant or not. Looking at the register might be construed as an invasion of my guests' privacy."

Charles leaned over the desk, rage sending the blood pounding through his head. "Johnny Reb, the only legal position that I can absolutely guarantee you'll have is that of suing me after I rip off—"

His threat whooshed out of his mouth along with his breath as he felt Lindman sink an elbow in his belly at the same time as Norwegian-accented English assaulted his ears, and those of anyone else in the vicinity of Texas. "Johnny Reb, what the sheriff means is that your whole motel is a crime scene and he doesn't need a search warrant. Actually, he can arrest you for obstructing justice, and that would be bad for business. Small town like this, folks might think you had a hand in what went on. Nobody would feel safe renting your rooms."

Johnny Reb dropped the register in Charles's hands as if it were a snake about to bite him. "Help yourself, Sheriff. If you have any questions, just ask. The staff of Carroll's Rest is proud to support its local police. Would you like to examine that back in my office? Maybe sit down and put your feet up? Can I bring you a cup of coffee and a danish? What about breakfast? Have you eaten yet? I'll be glad to serve you in my office. You can work and feed the inner man at the same time."

Charles looked over the desk at the hand-wringing manager. "Johnny Reb."

"Yes, Sheriff?"

"Shut up."

Charles watched Johnny Reb snap his mouth shut and perch on the edge of a high stool, exactly like an owl on a tree branch, then turned his attention to the register. He ran his finger down the names of guests registered since Friday night and finally looked up at Lindman in frustration. "Nobody. At least nobody I recognize, and I don't think I'm looking for a stranger. Johnny Reb, did anyone ask for Mrs. Hansford?"

"I hardly think whoever did that to Mrs. Hansford would announce himself, Sheriff," answered the manager; a smirk on his face as if he'd just scored off Charles. "But I might be wrong," he added quickly when he saw Charles's face.

Charles let his anger drain away. It was a stupid question, and even a twit like Johnny Reb recognized it. He rubbed his face as if to see if he were still skin over bone, or if his body had gone the way of his mind. "What about phone calls?"

"I did check on that, Sheriff," replied the manager. "Mrs. Hansford made one phone call about five-thirty yesterday afternoon—a local number—"

"To Ick Johnson," interrupted Charles. "To tell what story she'd told me."

"She received several phone calls beginning about ten o'clock—"

"After we talked to Ick Johnson," said Lindman.

"She, however, did not answer," continued Johnny Reb.

"I figure she was dead," remarked Lindman to Charles. "That body was already stiff from rigor mortis this morning.

"The calls stopped at midnight last night and did not resume until five this morning," finished the manager as he glanced curiously at the two men.

"Ick was at the store with Raul," said Charles. "Johnny Reb, did you see anybody go up to Mrs. Hansford's room?"

"Just you and your men, Sheriff."

"Did you see any locals at the motel between six last night and this morning?"

"Of course. The restaurant was full. Well, I'm exaggerating. Actually, most were hunters, but there were still a lot of locals. Your Miss Poole, for instance, and Mrs. Jenkins. I overheard them discussing higher mathematics—something about probability. Mayor Culpepper was here, he was very subdued. Didn't get up to shake a single hand. Jess was subdued, too.

Charles grabbed the manager's arm. "Jess who?"

"Jess Turner—and his wife, of course. Jess had his leg in a cast. He didn't look very well. I can't imagine why he wasn't home."

Charles released the manager's arm. "I can't either, Johnny Reb, but I'm concerned enough to find out."

CHAPTER 22

CHARLES WAS HALFWAY ACROSS THE PARKING LOT to his car before he heard Lindman finally catch up. "Damn stupid of the Turners when you think about it," panted the other sheriff. "What did they do? Whack the victim on the side of the head between the soup and salad?"

Charles slid into his car, flipped on the siren, and mashed the accelerator the second Lindman had his door closed. "I don't know, damn it, but I'm running out of possibilities. Bill Adams is last on my list because he had so obviously just finished dinner at his own home twenty miles away. Ick? I'll pass on Ick for the moment. Brad? I wonder what Brad's ever-loving secretary-fiancée would have said if I'd asked her about Saturday night instead of Saturday morning. But the Turners? They definitely had the opportunity, wouldn't you say? A rerun of Saturday morning. Marta does the dastardly deed and Jess covers for her."

"Why, Matthews?"

Charles turned to stare at the other man, then cursed as he felt the car swerve into the next lane. He refocused his eyes on the icy road. "If you're asking about motive, I don't have any idea. Maybe they thought she was as bad as Hansford. Maybe they thought she'd inherit his stock and continue screwing the farmers in this county. Or maybe—maybe they killed a potential witness."

"A witness to what, Matthews?"

"Ginny was the only one who told us that Marta was having an affair with Hansford. With her dead, all we have is her statement on tape."

"And it sure wasn't any secret what Mrs. Hansford was going to tell. She damn near put it on the loudspeaker in your squad room. Anybody that heard her could've told Marta Turner."

Charles slammed on the brakes, and the car skidded one hundred and eighty degrees before stopping in front of an old frame farm house, this one dating from the early Thirties. Rectangular, two story, peaked roof, and with a porch on three sides, the house looked solid, unpretentious, and shabby. It needed paint, shingles, window screens, and window panes to replace the cracked ones Charles saw. It also needed several new planks in the front porch.

The interior was equally shabby, but painfully clean. The Turners may have been short of ready cash, but there was no lack of soap and water and the will to use them. The woodwork was polished, the wood floors waxed, and the windows covered with crisply starched gingham curtains. The furniture was what Charles thought might be described as old but serviceable, if one meant that it couldn't be sold for a nickel on the dollar at a used furniture store, but had too much wear left to be simply thrown out.

Jess sat in an easy chair with his leg propped on a hassock, his fingers restlessly straightening a crocheted afghan across his lap. Charles noticed that the leather upholstery on both pieces of furniture was patched with tape meticulously painted to match. He sat down on a couch, careful to avoid looking at the worn spots on its cushions, and realized that he'd never hated Rich Hansford more than he did at this moment.

"Where's Marta, Jess?"

Pain had aged Jess Turner's face overnight, deepening grooves around his mouth and across his forehead and painting purple smudges beneath his eyes. "She's out with the hunters. I didn't want her to go, but she said we had a responsibility to the men who paid us."

His eyes unconsciously roamed over the worn furnishings. Charles knew Marta had another reason for going: the Turners couldn't afford to lose the hunting fees. "Jess, why were you at Carroll's Rest last night? A man with a newly broken leg should be home."

Pain hadn't lessened Jess's defiance. "I took my wife out, Sheriff. After what you put her through, I thought she needed something special, something better than coming back here and fixing supper for a cripple."

"Jess, you're not a cripple," objected Charles, feeling his conscience jab him.

"Might as well be. Who's going to check the stock, haul feed to them if it snows heavy? Who's going to check over the machinery, decide what can be fixed? I don't have a hired hand anymore. I had to let him go. Couldn't afford to pay him." He turned toward Charles, an ironic smile on his lips. "I'm not blaming you, Sheriff, so you don't need to sit there with that look like you just run over a puppy. The end's been a long time coming. This leg won't hurry it along any faster."

He plucked at the afghan, his face pensive in the lamplight. "I don't know why I'm worrying about it. Come Monday morning and the auction, the place won't be mine anyway, but habits are hard to break." He suddenly pounded his fist on the chair arm. "If that son of a bitch had just given me a little time, Sheriff. I've got good land here, and with the oil leases, I could've have kept my payments up, had a little left over. But he wasn't listening to anybody, and with the notice of foreclosure posted, or about to be, the oil company was talking to him, not me. I didn't have clear title anymore according to them. You know, it was like Rich Hansford wanted to hurt me—intentionally."

Charles nodded. "Hansford was capable of it."

The front door slammed open and Marta Turner burst in, a shotgun in her hands, and Charles didn't think it was open and empty, not judging by the hard reckless expression on the woman's face. "What are you doing here, Sheriff? I thought it was against the law to harass a witness."

Charles sat very still. He didn't think Marta Turner would shoot him, but he didn't want to startle her by moving either. After seeing Rich Hansford's body, he had a healthy respect for the kind of damage a loaded shotgun could do.

Lindman evidently didn't have the same kind of respect. Either that, or he didn't think he'd be Marta's first target. "Nobody's hassling your husband, Mrs. Turner. Now, you just lean that shotgun against the wall behind you, and let's talk a while. Shooting Matthews won't stop the questions; it'll just get you in more trouble."

"What questions? We already answered his questions, and we're not fixing to change our answers. We didn't kill Rich Hansford."

Lindman motioned Charles to be quiet, and leaned back against the couch and crossed his legs as if a furious woman with a shotgun weren't facing him. "You know, Mrs. Turner, I don't think you did either, but you're in a tight spot, and it got a hell of a lot tighter last night at dinner."

"Dinner? What's dinner got to do with anything? Is the sheriff accusing us of poisoning the soup at Carroll's Rest?"

"What time did you eat last night, Mrs. Turner?"

Marta's eyes narrowed as she considered the question. "Between six-thirty and seven-thirty."

"Did you leave the table during that time?"

"No."

"Can you prove it?"

"Why should I? Why are you asking me about Carroll's Rest?"

Charles felt the frustration building up and vaulted off the couch to face Marta, ignoring the shotgun aimed at his belly. A gunshot couldn't possibly make him hurt anymore than he already did. "Someone murdered Ginny Hansford, Rich Hansford's wife. Crushed her skull. She was smaller than you, lighter than you, not nearly so strong. She couldn't have put up much of a fight. Didn't, in fact, judging from the evidence. As if she didn't believe her murderer would hurt her, didn't expect to be attacked. I think she turned her back on her killer—as she might do if a woman stepped in that motel room!" He sank back on the couch and covered his face with his hands, taking deep breaths to ease the tightness in his chest.

Marta let the shotgun sag in her hands until it pointed at the floor. "She was nice to me once. And I don't think she was nice to very many people, because she had to step outside herself to do it. I think she was scared to death to do that."

"If you thought killing her would shut her up, you were wrong. I have her statement on tape. She testified that you were having an affair with Rich Hansford in exchange for his extending Jess's mortgage."

"No!" shouted Jess, struggling to get up.

Marta dropped the shotgun and rushed to push him back. "It's all right, Jess."

Charles watched the changing expressions on Marta's face, but he didn't see one of denial and felt as if all his illusions had finally died. "Marta?"

Marta patted Jess's shoulder, and turned away to pace the shabby room. "I don't know why Mrs. Hansford told you that except that I don't think Rich Hansford bothered to hide his intentions. He offered me that deal." Jess made another sound of denial but his wife ignored him. "I thought about accepting."

"Marta!" Jess's voice held more pain and disbelief than Charles thought a human could express.

She looked resolutely at Charles as if she couldn't bear to look at her husband's face. "I didn't, and not just because I wanted to vomit every time he came near me. If I had thought I could have saved Jess by giving in, I would have, but you don't stop a coyote by feeding him a chicken. He just wants another chicken."

"What the hell kind of man would I be if I let you sell yourself, Marta?" asked Jess.

"A dead one, Jess, on the inside, where it counts. My sleeping with Rich Hansford wouldn't have saved you; it would've killed you. That's the other reason I didn't do it."

"But you met him in that field, didn't you?" asked Charles. "Somewhere between four-thirty and five? An appointment you made by phone, an appointment you didn't tell Jess about?"

"No, she didn't!" shouted Jess. "Leave her alone!"

"Marta?" asked Charles.

Marta sat down on the arm of Jess's chair and wrapped her arms around herself. She stared across the room, her eyes unfocused for a moment, then looked up at Charles. "Killing Rich Hansford is one thing. I wouldn't help you find whoever did it. But killing his wife is different. Somebody went too far."

"You know who killed Hansford, Marta?"

Jess grabbed for his wife's hand. "Shut up, Marta!"

She didn't look away from Charles. "You're right, Sheriff. I did meet Hansford in that field a little after four-thirty. It was a stupid thing to do, but I felt like I had to try it. I asked him to give Jess an extension and he refused. He laughed at me. Then he said he was meeting somebody to 'talk over old times,' and would I like to entertain him while he waited. I spit in his face, and it felt good! Like something you dream about doing for years, and when you finally do it, it's as wonderful as you thought it would be. Sometimes dreams are better than real life, but not this time."

She smiled, and Charles felt stunned by a sense of awe. No one knew better than he how difficult it was to face past terrors and defy them. He decided that all the women, both witnesses and suspects, that he'd met while investigating this case demonstrated a hell of a lot more courage than any of the men involved—including himself. It was a sobering thought.

"What did you do then, Marta?" he asked.

"I got home about five-fifteen and told Jess what I'd done. He was furious. Stormed around the house for thirty minutes, yelling at me for being a fool, then left for the bank."

"You really didn't shoot him?" asked Jess in a dazed voice.

"Jess, I don't kill people!" retorted Marta in the same tone Charles had heard some women use when they say they don't do windows. "Sheriff, I don't know if what I said will help you or not, because he was alive when I left and I didn't see anyone else, but at least you know I didn't kill him. That eliminates two people for you to worry about."

"Sheriff?" Jess's voice was stronger, and Charles saw that the hopelessness was gone from his face. "Sheriff, I drove over to that field. I was so damn mad, I was fixing to beat the hell out of Rich Hansford. The way I figured it, I didn't have anything to lose, and he didn't have any business propositioning my wife." Jess stopped and swallowed several times. "He was sitting in that big Suburban of his as dead as last week's roast. There was a gun—a twenty-two—on the seat next to him. I own a twenty-two and I thought Marta shot him, so I faked that accident and hid the gun in the Waterman hydrant. I didn't know what else to do with it. I didn't want to take it to town with me, and I was afraid to just throw it away. I figured on going back later and getting it, maybe burying it in our dump behind the barn."

Marta started to laugh, then to cry, interspersing her words with jerky sobs. "My God, Jess! I thought you killed him! Otherwise, I would've told the truth. The sheriff can't prove murder if we didn't do it." She threw her arms around Jess and buried her face against his chest.

Jess rubbed her back, grinning and looking contrite at the same time. "I'm sorry, Sheriff. I guess if I'd left everything alone, maybe you'd already have your killer and I wouldn't have a broken leg."

"And maybe Ginny Hansford wouldn't be dead," said Charles. "Damn it to hell, Jess!"

"I guess you told them how the cow ate the cabbage, Matthews," said Lindman, relaxing in the front seat on the way back to town. "Yes, sir, even your Miss Poole couldn't have reamed out those idiots like you did. I should have been taking notes. Tell me something. Why didn't you layer on the guilt any better than you did? Why didn't you tell them that they were responsible for killing Mrs. Hansford? I noticed you tiptoed around that issue like it was a pile of steaming cow shit."

"If they're lying again, they wouldn't feel guilty, and if they're not lying, then. . ."

"Then what?"

"Nothing."

"You're a phony, Matthews. You know why?"

Charles glanced at Lindman and saw the other man tapping his fingers on the dashboard and grinning. "No, but I imagine you're going to tell me."

"What's that short story by O. Henry?" asked Lindman. "The one about the young couple who each sold the thing they loved the best to buy a Christmas present for the other?"

" 'The Gift of the Magi,' " replied Charles. "And it doesn't have a damn thing to do with why I didn't lay a guilt trip on Jess and Marta."

"Sure, it does. We got young love and personal sacrifice. Marta's ready to bed down with a snake who makes her want to puke to save her husband, and Jess makes a bloody mess of Hansford when the sight of blood makes him want to puke because he thinks he's saving his wife. Hell, it's even the Christmas season or near enough." Lindman scratched his nose and grinned again. "Of course, Marta decided it wouldn't do a damn bit of good to screw Hansford, and Jess messed up staging a fake hunting accident, so we can't carry these analogies too far. Still, a sentimental man might be a little touched by that scene in the armchair, two kids hugging and crying, their faith in each other restored. Might keep a sentimental sheriff from hauling their asses into jail on five or six counts of obstructing justice and at least one count of P.O.P.O. That's 'Pissing Off a Police Officer,' in case you ain't familiar with the term in Crawford County."

"I'm not sentimental."

"I suppose you had some practical reason for not following the letter of the law."

"The gun."

"What about it? Other than the fact that Jess's dropping it in an irrigation hydrant managed to ruin any fingerprint evidence, which in turn ruined any chance you might have had to land on your culprit before he beat Mrs. Hansford to death."

Charles shook his head. "I don't know that. Neither do you. When was the last time you sent someone to prison because you found a fingerprint on a gun?"

"Maybe five years ago, after a domestic shooting when the husband handed me the gun butt first after he shot his wife. Left a clear set of five prints on the barrel."

"Exactly. And other than a domestic shooting, when did you last find the gun left at a murder scene?"

"Once or twice maybe—when I was in the New Mexico State Police investigating a gang-type shooting. Since I've been sheriff—never. What's your point?"

"Why did the murderer leave the gun?"

"Hell, I don't know. Nervous, I guess. Blowing a hole in Hansford's face just might make somebody drop the gun and run like hell out of there."

"Maybe he wanted us to find it because it belonged to somebody else. Maybe he was setting up a scapegoat for us. When Jess tidied up the scene, the murderer was caught with his pants down and vulnerable to suspicion. Finally Slim finds the gun, but it's too late. The murderer doesn't want it traced now, so he steals the last six months' worth of Ick's records. Why? Because Ginny Hansford changed the equation somehow. Perhaps the scapegoat had a motive for killing Hansford, but not his wife, and the murderer decided it was safer not to risk presenting us with a false suspect. We might start asking questions. Even if Jess had not interfered with the evidence and we had arrested the scapegoat, Ginny would have remained a threat to the murderer. She had to die."

"So you had this sudden revelation after Jess told you he hid the gun? Sort of visitation from the Lord? And you decided our well-meaning couple should be let off with a verbal lashing?"

"What's wrong with my reasoning?" demanded Charles defensively.

"Not a damn thing. Your scenario sounds real logical. Of course, you've written logical scenarios about six times in the last twenty-four hours, and been wrong every damn time."

"And I suppose you would've arrested the Turners. Given them a reason to feel guilty the rest of their lives?"

Lindman pushed the heater up another notch. "No, I don't think so, but like I said, it's nearly Christmas. I get real sentimental this time of year."

Charles glanced through the window at a stubble field crowded with a line of hunters walking side by side down the rows of dead milo stalks. "It's not Christmas; it's pheasant season! And I get a little crazy this time of year."

Lindman reached over and punched his shoulder. "And sentimental, you stubborn son of a bitch!"

Charles grinned. "Maybe."

"Car thirty-two, come in."

The sound of Meenie's voice jolted Charles with an oppressive sense of fear. "This is the sheriff. What's wrong, Meenie?"

"Sheriff, get your butt back to the courthouse now. All hell's broken loose, and even Miss Poole can't keep these devils off your tail."

CHAPTER 23

THE SILENCE WAS OMINOUS, AND SO WERE THE faces. Even Meenie's normally placid features were screwed up in a tense expression, his tobacco a motionless bulge in one cheek. Worst of all, he wasn't wearing his hat. The last time Charles remembered Meenie not wearing his hat was at a funeral.

"What's happened?" asked Charles over the deafening silence. "Meenie? Miss Poole? Mrs. Jenkins? Slim?"

Mabel's face peered around the radio unit, her smeared glasses looking blank in the reflected light from the fluorescent bulbs overhead. She removed them, blinked like a suddenly awakened owl, and burst into tears.

"Mabel!" Charles took a step in her direction, halting when her tears changed to high-pitched yowling sobs, and she rushed past him toward the ladies' room, clutching her glasses in one hand and feeling the air in front of her with the other. He turned to watch her careen drunkenly through the reception area and around the corner. He felt his mouth gaping open and tried to regain control over his own features.

"Somebody tell me what's going on!" he demanded, turning back to the squad room and the silent figures standing there. "What's Mabel doing here on Sunday morning? What's she crying about?"

"She stayed overtime to man the radio, Sheriff," replied Miss Poole, her usual crisp, pressed, and spartan appearance showing fissures of stress. Several strands of hair had escaped from her bun and were straggling down the back of her neck, an occurrence so out of the ordinary that Charles couldn't think of an analogy. What was even more disturbing was the fact that Miss Poole didn't seem to notice.

"It's been an unsettling morning, Sheriff," continued Miss Poole. "Mabel, as you can see, is experiencing a temporary loss of emotional control. Slim suffered a similar loss earlier. Even I have had difficulty coping."

Charles barely avoided a loss of control himself. The idea of Miss Poole being unable to cope with anything less catastrophic than Armageddon was terrifying. "What in particular unsettled you, Miss Poole?"

"Hearing about Mrs. Hansford from Mrs. Jenkins was a shock, of course, since I couldn't imagine any practical reason why the murderer should have killed her after her interview with you instead of before. Then Slim returned from Carroll's Rest with Ick Johnson and Mrs. Ruiz." She stepped aside, and Charles's eyes zeroed in on a Hispanic woman in a crumpled uniform huddled in a chair by the dispatcher's desk.

"Mrs. Ruiz's comments in the patrol car upset Ick Johnson, who in turn made charges against you that upset Slim. If Ick hadn't grabbed Slim's arm first—which technically makes him guilty of assaulting a peace officer—I'm afraid Slim might have retaliated on your behalf—which would have made him guilty of assaulting a witness. As it was, Ick dislocated Slim's wrist, and the altercation ended in a draw. I sent Ick into your office and tried to send Slim to the hospital, but he refused. I was forced to call Dr. Wallace."

"I wasn't going to leave, Sheriff," muttered Slim, cradling his splinted wrist in his other hand.

"What comments? What charges? Damn it, Slim, it's unprofessional to respond to disparaging remarks made by witnesses," he said, turning to the white-faced young deputy.

"Perhaps you'd better listen to Mrs. Ruiz's statement before you chastise Slim," suggested Miss Poole.

Impatiently Charles turned to the maid. "Mrs. Ruiz, you found Mrs. Hansford this morning?"

"Sí," the Hispanic maid said, followed by an outburst in Spanish too fast for Charles to comprehend.

Lindman answered her, which prompted another longer speech. The New Mexican sheriff finally held up his hand to stop the flow of Spanish, and turned to Charles. "She says she was sweeping the upper hall and saw Ick Johnson knocking on Mrs. Hansford's door. She said Ick was looking worried, so she let him in."

"I bet Johnny Reb loved that—a maid unlocking a guest's door just because someone wanted in."

Lindman wiped his face. "From what I could understand—my Spanish is a little rusty—she'd been in that hall since yesterday afternoon. Seems that your Johnny Reb was a little worried since he found out about the fight in Hansford's room, and he stationed his employees around the motel—paid them double time. According to Mrs. Ruiz, Mrs. Hansford hadn't left that room since yesterday afternoon, and when Ick Johnson showed up and nobody answered the door, Mrs. Ruiz had a feeling that something was wrong."

"Mrs. Ruiz is very intuitive."

"Yeah, well, she ain't infallible though," said Lindman, looking disturbed. "She said nobody entered that room after you left it. Not a solitary soul."

Charles didn't need to look in a mirror to know that his face was colorless. He felt as if all the blood in his body had drained away, leaving him lightheaded and dizzy. "She's wrong. Someone had to have gone in that room. Someone murdered Ginny!"

"Well, that's part of the problem," said Meenie, speaking for the fist time. "Ick's saying you killed her."

Charles swayed before he sucked in a breath of oppressive air, but the lightheaded feeling remained. Voices seemed too loud and the light hurt his eyes. "That's ludicrous." He looked wildly around the room, then staggered to the phone. "I'll call Dr. Akin—get the preliminary autopsy report. See if he can pin down the time."

"I already done it," said Meenie. "I even ran back to Carroll's Rest to find out the exact room temperature so he'd know that. He checked everything six ways to Sunday with his calculator, his computer, even called a couple of other pathologists. Best he can say the time of death is six-thirty to seven-thirty. We was all in her room at six-thirty so we know she was alive then."

"But you left," said Charles.

"And you got back to the car at seven o'clock." Meenie leaned over the spittoon again. "We know that 'cause you asked what time it was."

Charles's sense of disorientation increased as he realized how Meenie's comment would sound in a court record. It would sound as if he was setting up an alibi—depending on the fact that Dr. Akin, or any other pathologist, couldn't determine time of death to the precise minute. "I didn't murder her! You can't believe that!"

"It don't matter a hoot in hell what they believe, Sheriff," said Fred Hansford, steering his motorized wheelchair through the door followed by Manuel, his companion.

"Mr. Hansford! What are you doing here?"

"I been waiting for you, sitting in that empty courtroom next door since I made everybody so damn uncomfortable in here. I heard that dispatcher of yours squalling and figured you'd shown up."

"I guess you already know about Ginny?"

The old man nodded, his eyes shadowed as if he were remembering a lonely young woman visiting him when his own son wouldn't. "I stopped by Carroll's Rest on my way here and that damn shit at the desk told me. Tried to dun me for hers and Rich's motel bills while he was at it. I told him the next time he wanted a bank loan, I didn't give a damn for what, I'd see to it that he had to put up his left nut for collateral. He was real accommodating after that."

"I'm sorry you had to find out that way, Mr. Hansford. I meant to tell you, but I felt I had to interview a suspect as quickly as possible."

"Couldn't pin it on your suspect though, could you?"

Charles shook his head. "No, but I'm continuing the investigation. I'm sorry you drove to town, Mr. Hansford. I don't have any information I can give you at this time, and there's nothing you can do."

"I can see where you'd like to think that, but you underestimated me. I may be a crippled-up old man in a wheelchair, but I'm not helpless—not as long as I've got my wits. I was going to be real fair—talk to Ginny before I came to you. I knew what a real bastard Rich could be, and my evidence was real one-sided, but I never got a chance to let Ginny round out the story. You saw to that."

"I never murdered Ginny," began Charles.

Hansford held up a hand crooked with arthritis. "I don't expect you to confess—smart man like you knows better—but I'm not here to listen to your lies either."

"I'm not lying!" exclaimed Charles.

"You can't jump a man until you've heard what he has to say," interrupted Meenie. "The sheriff at least has a reputation for having a nodding acquaintance with the truth, and you know your son was only honest when he needed to be—and he didn't feel the need real often."

"I know what my son was, Meenie, and he was vindictive

as hell. Nobody stepped on his toes without him striking back. I guess you figured I'd never find out about Dallas, didn't you?" Hansford twisted his head to look at Charles.

"I hoped you wouldn't," answered Charles. "I didn't think you needed to hear anything else detrimental about Rich."

"That's real kind of you," said Hansford, leaning forward, his crippled hands curling around the arms of his wheelchair. "Protecting an old man from dirt about his dead boy." He suddenly spat at Charles's feet. "The fact of the matter is, you were protecting your own backside."

Charles's stomach cramped, and he pressed his hand over it. "I don't know what you mean."

"I went to Amarillo yesterday, to the *Lone Star National*, to start looking over Rich's papers, see what I could salvage out of the mess my son was fixing to make of Crawford County, and I found a scrapbook full of newspaper clippings about your wife's murder."

Hansford folded back the afghan that covered his legs, picked up an ordinary brown scrapbook off his lap, and opened it. "Has a lot of other stuff in here, too. Gossip columns about how you divorced her for sleeping with my son, then damn near accusing him of killing her. There are some copies of police statements, too. Rich was good at getting hold of stuff he didn't have any business having. Anyway, in one of the statements, Rich told the Dallas detectives that he'd been messing around with your wife, but he didn't murder her. That's not such a dangerous piece of paper, but there's one that is. There's an affidavit from him that says you threatened to kill him—and he named two witnesses that he claimed heard you do it."

"The sheriff would never threaten a witness!" stated Miss Poole in outrage. "He just finished lecturing a deputy about that very subject."

"I don't hear him denying it, do you?" asked Hansford, looking at Charles with the expression of a man who never doubted his beliefs.

"Sheriff?" asked Miss Poole.

Charles braced his arm against the wall and tried to organize his thoughts. "I did it—threatened him. I went to his office one day after Carin's murder—to interview him again. He commented that whoever killed a drug addict drunk like her did society a favor. I lost my temper and told him I'd kill him if he ever said anything like that again."

"There ain't nothing in the affidavit about his saying anything," said Meenie.

"He said it, damn it!" shouted Charles, whirling around to face his deputy.

"I ain't doubting you, Sheriff," said Meenie, holding up his hands and backing away. "Sounds just like something Rich Hansford would say."

Fred Hansford stroked the cover of the scrapbook. "I figure Rich was vindictive enough to try to ruin you because you accused him of murder. But you got him first, didn't you? You killed my boy—and you figured as long as you kept quiet about Dallas, nobody would suspect you. Of course, that meant you had to kill Ginny, too. Well, you figured wrong all the way around. I know all about Dallas, I know why you killed my boy and Ginny, and I'm going to get you for it. Rich wasn't much good, but he was a damn sight better than you. At least he didn't strut around pretending to be a fine man. Everybody knew Rich would skin a customer if he could. He didn't make any secret of it."

"Mr. Hansford, I didn't kill your son, and I didn't kill Ginny." Charles heard the note of desperation in his voice and despised himself for it. He was innocent and still he felt sullied by the old man's accusations—sullied and shamed.

"What about your own wife, Matthews? You going to tell me you didn't kill her?" demanded Hansford.

Charles felt too numb to answer.

"I'll see you at the grand jury, Sheriff Matthews," said Fred Hansford as he turned his wheelchair around and rolled back through the door, Manuel silently following him.

Meenie shifted his tobacco to his other cheek and spat. "I looked at that scrapbook. It looks incriminating, Sheriff. There was a Sunday supplement kind of article in there—about you punching your boss. The writer was real nasty. Said Dallas was lucky to be rid of such a violent individual before he administered his own form of frontier justice—or some such words. I can't remember exactly, but that's close enough. Anyway, Rich was watching you closer than a badger watching a rabbit burrow. He's got everything that the paper's ever printed about you being sheriff. There was a bunch of notes with names of newspaper writers around the Panhandle. It looks like he was fixing to release his scrapbook to the papers come next election. It would've pretty well settled your hash as far as being reelected goes."

"I didn't kill Rich Hansford! I didn't know anything about his scrapbook!"

"I ain't the one you got to convince, Sheriff. It's the district attorney. Fred Hansford is asking the D.A. to call a grand jury to investigate you and indict you for murder."

"That scrapbook isn't enough cause for the grand jury to indict me!" exclaimed Charles.

"Maybe not," replied Meenie. "But Ick Johnson's backing up Hansford, and the evidence he's got might be enough to do it."

"That's my fault, Sheriff," said Miss Poole with a break in her voice that in the ordinary woman would be a prelude to tears. Miss Poole was not ordinary. Her hair might be escaping its bun, but Charles knew there were limits to what undisciplined acts the ex-schoolteacher would allow her body. She blinked several times and cleared her throat before continuing. "After Ick's violence, I should have searched him. I believe it would have been a legally defensible act. Barring a search, I should have stayed in your office with him. Of course, that would only have delayed the inevitable. Eventually, he would have examined his evidence, spoken about it with Mr. Hansford, but perhaps later he wouldn't have already been so angry. Although I'm inclined to believe it wouldn't make any difference. The evidence is damning."

"What evidence? Tell me, damn it!"

Meenie looked down at the floor, as if searching for an answer other than the one he had. When he raised his head again, Charles nearly gasped. The grizzled old deputy had tears in his eyes. "Ick Johnson found your goddamn cassette player in Mrs. Hansford's motel room."

Charles shoved an open file out of his way and propped his stockinged feet on the coffee table. Files were stacked on the couch, on the floor, on a nearby chair, both end tables, and spilled out of an open cardboard box lying on its side beneath the coffee table. Police files on Carin's murder. Rich Hansford wasn't the only one who knew how to get documents he had no business having. Somewhere in all that paper was a lead to Carin's murderer. But he couldn't find it.

Opposite the couch, in front of the fireplace and sprawled on his back with legs splayed in what Charles privately called his centerfold pose, lay a five-year-old registered beagle. An occasional snore erupted from the dog's half-open mouth, followed by a lip-smacking sound, as if its nocturnal emissions came in six delicious flavors.

"Hieronymous Bosch," said Charles, "you're a lazy, insensitive bum."

The beagle's head lolled toward Charles. One black-rimmed eye opened to peer at his master as if to say that anyone who named a self-respecting dog after a fifteenth-century Flemish painter of symbolic religious nightmares had very little business calling anyone insensitive.

"I'm in trouble, Hieronymous, and you're not offering me aid and comfort. Aren't dogs supposed to pick up on their masters' moods? Can't you tell mine's blacker than the inside of a snake's belly?"

The dog rolled over, stuck his hindquarters in the air, and stretched his front half flat on the floor. He then yawned, shook his head, rose on all fours, and padded over to Charles. He jumped on the coffee table, which bore several scratches and gouges from similar leaps, and sat on his haunches, long ears cocked as if prepared to listen to any confidences Charles might care to impart.

Charles felt his eyes burn and blur; he angrily wiped them. After stoically surviving the day without breaking down, a sympathetic look from a dog threatened to make him lose his composure. He swung his feet off the table and leaned over to stroke the beagle's soft fur. "Damn it, Hieronymous, I liked this country. I liked these people. I liked the way they welcomed me and didn't ask questions—or not many—about who I was or where I came from. They respected my privacy. Code of the West, Crawford County style." He laughed. "I doubt they'll make that mistake again. The next stranger who rides into town is liable to be met at the city limits with an invitation to move on. And speaking of moving on, where shall we go from here? That's assuming I have any choice in the matter. I'm a lawyer, you know, or used to be, and my legal training tells me that while the grand jury may indict me for Rich Hansford's murder, the odds are about sixty-forty that the trial jury will find me not guilty. Simply not enough evidence to convict."

He fondled the dog's floppy ears and continued. "However, my friend, an indictment for the murder of Ginny Hansford is an entirely different matter. I've bought the farm on that one.

Between Dr. Akin's testimony and the maid's, I don't think the best defense attorney in the world can raise enough reasonable doubt in the jury's mind to win an acquittal. And then there's Carin's murder. If the D.A. in Dallas wants to try for an indictment on that one, I certainly outlined his case for him on that tape. Carin wouldn't have left her apartment with anyone she didn't know, and that narrows the suspects down to me and Rich Hansford, and Hansford is dead. And I don't have an alibi—not since Ginny admitted on tape that she lied to give me one. Chances of conviction? Maybe fifty-fifty. But it doesn't matter one way or the other on any of the three. I can't stay in Crawford County."

The beagle cocked his head, then suddenly leaped off the table and ran whimpering toward the door. Pain knifed through Charles's belly until he doubled over. Hieronymous only acted like a neurotic baby begging to be loved with one person, and Charles wasn't prepared to face her—not yet—not until he'd had time to numb his sense of loss.

He drew a deep breath and straightened up, then rose from the couch, consciously tightening his features into an expressionless mask as Angie Lassiter walked in the room, carrying an ecstatic beagle whose paws were planted on her shoulders and whose long red tongue was enthusiastically engaged in licking her left ear. If Hieronymous Bosch loved Charles, he worshiped Angie.

"Hello, Angie," said Charles, sticking his hands in his back pockets so she wouldn't notice their shaking. "I was going to call you later."

Angie put the dog on the floor, where he immediately rolled over and implored her to rub his belly. "Not now, baby. I'll pet you in a minute." She stripped off her coat and dropped it on the couch. "How much later, Charles? After I read about your resignation in the paper?"

Charles evaded her eyes. "Later this afternoon."

"Now you won't have to; I'm here. Tell me something, Charles. I'm curious. Were you planning to break our engagement over the phone, or were you working up your courage to do it in person?"

His eyes snapped back to stare at her. "Are you doubting me, too?"

"I don't need to. You're doing such a good job of it all by yourself." She scooted files out of the way and sat on the couch, patting a spot beside her. "Sit down, Charles, and tell me why you're throwing away your life—and me."

He raked his fingers through his hair and dropped onto the couch. "Angie, I'm not throwing you away; I'm freeing you from a liability. I'll undoubtedly be indicted for murder. I covered up L. D.'s murder to protect you and your daughters from being publicly scorned as the wife of a killer. Do you think I'd let you expose yourself and them to the same scorn by going through with this marriage? No way, Angie. You're not marrying a triple murderer."

"In the first place, L. D. wasn't murdered. He was executed by the brother of the girl he strangled and buried—buried in a barbecue pit, for God's sake!"

"It's a matter of semantics, Angie! The fact is, I didn't arrest the killer."

"In the second place," Angie continued as if he had not interrupted. "L. D. was a murderer. He killed two people and tried to kill two more. If you had succeeded in arresting him, he would have seriously injured three more people: me and the girls. Because you're right; the finger pointing and name-calling would have been horrible—even in Crawford County. You let his executioner go and told everyone L. D.'s plane crashed by accident instead of being shot down. But L. D.'s case has nothing to do with this. He was guilty. You're not."

"Damn it, Angie, the effect will be the same. I can't prove I'm innocent."

Her hazel eyes glittered more green than brown as she pounded her fist on his chest. "Not by sitting out here, talking to Hieronymous, self-absorbed in your own noble gestures. If you want to tilt windmills, build one out in the front yard, but I'm not letting you go!"

The beagle cocked his ears at the sound of his name, and padded over to lean against his goddess's knees and put his head in her lap, gazing up at her with the soulful look his particular breed had been perfecting from the moment they discovered eons ago that it got them almost anything they wanted. Angie burst into tears. Hieronymous immediately turned to the cause of her tears and growled.

"Damn it, now even my own dog is mad at me!" exclaimed Charles, feeling ten kinds of a fool and wondering how he seemed to be losing a logical argument with a practical woman. He gathered Angie into his arms and began to kiss away her tears, then decided that her mouth wouldn't tremble so badly if he kissed it, too—which led to a natural progression of events that he blamed on overwrought nerves and his own desperation to reassure her that he still loved her in spite of his decision.

The second time had nothing to do with nerves or reassurance, unless Charles counted the sensitive nerves they kept discovering they each possessed—and the reassurances they gave one another that a particular act or touch was welcomed and indeed, mutually satisfying. The second time had nothing to do with desperation and everything to do with love.

Lying sweaty and replete on the couch, and holding an equally sweaty and replete Angie against his side, Charles failed to dredge up a single guilty feeling for breaking his self-imposed celibacy before the wedding night. He carried only one regret: that nothing had really changed; there wouldn't be a wedding night.

"Charles, I'm sorry I cried. I wasn't trying to manipulate you."

He stroked her arm. "I'm not sorry. And you can't manipulate me."

She pushed herself up on one elbow and leaned over him, her hazel eyes more brown than green as she studied his face. "At least you don't still look like you've lost your last friend." She untangled her legs from his and rose from the couch to gather up assorted pieces of clothing. She glanced back at him as she began to dress. "You were adamant this morning about keeping personal and professional lives separate, so you might want to put your pants on before we talk about your career. I don't mind at all if your personal half is showing, but I suppose I do need to keep my mind on business and not on what a sexy nude you are."

Charles felt himself turn red nearly down to his personal half, and grabbed for his pants. "Angie!"

"Besides, Miss Poole might be shocked—or maybe she wouldn't. I'm never too sure about Miss Poole."

"Angie! How in the hell did Miss Poole and my career get into this conversation. We're talking about breaking our engagement for God's sake, not about what Miss Poole might think of me buck naked." He was dancing around with one leg in his Levi's.

Angie pulled her sweater over her head and plucked a hair brush from her purse. Sitting down on the couch, she began to brush her tousled auburn hair, watching him with such a determined expression that Charles froze in the act of snapping his Levi's.

"You were talking about breaking our engagement, Charles. I was pointing out that there was no similarity between L. D. and you, and that your romantic gesture of giving me up to protect me from scandal is unnecessary. As far as I'm concerned there's nothing further to talk about."

"I suppose you think following me to prison isn't a foolish gesture?"

"If I decide to follow you to hell, it's my choice, not yours. You've always kept me on a pedestal. Angie Lassiter: wife and mother—a sort of two-dimensional figurine you could admire and protect and pet, but keep at a safe distance, too far away to see your flaws. You're not a saint, Charles. You're a flawed hero, and that's who I love." She dropped her brush in her purse and snapped it closed. "And by the way, I'm not climbing back on that pedestal. You'll have to take me the way I am, not the way you think I am."

He considered the woman on the couch, her head thrown back and a challenge in her eyes, and wondered if he'd live long enough to discover all the different dimensions of Angie Lassiter.

"Do I have a choice?" he asked.

"You can freeze me out, I suppose."

He pulled on his shirt and buttoned it. "Hieronymous would never forgive me. He'd pack up his dog bowl and run away from home."

She closed her eyes and sagged back against the couch. "Oh, God, Charles, I was so afraid."

He squatted down in front of the couch and grasped her hands. "Are you going to cry again?"

She opened her eyes and laughed. "If I do, you'd better just loan me a hanky this time. Your war council's on its way."

"What war council? What have you done, Angie?"

He was glad she had the decency to look guilty. Unfortunately, he didn't see any remorse in her expression. He had the feeling this was not the last time he'd see one and not the other.

"Miss Poole, Lindman, Raul, and Meenie. Did you honestly

think your friends were going to allow you to take off your badge and fight these charges alone? Fat chance, Sheriff Matthews!"

CHAPTER 24

CHARLES BRACED HIS HANDS AGAINST THE MANTEL over the fireplace and rotated his head from side to side in a futile attempt to relax his tense muscles. He could feel the eyes of the others in the room watching him. His war council. One sixty-year-old retired schoolteacher; one tobacco-chewing former cowboy barely tall enough and heavy enough to be hired as a deputy; one second-generation Hispanic in a case where the only Spanish-speaking witness told the same story in Spanish or English; one New Mexican sheriff out of his jurisdiction; one fiancée with no legal authority at all; and one forty-pound beagle. The beagle was the only one to serve any useful function; he padded from person to person to be petted, thus serving as a fur-bearing stress reliever.

Charles shook his head one final time and turned around, feeling his neck immediately stiffen again as he saw everyone staring at him.

"I appreciate all of you coming out here to show support or friendship or whatever." He abruptly stopped, realizing he didn't know what else to say.

"What do you want us to do, Sheriff?" asked Raul.

"I'm not the sheriff anymore," snapped Charles. "I resigned. Or had you forgotten?"

"Pretty hard to forget, Matthews," said Lindman, sitting on the couch and leaning over to rub Hieronymous's belly. "I never heard such a pile of crap since my wife's cousin's brother-in-law got caught romancing the widow Lopez and claimed he'd just stopped by her house to comfort the grieving. It was a convincing explanation—except that *Mr.* Lopez had been dead for going on six years. Your speech was convincing, too—except you were acting out another false scenario, like you been doing the last two days."

"It was a beautiful speech, Sheriff," said Miss Poole. "You expressed such admirable sentiments."

"I wanted to cry for you," said Raul.

"It was another damn noble gesture," cried Angie.

Meenie spat in an empty coffee can that Angie had provided. "It made me mad as hell. All that talk about—what was it, Miss Poole—dishonoring your office, and knowing we wouldn't be human if we didn't doubt you. We ain't doing no such of a thing, and I'd like to hit you between the eyes with a fence post like Lindman told Miss Angie she might have to do when you got contrary. Besides, the fact is you're still the sheriff—and will be until the county judge and at least two of the commissioners convene a meeting and accept your resignation. That ain't likely to happen for a while."

"Why not?" demanded Charles. "I told you to call the county judge."

Meenie scratched his beard and looked at Raul. "He's out hunting. So're the county commissioners. And the D.A."

"Tell Mabel to radio the deputies to find them," said Charles.

Raul looked at Miss Poole. "We can't, sheriff. The radio's down, and Mabel says it will take a while to fix."

"How long?"

Miss Poole looked at Lindman. "Perhaps a week."

"A week!" exclaimed Charles. "I don't intend to leave the county in limbo for a week. Send someone out to find them."

Lindman looked at the ceiling. "We did. Or rather someone volunteered."

Charles berated himself for feeling a sense of betrayal. What did he expect? Knowing your sheriff was accused of triple murder was enough to shake any deputy's faith. Isn't that what he'd known would happen? Everyone would begin to doubt.

"Who volunteered?"

Meenie shifted his tobacco. "Slim did. Said he'd take care of it."

"Slim! You trusted Slim?"

"Seemed like the best man for the job," replied Meenie.

"Only if you didn't want them found, or—" Charles stopped abruptly and studied the blank faces that stared back at him. He sat down suddenly on the hearth, rubbed his hands over his face, and looked at his war council again. He ought to be furious; instead he felt like—an insider.

"That's it, isn't it?" he asked finally. "Slim won't find the county judge or any of the commissioners, will he? On purpose?"

Meenie looked worried for the first time. "To tell you the truth, Sheriff, we kind of hope he don't. See, we ain't too sure what he planned to do with them if he did find them. He just said not to worry. He'd make sure nobody got back to town for a while."

Charles turned to Miss Poole. "There's nothing wrong with the radio, is there?"

Miss Poole looked uncomfortable. "I'm not certain, Sheriff. Mabel did something to it when Mr. Hansford and Ick Johnson demanded that we track down the district attorney. However, Mabel is quite knowledgeable about our system. I assume she can fix it when the time comes."

"And when might that be, Miss Poole?"

"Whenever you arrest someone for Rich and Ginny Hansford's murders."

"Mabel is deliberately helping me?" asked Charles in amazement. "Mabel, who has spent nearly all of my term being what I might charitably describe as a thorn in my side, is helping me? What brought about this transformation?"

Miss Poole looked even more uncomfortable. "I believe the fact that Fred Hansford is not a Crawford County resident weighs heavily in your favor, Sheriff. Mabel has a strong sense of loyalty."

"Yes—to the former sheriff."

Raul shifted his feet and stroked his silky black beard. "Miss Poole did tell Mabel that if you hadn't murdered her, you weren't likely to murder anybody."

"I believe she's very fond of you, Sheriff," said Miss Poole. "But she lacks social skills, so she tries to win your attention by irritating you—like a schoolgirl with a crush."

"A crush?"

Miss Poole nodded. "As a teacher, I observed many instances of similar behavior in adolescent girls. In many ways, Mabel's emotional development is arrested."

"Oh, God," said Charles. "I think I'd rather have Ick Johnson after me than Mabel."

"Ick Johnson's a hell of a lot more dangerous," observed Lindman, giving Hieronymous a final scratch and straightening up to give Charles a level stare. "So what are we going to do about him?"

Charles returned his look. "I appreciate all that you, all of you, have done. It—it humbles me."

"Crawford County takes care of its own, Charles," said Angie, making room in her chair for Hieronymous, who settled his front half in her lap.

"But the situation hasn't changed," continued Charles. "I'm still my own best suspect for three murders. I killed my wife and blamed Hansford for it. When that didn't work out, I left Dallas, and when Hansford came back to the Panhandle, I waited for my opportunity and killed him, apparently for sleeping with my wife. Then I killed Ginny because she was the only person who knew I didn't have an alibi for Carin's murder. I have the best motives of anybody, and so far as I can determine, I'm the only one who had a motive for murdering Ginny. I don't know how all of you can be so sure I didn't do it. In your position, I don't know that I'd be so certain."

Meenie exchanged glances with Raul, then pulled a piece of paper out of his pocket. He got off the couch, hitched up his trousers, and walked over to Charles. "Ick played the tape for us when Fred Hansford came to the office this morning, ranting and raving about you killing Rich, and we told Lindman about it after you resigned. Ick wanted us to know what kind of a man we worked for. But we don't worry much about them motives. Raul and me figured that you aren't the kind of man to kill for revenge, and you sure aren't the kind of man to kill Mrs. Hansford just to cover your own behind, so we eliminated your wife's and Mrs. Hansford's murders. What worried us was Hansford's murder. You ain't got an alibi. And you damn sure had a motive—a lot better one than Ick Johnson or Fred Hansford knows about. Rich Hansford was fixing to get you indicted as a party to L. D. Lassiter's murder."

"Oh, my God," cried Angie, her face draining of color until even her lips looked bloodless.

"What!" exclaimed Charles hoarsely, shock freezing him until he felt himself start to shiver.

Lindman got up. "I think I'll go in the kitchen, Matthews. I don't think whatever's coming next is any of my business."

Charles motioned the other sheriff to sit down. "No, Lindman. You've got a right to know what kind of a man—what kind of a sheriff—you're trying to help. You may decide to withdraw from the coalition. You may decide to go to the grand jury yourself. But whatever you do, please don't hurt Angie."

Lindman sat down again. "I don't believe in justice hurting the innocent, Matthews. Goddamn criminals do enough of that."

Meenie handed Charles the creased document he'd taken from his pocket. "Hansford got hold of the insurance company's report on their investigation into L. D.'s plane crash. They didn't pay Miss Angie's claim because they couldn't find a chunk of the fuel tank. 'Course we didn't want them to find it, because it had a bullet hole in it. Anyway, the insurance company ruled the accident as probable sabotage, and Miss Angie dropped her claim. Raul and me figured it was just a matter of time before Rich Hansford put all the pieces together. Once he knew that plane crash wasn't no accident, it wouldn't take a fool long to backtrack to all them murders we had that summer and decide L. D. committed them and that you knew it. Put that together with Mrs. Hansford's talking about how Rich seemed so tickled about your engagement announcement to Miss Angie—and the picture gets real clear. Rich Hansford found his last piece to the puzzle. He figured you covered up L. D.'s murder so you could marry the widow. That's how *he'd* do things. I don't think it ever occurred to him that maybe you did it to protect Miss Angie from all the ugly talk. And see, that was the problem Raul and me had when we found that report mixed in with Rich Hansford's papers in his motel room. We knew you'd never kill him to protect yourself, but you sure as hell wouldn't think twice about doing it to protect Miss Angie."

Charles licked his lips, noticing how cold and numb they were. "That's what you meant, Raul, when you mentioned a test of faith when you were searching Hansford's motel room. Believing I was innocent was a test of faith for you and Meenie."

Raul nodded. "It wasn't a difficult test to pass, Sheriff."

Charles looked away. His throat ached with suppressed sobs. Maybe he was an unconverted macho son of a bitch, a cold, self-controlled Anglo-Saxon, but he'd be damned if he'd cry. There was a limit to how much of himself a man could expose to other men without losing his dignity. Besides, there was a time to cry and a time to fight, and this was a time to fight.

"I suppose you brought my badge with you, Meenie?" he asked.

Meenie grinned, exposing the gaps where several molars should be and weren't. He reached in his pocket and handed Charles his badge. "We figured maybe you'd change your mind once you had a chance to get real mad. You wouldn't let Rich Hansford beat you if he was still alive. I don't think you're gonna let him beat you when he's dead. Besides, you just plain don't like murderers. Makes your belly hurt worse."

Charles touched his badge, tracing the star on its surface, then dropped the leather flap inside his shirt pocket, leaving the metal emblem on the outside. He looked over at Angie and smiled. "Rich Hansford doesn't have anything to do with it. I'm making a gesture. You see, Meenie, what didn't occur to you or Raul is that if I had been indicted as a party to L. D.'s murder, so would have the two of you. You were with me when L. D. was killed, and you knew about the cover-up."

"Knew, hell," said Meenie. "We helped." He stopped in mid-chew, squinting at the sheriff. "I guess me and Raul had as much reason to kill Hansford as you did. We didn't think about that."

Charles rose and slapped his deputy's shoulder. "I know you didn't. That's why I'm taking my badge back. If you two are more concerned about saving my butt than you are of watching out for your own, then I guess I'd better do it for you. Besides, even flawed heroes can't cop out on a test of faith."

He looked at Lindman and raised one eyebrow. "What's it going to be, Lindman? Are you in or out?"

The other sheriff rubbed his jaw and studied Charles, then shifted his attention to Angie. Finally, he sighed and shook his head. "I don't like vigilantes, Matthews. I don't like anybody, particularly a peace officer, playing judge and jury. It goes against the grain."

Charles flinched, then squared his shoulders, and walked over to the other man, holding out his hand. "I understand, Lindman, and thank you for sticking around this long. I don't expect you to go against your conscience, so I'll say goodbye. If you'd rather I detour around Union County the next time I got to New Mexico, I'll understand that, too."

Lindman shouldered him aside and walked over to Meenie. "Give me that insurance report."

Charles glanced at Angie and drew a breath that shuddered through his chest. He'd tried to protect her, but he'd failed.

He'd broken his oath of office, broken the law, and now he had to pay the piper. He wished that the price didn't include Angie and Meenie and Raul.

Meenie clutched the paper while he studied Lindman, then held out the report to the other man. "Don't do wrong while you're worrying about doing what's right."

Lindman nodded, stepped past Meenie, and threw the insurance report in the fireplace. He watched it blaze up, then turned around. "It's real easy to follow the rules like they're written, Matthews. A man could do that his whole life and never have to make any moral judgment. He could die knowing he'd always done just what he was supposed to and never worry a day about whether he was right or wrong. He'd left those decisions to whoever wrote those rules. Ninety-nine point nine percent of the time the system works and justice is served. The other nine-tenths of one percent it fails because the law's an abstract, and people aren't. That's when a man—a sheriff—has to make a judgment call. He has to decide if obeying the law as it's written is right—or wrong. There aren't many men I'd trust to make that judgment, but I believe you're one of them. You might say I conducted my own test of faith, and you got a passing grade."

He pulled his coat open to expose a shiny new Crawford County deputy's badge hanging from his shirt pocket. "So how the hell are we going to haul your ass out of the creek without getting our feet wet, Sheriff?"

Charles walked over to the older man and clasped his shoulders. His eyes blurred, but not before he noticed that Lindman's looked suspiciously red. He blinked to clear his vision. "We're going back to Carroll's Rest to talk to Mrs. Ruiz. If I didn't murder Ginny Hansford, then there has to be a reason why she didn't see who did."

"If we find that reason, then what? If she didn't see anybody, we still don't have a witness."

"We've got reasonable doubt," answered Charles. "And that may be enough to persuade Ick Johnson to cooperate."

"The only way Ick Johnson is going to cooperate with you, Sheriff, is to lock the cell door behind you," said Miss Poole. "He was obsessive about your guilt."

"Charles!" cried Angie, pushing Hieronymous off her lap and rushing over to grab him around the waist. "Charles, Ick isn't rational about this. He might try to kill you."

Charles tipped her face up and kissed her, wishing he had

the time and privacy to do it right. He lifted his head and smiled. "Ick's a romantic, Angie, just like me, and we romantics understand the grand gesture."

"Oh, God, that just means you're both fools."

An hour later, Charles wished Ick's grand gesture hadn't involved an upper cut to his chin. Wiggling his jaw, he concluded it wasn't broken, but he was seeing stars where there weren't any. He shook his head to clear it, then wished he hadn't. He felt as if there were all sorts of loose places in his head, and every one of them hurt. He looked up from his prone position on Ick's front porch and saw his three deputies wrestling the former roughneck back inside his house.

"Son of a bitch!" yelled Lindman. "You just assaulted a peace officer."

"Then I don't have anything to lose if I do it again," panted Ick. He butted Lindman in the stomach, knocking him back outside.

Charles rolled over just in time to avoid becoming a landing pad. "You all right, Lindman?"

Lindman's mouth opened and closed several times before he finally managed to wheeze out a sentence. "You and your grand gestures."

"Ick, I didn't kill Ginny Hansford and I can prove it!" Charles yelled at the figure struggling to shake off Meenie and Raul, who were clinging to his arms and dancing around to avoid his wildly kicking feet. "Mrs. Ruiz couldn't watch Ginny's door every minute because of the banana tree."

Ick froze, and Meenie pulled out his handcuffs and snapped them closed over the man's wrists in a motion faster than Charles had ever seen the laconic deputy make. "Banana tree? What the hell are you talking about?"

"Ick?" Joella Hammond's voice was high and frantic-sounding as she ran up the sidewalk carrying one baby and dragging another. "Ick, what's wrong?"

She saw Charles trying to pull himself upright by grabbing onto the porch railing. Lindman was on his hands and knees making retching sounds as he tried to get his breath back. Then her eyes darted to Ick Johnson, standing in his doorway in all his handcuffed glory. "Let him go! He didn't kill anybody!"

Charles finally managed to stand up without swaying. He turned around to see little Bobby escape his mother's clutches and launch himself against Ick's legs, hanging on with hands and feet like a baby monkey.

"Bobby!" his mother wailed, and tried to free Ick from the clinging little boy, but Charles decided she'd have more luck trying to pry a limpet from a rock.

"Meenie, unlock the cuffs. I don't think Ick will assault anybody else with Bobby watching. He doesn't want to set a bad example."

Joella gave up trying to pry her son from Ick. "What do you mean, assault?"

Charles shrugged. "Ick's a little upset with me. Tell me, Mrs. Hammond, why are you so certain Ick didn't kill anyone? You don't know any facts about the case."

She looked at Charles for a moment, then back at Ick. "I just know."

"I think that's called a test of faith, Ick," said Charles. "Now, why don't we go inside out of the damn sleet and talk about this. Mrs. Hammond can take her children home before they catch pneumonia."

"I'm not going anywhere," said Joella firmly. "Not until I learn what this is all about. Although I bet it has something to do with that blonde you've been sneaking around with, Ick Johnson."

Ick rubbed his wrists and leaned down to pick up Bobby. "It's none of your business, Joella, and don't say anything about Ginny. She's dead, and I think the sheriff killed her!" His voice broke, and he turned and stumbled inside.

"Oh my," said Joella as she followed him in.

Charles leaned down and grasped Lindman's arm to pull him up. "Come on, Deputy Lindman. My instincts tell me this is going to be an interesting confrontation."

Lindman staggered to the door and inside to fall onto Ick Johnson's couch. "I ought to get combat pay, Matthews."

Joella whipped a diaper off her shoulder and dried Lindman's sweaty face, then turned and gently touched Charles's split lip. "Did Ick do this?"

"Damn it, Joella, I told you—I think the sheriff killed Ginny. Don't you think I've got a right to hit him?"

"Ginny's the blonde? The one who didn't give you an alibi?"

"How do you know that?" asked Ick, looking thunderstruck.

"Because I'm a witness," announced Joella. "I told the sheriff about her. And by the way, Ick Johnson, the sheriff never killed anybody either. A man who'd leave five hundred dollars pinned to my screen door isn't going to kill a woman."

"So that's why it took you so long to close her door and get back to the car last night," mused Lindman.

Charles felt himself flush. He didn't like his charities announced as if they were a score at a baseball game.

"One doesn't have anything to do with the other, Joella," said Ick, sitting down and shifting Bobby to his lap.

"Of course it does. A man who does good things when he doesn't have to isn't going to do bad things just because he can."

"Tell him about the banana tree, Sheriff," said Meenie.

Charles dropped onto the couch beside Lindman. "Mrs. Ruiz was patrolling the second story hall, which is nothing but a balcony opening onto the atrium full of all that tropical vegetation—including banana trees. She circled the balcony about every seven minutes. Meenie and Raul timed her. When she came opposite Ginny's room she couldn't see the door, because one of Johnny Reb's banana trees is two stories tall and completely hides room 243. Mrs. Ruiz wasn't lying; she didn't see anybody else leave Ginny's room, but for a period of ninety seconds to two minutes, she couldn't see the door. Neither could she see the door to the staircase leading to the first floor, which was right next to Ginny's room. She saw me leave because she was on the same side of the balcony and I took the elevator. Whoever killed Ginny used the staircase and waited until Mrs. Ruiz was on the opposite side of the balcony."

"That doesn't prove anything," said Ick.

"Then think about this, Ick," said Charles. "Would I kill the only alibi I had for my wife's murder? Would I kill a woman who continued to live with Rich Hansford at least partly to prevent his questioning whether his wife's lies were to protect him—or me? Would I wait nearly four years to kill Rich Hansford? And finally, to quote you, *if* I'd killed him, I wouldn't have screwed it up."

Joella listened open-mouthed, then turned to Ick. "You think the sheriff killed three people? He'd really have to like killing—and he doesn't strike me as the type. You're not thinking straight, Ick. Grief and all, I guess."

"There's something else, Ick," said Raul. "The sheriff didn't break into your hardware store. He was with somebody every minute last night."

"Maybe that didn't have anything to do with the murders," said Ick.

"That's about as likely as Rich Hansford walking through that door," said Lindman. "The lady's right. You're not thinking straight."

"I'm right about something else, too," said Joella, her cheeks flushed and her gray-green eyes glittering with impatience. "That Ginny woman should've stood up for you."

"Christ almighty, Joella, she couldn't! She would've been on the sheriff's shit list right along with me."

"Watch your language, please. Kids Bobby's age pick up those four-letter words awful quick."

Ick glanced quickly at Bobby, and Charles was amused to see a blush stain the man's blunt features. "Sorry, Joella."

"I still say that she should've stood up for you," said Joella, returning to the subject as if it were a sore tooth she couldn't resist prodding. "If she wouldn't stand up for you, she wouldn't stand up for anybody. Too busy looking after her own skin."

"Shut up, Joella!"

Joella bit her lip and straightened her thin shoulders, but she didn't retreat. "You think about it, Ick Johnson, and don't sit over here and make her into some kind of saint. There's no woman God ever put on this earth who's that. I'm not saying she was bad—she must have had something good about her for you to be crying over her—but she was just a woman and had her weak points. Now, I've had my say and I'll go home. Sling Bobby over my other shoulder. He's fast asleep and I don't want to wake him up just to make him walk across the street."

"I'll carry him," said Raul, lifting the little boy off Ick Johnson's lap.

"Thank you. I'd appreciate that. Thank you, too, Sheriff, and I'll pay you back your money as soon as you catch Lance Wayne and pick his pockets for my child support. I don't take charity when I can help it. Of course, I can't help it right now. Good night, Ick, and I really am sorry about your Ginny. A man's weak point is usually a woman, and I guess she's yours. I never found a man who had a weak point for me. It must be nice."

Ick glowered at her. "Go home, Joella, and don't bother coming back."

Joella flinched. "I guess I can't blame you, but I had to try to shake you up. You're too nice a man to turn into a hermit, and that's what you'll do."

"That's because he's a romantic, Mrs. Hammond," said Charles.

She nodded. "I think you're right, Sheriff. Men like that are nice to love, I guess, but I figure there would be times when they'd just wart a woman to death. Just not practical about some things."

She walked out the door behind Raul, and Lindman stood up and carefully removed his Crawford County deputy's badge. "Stand up, Johnson."

Ick rose, his eyes bright with frustration and anger. "You want to try to pay me back for hitting you, Lindman?"

The New Mexican sheriff stepped close and buried his fist in Ick Johnson's belly. "Nope, I want to pay you back for her," he said, nodding toward the door and observing the other man writhing on the floor. "Don't go insulting nice women like her anymore, and if she comes to your front door needing help and you turn her down, Matthews here will call me, and I'll take a drive down from New Mexico and beat the shit out of you."

"That's assaulting a witness, Lindman," said Charles.

"No, it's not. It's assault, period. I didn't have a badge on when I did it."

Ick pulled himself back into his chair, holding his belly and looking pale. "I won't turn her down, Lindman. I was just pissed at her. She can make me madder than any woman I ever knew—and she makes me want to pat her on the head at the same time."

Lindman grinned. "It appears to me that you were chasing the glitter when the gold was right across the street waiting to be picked up. Maybe you'll think so, too, when you get your crying over with and your head back in order."

"Butt out, Lindman," Ick said savagely.

"Ick, I want to listen to that tape you stole," said Charles.

"Why? Because you want to gloat?"

Charles catapulted off the couch, grabbed the neck of Ick's shirt, and jerked him half out of the chair. "Taking evidence from a murder scene is a crime, Johnson. I haven't pushed it yet because I was too busy feeling sorry for myself and you, but I'm over that. You and Fred Hansford are about to louse up my life and Angie's life because you both want vengeance, and I look like an easy target. Image and reality. Remember you told me how people confuse the two. That's what you and Fred

Hansford are doing. And before you and he count me out on the basis of that tape, check with a lawyer. It's inadmissible in court because it was illegally obtained. Now, get it out and let me listen to it. Somewhere on that tape is the reason Ginny Hansford was killed."

He felt Lindman and Meenie tugging at him and he let go of Ick's shirt. "Matthews, if you're gonna touch the witness," said Lindman under his breath, "for Christ's sake, resign again first."

CHAPTER 25

"MABEL, ANY WORD FROM SLIM?"

Mabel looked up, her eyes indistinct blobs behind her thick, smeared lenses. "Sheriff!"

"It is I, in the flesh, Mabel." Charles swallowed and gathered his social resources. "I want to thank you for helping me. In view of our past disagreements, it was very generous."

Mabel sat gaping at him, then her face turned an ugly, splotchy red. Whatever the dispatcher's attractive assets might be, none were physical, thought Charles sympathetically. She giggled, a high-pitched sound that made him wince, and he decided none of her assets were verbal either.

"When Sheriff Johnson lost the election to you, he patted me on the shoulder and said not to worry, that you were dumb about how we did things in Crawford County, but you weren't mean. You still don't do things the right way, but you haven't gotten mean either. Sheriff Johnson always said it took a mean man to kill somebody."

Charles bared his teeth in a smile. He might have known Mabel would evoke the former sheriff's name. "I appreciate his belief that I'm harmless."

"You yell a lot," said Mabel. "Sheriff Johnson never yelled."

Charles controlled his urge to yell. "Have you heard from Slim?"

"The radio's broken."

"Please fix it, Mabel, and call Slim. Tell him I'm not resigning, and he can let the D.A. and the county commissioners get back to their hunting."

"You might change your mind."

Charles counted to ten as he reminded himself that this woman was the only living human being in Crawford County who could fix the radio. As such she not only had absolute job security, but on this occasion at least, absolute power. So he did the only thing he could. He knelt down, ignoring the various snorts, gasps, and other indications of poorly smothered laughter, and took Mabel's hand. "Mabel, I give you my solemn oath as your sheriff that I do not intend to resign, and that I shall try very hard not to yell at you in the future."

Mabel blushed again and reached for a screwdriver. "I'll fix it, Sheriff."

"Thank you, Mabel." He rose from his knees, glared at his deputies, and turned to Miss Poole. "Do you have Raul's and Meenie's notes typed up from the interviews we did last night?"

Miss Poole frowned. "Of course, although Meenie's presented some difficulties. In all my years of teaching, I never saw such a consistently poor speller."

Meenie spat. "I spell just like the word sounds."

Miss Poole sighed. "Yes, I know, but your phonetic spelling has a Panhandle drawl. At any rate, Sheriff, I have the interviews, but I must say that I can't see how they help you." Her eyes turned suddenly watery.

He hugged the ex-schoolteacher. "Don't worry, Miss Poole. It's all a matter of changing my perspective."

She disengaged herself, her wrinkled cheeks an attractive pink. "What do you mean?"

"Alibis, Miss Poole, alibis that are confessions if you turn them around. Now, do you have the list of everyone you saw eating dinner last night at Carroll's Rest?"

She handed him another sheet of paper. "It's incomplete, Sheriff. I left around seven-fifteen, and I have no idea who came in after that. Also I wasn't as attentive as I might have been. Mrs. Jenkins either talked about the poker game or her niece. She's quite worried about the young woman. Well, you heard it from the girl's own lips. She and Brad seem to be celebrating the honeymoon before the wedding. Although to be perfectly honest, I suspect Mrs. Jenkins is more upset about her car. Maggie can't drive a standard shift pickup and takes Mrs. Jenkins's car."

Charles scanned the list of names, with Miss Poole's meticulous notes after each one she had observed leave his or her table and return. What was most interesting were the names not on the list—one without a motive, and the other without an alibi. Protection and self-protection—the two threads woven together like steel braid—were shielding a murderer. He closed his eyes. Mrs. Jenkins was right. In a county so sparely populated as this, it was impossible not to hurt someone you liked.

He turned abruptly and walked into his office. He heard the click of heels as Meenie, Raul, and Lindman followed him. "Close the door and don't talk to me. I want to read these interviews and reflect. I have to be absolutely sure this time. No more false scenarios."

"You know who done it, Sheriff?"

Charles nodded. "I think so, Meenie, but whether I can prove it or not depends on Crawford County. I'm the outsider going after an insider. I don't know if the county will give up the killer." He picked up the interviews and started to read.

Finally he laid down the typed sheets and aligned the pages. He had to be right. The motive; the opportunity; only the means was lacking. He picked up the phone and dialed a number, feeling a spasm of sympathy at the tired, grief-filled voice that answered. "Ick, this is the sheriff. Has your memory improved?"

"Jesus Christ, Sheriff, isn't there any way out of this?"

"I take it you've exonerated me?"

"Yeah, finally, but not because of any of your bullshit arguments. You could've been lying about why you wouldn't have murdered Ginny. And Mrs. Ruiz might not have seen anybody else because there was nobody else to see. Negative evidence, Sheriff. It was the tape that did it. I listened to it again after you left, except I listened all the way to the end this time. If I hadn't been running around with my head up my ass since Ginny was killed, I'd have done it before. Anyway, there was about ninety seconds of silence after she told you she lied to give you an alibi, then the sound of movement, then the door closing, then more movement, then somebody turned off the tape. If you turned off the cassette before you killed her, then why didn't you take it with you? But if that was you going out the door, then Ginny was still alive after you left. I'm not Sherlock Holmes, but I'm a logical man."

"Then you know whoever killed Hansford also killed Ginny and robbed your hardware store. How many twenty-twos did you sell in the last six months? More importantly, who bought them?"

There was a frustrated sigh on the other end of the line. "I didn't tell your deputy, but I had the serial number of that gun on computer. I ordered it eight months ago. I didn't say anything because—well, because I wasn't turning anybody in for killing Hansford. There ought to be a bounty on men like him. But Ginny, that's different. So I'll tell you what else I know. I don't have a record of its sale, so it was one of three I've sold in the last six months."

There was silence on the other end of the line, but before Charles could prompt him, Ick continued. "There's got to be another explanation, Sheriff, because I only sold one of those guns to a Crawford County resident, and I'd rather believe Santa Claus shot Hansford."

"Who was it, Ick?" asked Charles, and closed his eyes when he heard the name.

"Sheriff?" asked Ick before Charles could hang up.

"What is it, Ick?"

"About that tape. I talked to Fred Hansford, told him what you'd said about Mrs. Ruiz, and what I'd decided. He sounded real bad, Sheriff, sounded like he'd lost interest in living. Said he should've figured that Rich being killed wasn't enough to stop his lying and causing trouble for the hell of it. He wants to talk to you about your wife's murder. I think he feels real bad about that." Ick hesitated, and Charles heard him expel a loud breath. "I'm sorry about it, too."

Charles clutched the phone harder. "Fred Hansford will have to wait."

"Don't make him wait too long, Sheriff. He's a sick old man."

"As soon as I know the end of the story, I'll tell him."

"I'll drop that tape by your office, Sheriff. I wish I'd never taken it. And don't bother coming by here after you make your arrest. I know the end of the story."

"All of it?' asked Charles.

"What I don't know for sure, I'll guess at. I'll be all right, Sheriff. I just need to be alone for a while, try to put things in perspective. Then maybe I'll go across the street and see if that story might end a little better."

"Tell Mrs. Hammond I'll try to find Lance Wayne," said Charles.

"Check at the pool hall around the corner from the movie theatre. That's where I found the son of a bitch the last time I went looking for him."

There was a click. Charles sat holding a dead phone. He looked up to see the other men watching him with expressionless faces. "Almost there. Another couple of calls."

"Why don't you tell us now?" asked Lindman.

"Because I might be wrong, and if I am, I'll be the only one to know the name. Suspicion hurts, Lindman. If I've learned nothing else during this investigation, I've learned that. I don't want to hurt anyone else with my unfounded suspicions."

He dialed the phone, listened to the ring, and was ready to hang up when a sleepy, impatient voice answered. "This is Dr. Wallace. If you're an adult and not bleeding, having a baby, and don't think you're suffering a heart attack, why don't you take two aspirins and call me in the morning? On the other hand, if you're calling about a child or an elderly person, talk to me."

"Dr. Wallace, this is Sheriff Matthews."

"That ulcer finally started bleeding? From what I heard at your office, today, I'm not surprised. Well, don't take any aspirin. That'll make it worse. Meet me at the hospital, and we'll try to get the damn thing stopped."

"Doctor, there's nothing wrong with me—"

"Of course, there is. You just won't admit it. By the way, while I was in your office today, I confiscated all that across-the-counter crap you had in your desk and left you some tablets. Take them, goddamn it, or I'll stuff them down your throat. I also told Ick Johnson that if he mentioned that damn tape before you had a chance to defend yourself, I'd treat his colitis with speckling compound and water the next time he had an attack. I'm getting tired of my patients aggravating one another, and I want it stopped." He took a breath. "Now, that we've cleared the air, what did you want, Sheriff?"

"Does Brad Masters have high blood pressure?"

"You're asking me questions about my patients? Sit down and put your head between your knees. Let some blood get to the brain—because you damn sure are suffering some kind of deprivation in your upper story if you think I'm going to divulge one damn thing about another patient without a court order."

Charles rubbed his belly and wished the doctor a quick trip to perdition. "Dr. Wallace, I'll get one if I have to, but I'd rather not. Let's classify my questions as secrets that hurt and let it go at that."

"Is my answer going to get him into or out of trouble?"

"I won't know until you answer," said Charles through clenched teeth.

"Stop gritting your teeth, Sheriff, or you'll be toothless before you're forty. All right, I'll trust you to know what you're doing. I'm treating Brad for high blood pressure, for all the good it does either one of us. I kept altering his blood pressure pill and I finally threw in an anti-anxiety medication, but nothing is working very well. With Hansford gone to his reward—and I hope it's shoveling coal in hell—maybe I can get Brad under control." The doctor fell silent, and Charles could almost hear his brain clicking away like a calculator. "Is this about Hansford's murder?" he finally asked.

"Yes," answered Charles and hurried on to his last question. "What happens if Brad drinks while taking all this medication?"

"At worst, I suppose it could kill him. At best, he'd sleep heavily. The answer's probably somewhere in between—meaning I don't know. He might just be groggy and disoriented—depending on how much he drank, of course. But he's a fool to drink any at all in his condition. Now, did my answers help him or hurt him?"

Charles hesitated. "Doctor, at this point, every answer hurts." He hung up the phone before he was faced with another question.

"So it's the banker after all," mused Lindman. "That's fitting, at least. One banker killing another banker."

"Shut up, Lindman!" said Charles, pushing himself slowly out of his chair. He picked up his hat and walked to the door, hesitated a moment, then jerked it open.

Bill Adams, dressed in worn Levi's, flannel shirt, orange down-filled vest, and a stoic look, sat by Miss Poole's desk watching Charles's door. He rose with the unhurried motion that Charles associated with farmers. Faced with a lifetime of physical labor, they learned to husband their energy as they husbanded their land.

Adams nodded at Charles. "Sheriff."

Charles returned his laconic greeting. "Mr. Adams."

The elderly farmer looked at his gimme hat, with its grain company logo, that he held in his gnarled hands, then raised his head to meet Charles's eyes. "I reckon I got something to tell you."

Silently Charles motioned the man into his office and closed the door. He nodded at Raul to take notes. "Sit down, Mr. Adams."

The old man sat in the middle of the three chairs in front of Charles's desk, while Lindman and Raul took the ones on either side. If Bill Adams felt intimidated by being flanked by the two men, he gave no indication of it that Charles could see. In fact, he seemed not to notice them or Meenie, who leaned against the end of the desk nearest the spittoon. To the farmer, there was only one other man in the room. Bill Adams had spent a lifetime doing business with the man in charge, whether he was the president of the bank, the seed company manager, the head of the combine crew that cut his wheat, or the Crawford County sheriff.

"I was lying the other night, Sheriff."

Charles folded his hands and rested them on top of his desk. "I know that, Mr. Adams, but there wasn't a lot I could do about it."

The old man nodded. "I don't approve of lying. It's a low-down thing for a man to do, but I'll tell you straight out, Sheriff, I would've gone silent to my grave to protect anybody who shot Rich Hansford. But that's changed now. I ain't about to risk my immortal soul to protect some fellow who runs around killing women to save his own hide from going to jail—and I reckon that's the only reason he did it. That ain't the way we do things in Crawford County. You get caught doing something against the law, you take your chances with your neighbors on the jury letting you off easy, and not holding it against you. You don't, by God, keep on killing."

Bill Adams leaned forward in his chair. "And you don't let somebody else take your licks for you. That ain't the way we operate in Crawford County either. You protect your neighbors and your friends and your family the best way you can, but not if it means somebody else has to pay the piper when they didn't hear the music. I heard how Ick and Hansford figured you done all the killing. He called me to let me know I was off the hook. I let my hired hand take out my party of hunters, and I stayed home and studied on what I was going to do. He called back a little while ago to say he was wrong, but it didn't make no difference. I'd already made up my mind. I figured that you're innocent, Sheriff, because anybody who won't shoot a pheasant and hates guns as much as you ain't likely to shoot a man. Everybody else is going to think the same. But we can't none of us leave it there. You been accused, and it's our responsibility to help you clear yourself."

"Even if the price is my arresting one of your friends and neighbors?" asked Charles, swallowing to ease the tight feeling in his throat.

"We're mostly farmers and ranchers in this county, Sheriff. We know you can't let weeds choke out the crop or ruin your best pasture."

Charles wasn't able to answer.

Adams looked over Charles's shoulder, a silent acknowledgment that one man doesn't watch another man while he's struggling to control himself. "My dogs woke me up the other night just like you figured. I saw a car go by. It was dark as the inside of my henhouse, so all I could do was judge the size of it by the distance between the headlights and the taillights, and I figure it was Hansford's Suburban. Dogs didn't even have a chance to slow down to less than a yap or two when a pickup drove by. I ain't lying when I tell you I don't know whose it was. Pickups look a lot alike in the dark. Maybe ten minutes later the pickup came back by my house. I was getting curious and looked at the window toward my fields, but I couldn't see nothing, so I went back to bed. Twenty minutes later, at five o'clock according to my old Bendix, a car with a damn noisy muffler drove by. A few minutes later, maybe less than five, I heard a shot. I got up again but I wasn't moving real fast. It's pheasant season, and the shootings start early. Mostly city boys hoping to get a jump on everybody or bag more than their limit before the game warden starts counting birds. Anyway, before I got my pants buttoned, that car drove past again. There wasn't no more sounds after that, and the dogs quieted down. It was time to get up by that time, so I got myself some breakfast and came on to town. Got to the bank about the time Brad Masters drove up in that fancy sports car of his, grinding his gears like usual. Ick was already there, and Jess Turner got there about fifteen minutes later. I jawed with them for a while and never thought no more of the goings-on out at my place until I seen Rich Hansford lying in the field. And that's the honest-to-God truth."

Charles sat staring at his hands for a moment, then slowly leaned over and pulled out his bottom drawer. The .38 police special was lying there undisturbed, just as if it had been for nearly three years. He rubbed his hands on his trousers, then picked it up. He heard Meenie suck in a breath, just as Raul whispered a sentiment in Spanish. Charles hoped the mother of God heard his deputy's prayer.

He dropped the gun in his coat pocket and stood up. "I'm going out there."

Meenie spat. "The hell you say. We're all going."

Charles pulled on his sheepherder's coat, leaving it unbuttoned. "You're my blockers. As I recall, there are two roads into that place. I want each of you in a car blocking those roads. Lindman, you stay here. This is Crawford County business now."

Lindman got up and pulled his coat back. "And I got a badge on that says I'm a Crawford County deputy. I'm going with you. Somebody needs to watch your back. A man who hates to use a gun as much as you do is liable not to defend his ass as quick as he should."

"You already knew who it was before I come in here, didn't you, Sheriff?" asked Bill Adams.

Charles nodded. "But I had to be certain. You gave me the last bit of information I needed."

"What was that, Sheriff?"

"That Brad's sports car has a standard transmission."

CHAPTER 26

THE HOUSE WAS THE MODEST RANCH STYLE SO POPular in the late Fifties, red brick with white trim, with dormant flower beds filled with dead chrysanthemum stalks and leafless rose bushes on either side of the door. An ice-encrusted willow in the front lawn sang a high-pitched song with each gust of wind, while the red cedars that lined the circular gravel drive furnished a rustling accompaniment. The outbuildings—barn, single-car garage, and a large wire enclosure surrounding several dozen small pens—stood a hundred feet or so from the house, far enough to give the illusion that work space and living space were separate when in fact Charles knew they were not. At one time or another most farmers ended up nursing various offspring of their livestock in the warm confines of their kitchen or glassed-in back porch. The runt of a sow's litter, baby chicks who needed a little more warmth than the henhouse in midwinter provided, puppies, kittens, occasionally even a calf whose mother for one reason or another refused to feed it—all found refuge for a few days or weeks until each was strong enough to survive out-of-doors.

"Pretty place," remarked Lindman, removing his gloves and flexing his fingers.

Charles shuddered at the other man's action, knowing that Lindman didn't remove his gloves because he was hot. A man who might have to use a gun didn't want his fingers restricted by heavy gloves.

"Goddamn shame, Matthews."

Charles nodded and got out of the car to walk slowly toward the short plump figure replenishing the feeders scattered inside the wire enclosure. Several hundred quail scurried about her feet and waded through the muddy slush created by a dripping pipe from a stock tank. He lifted the catch on the gate and stepped inside the enclosure.

"Mrs. Jenkins."

Viola Jenkins dropped the scoop back inside the gunny sack of birdseed and brushed off her hands. "I didn't know when you'd figure it all out, but I knew you would. I've been expecting you. I'll come along peaceably, Sheriff. I was figuring on turning myself in anyway. Couldn't let you take the blame. That wouldn't be right."

"Why, Mrs. Jenkins?"

"A couple of reasons, Sheriff. I got tired of all the dead bodies, some of them suicides, because of Rich Hansford."

"Suppose you tell me the other reason."

"Maggie Pace is my sister's girl. She's the only kin I got except for my husband, and he never notices if I'm around or not, mainly because he's never around—like now. I ruled her daddy's suicide an accident, and Doc Akin didn't go against me because I never showed him the note my brother-in-law left. I guess Doc Akin might have had his suspicions, but when a man gets drunk and drives into a tree, it's debatable whether it's suicide or stupidity, and Doc decided to save the family the embarrassment. But it was really murder in a way, Sheriff. Hansford forced Brad to foreclose on his land, and my brother-in-law didn't see any way out. I thought everything was going to turn out all right after all, because she and Brad decided to get married. But Hansford turned up again. He was going to force Brad into foreclosing on his neighbors. Worse than that, he was going to force Brad into insolvency. Brad's a nice enough man, but he's a lot like Maggie's dad. He's not lucky and he's not tough, not like me, anyway. I guess the women in my family gravitate toward that kind of man. Seems that's the only kind we marry. But Brad's honest and hardworking, and they'll make out if they have a chance. I gave them a chance and I'm not sorry. Blood ties are strong in Crawford County."

"What about Ginny? Why was Ginny murdered?" asked Charles, amazed at the amount of pain he heard reflected in his own voice.

Mrs. Jenkins flinched and closed her eyes for a moment. She looked old, Charles thought, much older than yesterday. When she opened her eyes again, they too looked old. "I feel bad about that, Sheriff. I heard her causing trouble between you and Angie, and then she threw dirt on Marta Turner. She wasn't a good woman, but that's not why I killed her. I was afraid she was going to tell lies about Maggie like she'd done to Marta Turner. I didn't know how much of it you'd believe, but I couldn't take a chance."

She rubbed the back of her neck and straightened her shoulders as if she'd finally let go a heavy burden. "I guess it's lucky you found me out. Killing is too easy if you're tough. It could get to be a habit."

Charles reached out and clasped her hands. He could feel their coldness through his gloves, and rubbed them to restore the sluggish, cold-inhibited circulation. It was the only comfort he had to give her. "Aren't you afraid it's already a habit, Mrs. Jenkins?"

Her wind-chapped face went white and pinched. "I haven't killed anybody else, Sheriff."

"You haven't killed anybody at all, Mrs. Jenkins. You're only protecting the one who has, and if your niece knew how to drive a standard shift car, I might have almost believed you."

She turned even paler. Charles caught her as her legs folded up. "Oh, God," she mumbled.

Charles helped her toward one of the wooden feeders, easing her down until she sat on its edge. "Your niece lost everything and blamed Hansford. When it looked as if she were going to lose everything again because of the threat to Brad, she arranged to meet him in Mr. Adams's field. She shot him with the twenty-two you'd bought last summer from Ick Johnson."

"Wouldn't you go a little crazy if Rich Hansford threatened somebody you loved after he'd already driven your father to killing himself?" she argued. "Wouldn't you kill him if he laughed at you when you begged him to stop?"

"Yes, and if that had been her reason, she could've taken her chances with the jury. But that was only part of the reason. She didn't commit this just to protect Brad Masters, although I'm certain that's what she told you. She did it out of revenge and hurt pride. What she was so afraid Ginny Hansford would tell me was about her affair with Rich Hansford—before he foreclosed on her father's land. A trade-off: sex for land. Ginny mentioned Hansford did that regularly and that he'd had that kind of arrangement with another Crawford County woman. But she never told me who. That woman was your niece, Maggie Pace. That was the lie she told you she feared."

Viola Jenkins shook her head. "No, she wouldn't do that."

"She's not the first woman to be tricked by Hansford, but

she is the toughest. When he reneged on their agreement and then threatened Brad, she decided to retaliate. She wanted revenge, but she also wanted to make sure she never got caught. She took Brad home and spent the night, the first time she'd ever done so. She fed him his medication, including an anti-anxiety drug. She followed that up by persuading or allowing or encouraging him to drink beer, a potentially lethal combination. And she knew it! She told me that alcohol and his drugs would put him to sleep. I left Brad's house suspecting that she lied for him, when actually she lied for herself. She was not his alibi, as I had suspected. He was hers. If he was unconscious, he wouldn't know that she left the house in your car, shot Hansford, and returned to wake him. The best alibi is one that involves a totally innocent and gullible party. I'm certain he's convinced she spent the night with him and will swear to it, when in fact he only has her word for it."

Mrs. Jenkins wrapped her arms around herself. "It's not true. It wasn't like that at all. She loves Brad."

"Mrs Jenkins," said Charles softly, "she left the gun at the scene—your gun—an inexplicable mistake for one who had planned a crime to the last split second and concocted such a clever alibi. When the gun was found, I would trace it, and then arrest you. She was depending on you not to give her away. Blood ties are strong, you said. Then Jess Turner interfered, and Ginny made vague threats. I'm certain Maggie was shaken. She didn't know where the gun was, didn't know what I believed, nor what Ginny might tell me next. If Ginny told me about Maggie's affair, I would add Maggie to my list of suspects immediately, and she couldn't afford that. I might notice that her alibi and Brad's were in fact only his. Self-protection had become Maggie Pace's ruling passion, if indeed, it had ever been anything else. Ginny Hansford had to die."

He had barely bent his knees to squat down in front of Mrs. Jenkins when the first shot echoed in the chill air. He heard Lindman scream a curse.

"Goddamn it, I'm hit!"

Charles sprawled flat on the ground in front of the feeder, pulling Mrs. Jenkins down beside him. Another bullet punched a hole through the wooden side of feeder a few inches above his head, and he crawled on his belly around to the back of it, dragging the unresisting woman with him. The chirps of several hundred frightened quail, as they first scattered, then froze in instinctive little tableaus of short-tailed mottled brown terror, added a surrealistic element that Charles thought Steven Spielberg would appreciate more than he did.

"Matthews!"

Lindman's voice was barely audible over the sounds of the quail. Charles raised his head just slightly to look for the other man. He saw him about fifteen feet away behind one of the wooden pens, huddling against its back wall. Originally designed for pigs, the pens were actually more like small sheds with wire mesh doors, poles for roosting, and floors covered with hay and dried grasses. They wouldn't stop a bullet much better than the feeding troughs, but they were bigger, and a man could at least get his whole body behind one and enjoy an illusion of safety.

"Lindman!" called Charles. "Flat in the dirt! You're less of a target that way."

Another bullet thudded into the feeder, punched its way through and whined by Charles's face. "Mrs. Jenkins, we can't stay here. She's trying to kill us!"

He lifted his head just enough to turn his other cheek to the frozen ground and looked at the prone justice of the peace. Mrs. Jenkin's face was slack and white, her breathing shallow, her eyes wide and confused, symptoms of emotional shock. Charles cautiously pulled his flask out of his hip pocket. "Mrs. Jenkins, brandy is probably exactly the wrong thing to do from a medical point of view, and any kindly human being would condemn me for what else I'm about to do, but I don't have a choice."

Pulling off his glove with his teeth, he swung his hand in a shallow arc and slapped her across the face as hard as he dared, feeling almost sick with relief as she shook her head and blinked furiously, her eyes gradually focusing. Lifting himself as much as he dared, he slipped his hand under her head to elevate it, unscrewed his flask with his teeth, and dribbled the brandy into her slack mouth. "Drink up, Mrs. Jenkins. We're in a hell of a mess, and unless you want two dead sheriffs cluttering up your quail pen, you're going to have to be tough."

She coughed, took the flask, and drank, grimacing as the liquor burned a path down her throat. She handed it back and rubbed her cheek. "There'll be three dead bodies, Sheriff. I can't fool myself any longer. I'm a danger to her, and you saw what she did to Mrs. Hansford for the same reason. I can break her alibi, you see."

She angrily wiped away tears running from the corner of her eyes. "When I got up at five yesterday morning so I could get down to the bank to pick up my own party of hunters, I found out she wasn't home. I called Brad. Nobody answered." She stopped and took a breath. "Nobody answered until five-thirty when Maggie picked up the phone. When Hansford's body showed up, I *knew*, Sheriff, whether I wanted to admit it or not. That's why I spent all day yesterday playing the worst poker I've ever played in my life. I had to know what was going on. I had to know if you were suspicious. Then Slim found my twenty-two with the cracked grip, and I couldn't avoid facing it. I broke into Ick's store and stole his sales slips so you couldn't trace the gun. I knew, you see, that nobody in Crawford County would help you catch Hansford's killer, so Maggie would have a chance. But then she killed Mrs. Hansford."

"Matthews."

Lindman's voice sounded weaker, and Charles lifted his head and stared in alarm. The other man's coat was soaked with blood, and his skin had turned from olive to gray. "Hang on! I'm coming over."

Cautiously Charles raised himself to a kneeling position, tensed his legs, and took off in a zigzagging run to the wooden pen. He felt a bullet rip across the shoulders of his coat, and another sent his hat whirling across the enclosure. He hit the ground and rolled the last two feet to lay flat by Lindman's side. Raising himself on his elbows, he pulled open the other man's coat and shirt. Judging from the size of the hole high on the right side of Lindman's chest, and the amount of blood seeping from it, Charles knew Maggie Pace might cut another notch on whatever stick she kept score on if he couldn't get the New Mexican sheriff to the hospital.

He slipped off his sheepherder's coat, then his suit coat and shirt, shivering as the icy wind blew across his sweaty chest. Tearing half his shirt into strips and using the rest for padding, he made a crude bandage. "Hang on, you tough bastard. Meenie and Raul ought to be here soon."

Lindman shook his head. "Don't count on it. Too many guns going off all over the goddamn place. Pheasant season, and I never bagged a single one." He drew a bubbly sounding breath and grabbed Charles's forearm. "You're gonna have to take her out, Matthews, or I'm not going to make it. I know it'll eat a hole right through your guts to do it, but damn it to hell, don't let me die in a pile of quail shit in the middle of goddamn

Texas. The folks back in New Mexico would probably refuse to bury me in consecrated ground.

He sank back to the ground. "Let me have the rest of whatever Mrs. Jenkins was drinking."

Charles tucked both his coats over Lindman, although how much good they would do a man lying on ice-cold ground, he didn't know. "I don't think brandy is prescribed for a gunshot wound."

Lindman grinned. "Always knew Texans weren't civilized. What the hell kind of people would let a man die sober?" He held out his hand as a groan forced its way from between his teeth. "Give me the brandy, Matthews. It's the only damn anesthetic we've got."

Charles unscrewed the cap and gave it to him. He removed his gun from his suit coat, which he noticed was already noticeably stained with blood. "Hang tight, Lindman. I'm going over the top, as they used to say in World War I."

"They fucking died in World War I, too, Matthews. How about you think of something clever—like a smart bomb or something?" He groaned again and bit his lip as his body shuddered. "Jesus, Joseph, and Mary, why did she shoot *me*, anyway? We were all standing out in the open, and I'm damn sure not the threat to her that you are. The woman's crazy."

Charles rose to a half-crouch. "No, she's not. She has a reason for every thing she does." He eased over to the side of the pen. "Maggie Pace, can you hear me?"

"Yes!"

Charles saw Mrs. Jenkins raise up and peer over the feeder, then duck down again. "It's over, Maggie. Time to give up."

"I don't think so, Sheriff. With the three of you dead, I figure I've got a chance to persuade everybody that Aunt Viola did it, and that when you came to arrest her, she went crazy and started shooting at you. I killed her trying to save you, but it was too late."

"It won't work, Maggie. Everyone in my office knows I came out here to arrest you."

"Like you tried to arrest Marta Turner? How many times have you been wrong? Don't you think folks might wonder if you weren't wrong again? It was Aunt Viola's gun, and she was trying to protect Brad and me from Hansford. And everybody in your office heard how she jumped Hansford's wife for talking about me. Then there's Daddy's suicide note. She kept it. That's just one more reason for everybody to wonder if maybe she didn't do it after all."

"I've got a witness that heard you drive by in your aunt's car on your way to that field. The witness also heard the shot. That car has a noisy muffler. I don't think there's another like it in the county."

"But did he see me in the car? If he didn't, then you can't prove anything. I have an alibi, remember? Do you think Brad will ever believe I wasn't in bed with him the whole night?"

Charles let his shoulders sag. He knew the answer to that question. It was no. Brad would never believe it, and he would tell a lie with convincing honesty. But it wouldn't matter.

"How did you get to the bank yesterday morning, Maggie? Whose car did you drive? You didn't drive Brad's because I have a witness that saw him drive up by himself. Besides, it's a standard shift. How many people saw you drive your aunt's car? Your aunt drove to town in the pickup—a standard shift pickup—one you can't drive. How many people saw her? You can't kill everybody, Maggie."

"Nobody will care that I killed Hansford, and after Aunt Viola got so mad at his wife in your office yesterday, they'll think she killed her. You don't have any proof on that killing except the maid who says you did it."

"Yes, I do, Maggie. No one asked at the desk for Mrs. Hansford's room. Outside the sheriff's department, only four people knew which room was hers: Angie, who had no motive to kill her; Brad Masters, to whom she posed no threat; Mrs. Jenkins; and you. Mrs. Jenkins was at Carroll's Rest last night, dining with Miss Poole until seven-fifteen, and I believe Miss Poole would have noticed your aunt sneaking back into the motel after they paid their bills and went out to the parking lot. And seven-thirty is the outside—the absolute outside limit on the time of death. Your aunt didn't have time to murder Ginny Hansford, and I'm certain Miss Poole will testify to that. But you were in town, Maggie. What time did you get to Brad's, and don't you think even he would wonder if you asked him to lie?"

He shivered, his bare chest and back numb from the cold. "There's no way out, Maggie, none at all. Give up the gun, and let me get help for Lindman so you won't be tried for triple murder."

"He's not dead yet? I aimed for a solid lung shot close to the heart."

"You're crazy, Maggie. Meenie will request that Potter County send over its Special Crimes unit. You can't win."

"I will win! I will!" For the first time Charles caught a note of uncertainty in her voice.

He ducked as a barrage of shots shattered the corner of the pen. "Tell me something, Maggie. Why did you shoot Lindman first? Why didn't you shoot me?"

"He had the gun. Everybody knows you don't carry one. I didn't want anyone shooting back at me, and with him dead, I don't have to worry."

"I'm with Lindman. I can use his gun."

She laughed, all sounds of uncertainty gone. "You won't even go pheasant hunting, so I know you won't shoot me. Are you coming out, Sheriff, or do I come after you and shoot you down like a dog?"

Charles fell back beside Lindman. "Now we know why, and now I have a chance."

Lindman opened his eyes. His body shook continuously with chills, and he had to make an effort to concentrate. "I don't see one. I just hope she takes you out with a clean shot, because I'm here to tell you that dying by inches ain't the most fun I've ever had."

Charles sat up and clicked the safety off his gun and tucked it in the small of his back. "She's going to have to come after me in the next few minutes or risk my getting away in the dark. She doesn't think I'll use a gun, so she won't be watching me as closely as she should. If I keep her talking, I should be able to get within twenty-five or thirty feet of her before she feels threatened and shoots. With my gun, I have to be at least that close to have the kind of accuracy I need."

"You're going to try to wound her? You're crazy as hell, Matthews. Go for the body shots, or we'll both be dead. She'll punch so goddamn many holes in that hide of yours that there won't be a big enough piece left to make a condom for a pissant."

"You've got a way with words, Lindman," said Charles as he slipped his suit coat off the wounded man and rubbed it over his face and chest, gagging at the sweet coppery scent of blood. It was the best way he could think of to darken his skin to blend with the gathering darkness.

"She'll kill you, you stupid son of a bitch."

"I have another advantage besides the fact she likes to talk too much, Lindman. She aimed for the middle of your chest and hit your upper right shoulder. That rifle of hers shoots high and to the left, and she doesn't know it." He cupped his hands around his mouth, his words barely carrying over the muted chirping of the quail. "Mrs. Jenkins, I'm going out. When I get within fifty feet of her, you start talking to her."

"Don't do it, Sheriff," Viola Jenkins warned. "That's not my niece. I don't know what happened to her, but she's gone. That's some kind of a monster out there."

"She's still your niece, Mrs. Jenkins. You just never saw the black spots grow until they crowded out all the white. You just do what I say, and don't try to be heroic. I'm the one who makes all the romantic gestures. You're a practical woman. If this doesn't work, you use the confusion to run like hell, try to make it to one intersection or the other. Meenie's at one and Raul's at the other." He raised his voice. "Maggie, I'm coming out, but I've got one more question. May I ask it before you use me for target practice?"

"Is that a last request?"

Her voice sounded closer, and Charles flattened himself on the ground and peered cautiously around the corner of the pen, trusting his bloody camouflage to keep from getting his head blown off. She stood about seventy feet away, a petite, indistinct figure in the darkness. He wondered at her stupidity and confidence. She was walking toward him, shoulders straight and rifle held ready as if she were in a stubble field hunting pheasant.

Someone should have warned her that a man is not a pheasant.

"I guess that's my last request," he finally replied.

"Come on out. I won't shoot until I answer—if it doesn't take too long. And I want to see your hands," she belatedly added, as if some rudimentary caution had suddenly bestirred itself.

Charles rose and stepped away from the pen, walking slowly, but with longer than usual strides, toward the enclosure's gate. Fifteen feet, ten feet, five feet, and he touched the latch. "Your aunt took you in when you didn't have a place to go. She fed you and clothed you, helped you through the foreclosure when you lost your land."

Through the gate and five feet beyond it, feeling clumsy, as if he was walking hip-deep in thick mud. "Why are you trying to murder your Aunt Viola?" he asked, deliberately using Mrs. Jenkins's name, deliberately personalizing her.

"She knows I killed Hansford—and his wife. She didn't like that. I could tell. I saw her looking at me. She didn't understand that I didn't do anything wrong. They deserved it."

Charles wondered if Maggie realized how much like Rich Hansford she sounded. He never thought Carin's murder was wrong, either. Classic sociopaths, both of them. People weren't people; they were things to be used, discarded, or if necessary, killed.

Maggie suddenly jerked the rifle up to her shoulder and sighted it. "That's enough. Don't come any closer."

Too far. He was still too far.

"Maggie."

Maggie's head jerked slightly as Viola Jenkin's voice broke the silence. A flurry of soft feathered bodies further disturbed the quiet as the quail scurried away from unexpected new sound.

"I hate those ugly birds," screamed Maggie as she fired mindlessly into a small covey by the gate.

Charles whipped his hand around to his back and drew his gun, running forward at the same time. He saw Maggie shift her rifle from the quail to him and ducked to his left. He felt the hot sting of a bullet graze the top of his right shoulder as he dipped to his left again, raised his gun, and fired in that instinctive manner all marskmen strive for and so few attain.

His bullet paralyzed Maggie's right arm.

Lindman's shattered her left shoulder.

CHAPTER
27

CHARLES AND VIOLA JENKINS SAT SIDE BY SIDE IN THE hard plastic chairs outside the operating room. Maggie had already been transported under guard to Northwest Texas Hospital in Amarillo, where an orthopedic surgeon would attempt to repair her arm.

Lindman had not been sent to Amarillo. It was too late by the time the ambulance had arrived at Viola Jenkins's. He was unconscious, his blood pressure was nearly nonexistent, and his breathing was shallow and irregular. He didn't have the hour left that the trip would have taken. His life was in Dr. Wallace's hands, and the doctor had not been optimistic.

"I'll do the best I can, Sheriff, but I've never seen anybody lose so damn much blood and live," said the doctor, standing just inside the operating room, masked and gloved and waiting. "I think the damn bullet nicked an artery, took part of the lung, and I won't know what else until I open him up—providing we can keep him alive long enough for me to operate."

"He's tough, Doctor."

"He'd sure as hell better be," said the doctor grimly as he turned away and the doors closed behind him.

That had been four hours ago.

Viola Jenkins shifted her weight and the chair creaked. "I'm resigning, Sheriff, as soon as the commissioners' court meets."

"The commissioners!" exclaimed Charles. "Oh, my God. Slim's still holding the commissioners."

"We found him, Sheriff," said Miss Poole from her position on the other side of Viola Jenkins. "He told them the best pheasant hunting was on a ranch near the Canadian, and that the rancher had given him permission to take a party in."

"They believed that?" asked Charles. "No rancher in his right mind would let hunters escorted by Slim on his property."

"Slim can be persuasive," replied Miss Poole. "At any rate, Slim drove them out to a pasture, punctured the oil pan on the patrol car trying to cross a gully, and left the commissioners and the D.A. stranded while he went for help. Unfortunately, he got lost, and a cowboy found him before he tried to climb over an electrified fence. As soon as it's light, I'll call the Department of Public Safety and ask if they'll send a helicopter to look for the patrol car. Slim doesn't know exactly where he left it."

"Ain't surprising," said Meenie. "Slim can just barely find the courthouse."

"I'll miss all you boys," said Mrs. Jenkins. "It won't be the same not dropping by the courthouse every week or so."

"I think you're being precipitous, Mrs. Jenkins," said Miss Poole. "You are hardly responsible for your niece's transgressions."

"I should have stopped her when I first suspected her," said Mrs. Jenkins. "For the rest of my life I'm going to carry the burden of knowing I'm responsible for Mrs. Hansford."

Charles turned his head to look at the justice of the peace. "That's an adequate punishment and you're alive to suffer it. If you had confronted Maggie sooner, you'd be dead, and you still wouldn't have saved Ginny Hansford. You tried to protect your niece. As Miss Poole says, that's human nature. The law takes into account the intent of the accused, and you didn't intend any harm. You can resign, turn yourself in to me or the D.A., demand to be charged for obstructing justice and just add more to the waste your niece has made. You're the best justice of the peace in the county, maybe in the Panhandle. I don't want to see Maggie Pace bring any more destruction to Crawford County and its people. So live with guilt, Mrs. Jenkins, but don't quit."

The double doors opened and an exhausted looking Dr. Wallace walked out, his green scrub suit soaked with sweat and his shoulders bowed. "Sheriff, I've put all the pieces back together that I could, took out what I couldn't put together and he could live without. We pumped him full of blood when I finally got all the leaks patched. Now we'll see what happens. You can take a look at him when they roll him by on the gurney, then go home to bed. No visitors until he's conscious, and I don't know when that will be. Maybe tomorrow, maybe the next day, but I'll call you." He turned to the silent woman holding Charles's hand. "Angie, take him home, stuff some of those antibiotics down him to ward off infection. I don't know what kind of bacteria lives in quail shit. Good God Almighty, quail shit!" He pulled his surgical cap off, glared at Charles, and walked away muttering under his breath.

Angie tugged on his hand. "Come on, Charles. You look awful—and you don't smell much better."

He leaned over and kissed her, feeling that sense of homecoming again. He wished he could go home, shower, eat, make love, and find some peace. But he couldn't. Not yet. The story hadn't ended.

"I'll be home in another hour or so."

Angie caught his hands before he could leave, and studied his eyes. "Will you tell me where you're going? Not that I'm nosy, but I don't have myself back together yet. Every time someone shoots at you, my insides quiver for a while afterwards. Like a bowlful of Jell-o that someone bumps. I think it was worse tonight because you had all that dried blood all over you. I thought it was yours, and I . . ." She looked down at the floor, and Charles saw her lips tremble. Finally, she glanced back up. "I'd like to know that you'll be safe. If you'll humor me, the quivers will be gone in a few days, and I'll be fine—until the next time."

He kissed her hands. "I have to go tell a man about his son."

Fred Hansford looked up as Charles walked into the living room. "Sheriff."

"Mr. Hansford. Thank you for agreeing to talk to me so late. The news could have waited, but I couldn't. And I don't think you could either. I arrested Rich's and Ginny's murderer this evening. It was Maggie Pace, and she was a lot like Rich." Charles sat down on the couch and laid his hat on the coffee table. His eyes burned, and his chest and back felt itchy. The room whirled around for a second. He knew he hadn't much energy left.

Hansford lit a cigarette and inhaled a puff of smoke. He let it slowly trickle out of his mouth, and Charles knew the older man found the words more difficult than he had anticipated. "I'm sorry I accused you this morning, Sheriff. Grieving people do that, I guess. Anger, mostly. The folks that the dead leave behind are always a little angry. Death didn't consult us, and we still had some unfinished business with the deceased, some debts not paid. I figure Rich died owing you a big debt, and I can't pay it. That's another reason the living are angry at the dead. We have to clean up their messes, and most of the time we can't."

The old man wiped his eyes with a red bandanna and tucked it away in the pocket of his robe. "My son was everything I hated. He was a liar, a cheat, a thief, an adulterer, but I never thought he was a murderer. That's why I struck out at you so hard. Rich had one virtue, and you were threatening it. I didn't want to consider that of the two of you, *he* was a damn sight more likely to kill somebody. I could deny he killed your wife as long as I could believe *you* did it. He was innocent because you had to be guilty. But that ain't the truth, is it? You're innocent, so he had to be guilty. But I didn't want him to be. Still don't. But he is, and I'm real sorry you're the man he hurt. I can't say anymore. There's nothing else to say."

Rich was not a murderer, Mr. Hansford," said Charles, watching the shock on the other man's face—shock and uncertain hope. "I thought he was for reasons you heard on the tape, but I was wrong. It wasn't until I was investigating his murder and considering alibis and motives, and how often protection turns to self-protection, that I realized what I should have known all along. Ginny's alibi protected Rich and me, but it also protected her. I never thought to ask her where she was that night, and neither did the police. Besides Rich and myself, Ginny was the only other person who could have persuaded Carin to go out at night. But I never suspected her. I never reversed the alibi. And I should have, because her motive was the strongest of all. If I felt betrayed by my wife, imagine how Ginny must have felt. She was betrayed twice. Carin was her sister."

Charles rested his head against the back of the couch. He had given back Fred Hansford's son. Now, he only had to forgive Ginny.

The old man broke the silence, his hoarse voice firm. "I burned that scrapbook, and now I'll bury my son and his wife. I figure that if she killed for him, then she at least ought to rest beside him. I hope it's true that the spirits of the dead stay close to their graves, because I think it's only God's justice that Rich has to sleep beside the same woman for eternity."

He stubbed out his cigarette, and folded his hands across his lap. "Go home, Sheriff. It's finally over."

Charles picked up his hat. "Lindman got shot tonight when

we arrested Maggie Pace, so the hurting isn't over yet. But I have one more visit to make. To a pool hall. You might call it Charles Matthews's attempt to restore the balance between good and evil in Crawford County. I can't heal Lindman, and I can't undo what your son and Ginny did, but by God, I can see to it that Lance Wayne Hammond pays his child support."

As Charles climbed stiffly out of his car, he saw Hieronymous poke his nose between the drapes in the dining room. He glimpsed a table set with crystal and china and a slender figure lighting candles.

The front door opened easily. Charles wondered if anyone in Crawford County would ever learn to lock their doors.

He hoped not.

He stepped inside and closed the door. "Angie, I'm finally home."

ABOUT THE AUTHOR

The Sheriff and the Pheasant Hunt Murders is the fourth in D. R. Meredith's successful crime fiction series featuring Sheriff Charles Matthews. It was preceded by *The Sheriff and the Panhandle Murders*, *The Sheriff and the Branding Iron Murders*, and *The Sheriff and the Folsom Man Murders*. Among Ms. Meredith's other acclaimed novels of the New West are *Murder by Impulse*, *Murder by Deception*, *Murder by Masquerade*, and *Murder by Reference*. Ms. Meredith lives in Amarillo, Texas, with her husband and their two children.